Also by BILL BRODER

FICTION

Remember This Time
with Gloria Kurian Broder

The Sacred Hoop

Taking Care of Cleo

The Thanksgiving Trilogy:
Crimes of Innocence
Esau's Mountain
What Rough Beast?

Two Russian Bicycles:
Tolstoy's Wife and
The Sphinx of Kiev (novellas)

Belief, A Novel

The Teeth of God

Six Hands Clapping

NONFICTION

A Prayer for the Departed:
Tales of a Family Through the
Decades of the Last Century

What Do We Do with Our Dead?

A Man of No Rank

NEGLECTED WORKS

Volumes One, Two and Three

YET IN ARCADIA
A NOVEL

YET IN ARCADIA
A NOVEL

BILL BRODER

THE AINSLIE STREET PROJECT

Copyright ©2020 The Broder Family Trust UA 08-07-1989

All rights reserved. No part of this publication may be reproduced or transmitted in any form, or by any means, electronic, or mechanical, including photocopying, recoding, or by any information storage or retrieval system, without permission from The Ainslie Street Project, except in the case of brief quotations in reviews for inclusion in a magazine, newspaper, broadcast, or podcast.

Yet in Arcadia is published by The Ainslie Street Project, 68 Central Avenue, Sausalito, CA 94965

Cover and interior design by Barbara Geisler

PHOTO CREDITS
page *vii*: Detail of "Et in Arcadia Ego" by Giovanni Francesco Barbieri
back cover: Bill Broder and Sophie by Gilbert Robinson

ISBN: 9798686305632

Library of Congress Cataloging-in-Publication Data
Broder, Bill, 1931 –

1. Fiction 2. Death 3. Eulogies 4. Family life 5. Sausalito and the San Francisco Bay Area 6. Cremation 7. Friendship

Printed in the United States of America

ET IN ARCADIA EGO

"Against you I will fling myself unvanquished, unyielding, O Death!"

—*The Waves,* Virginia Woolf

PROLOGUE

We live in a beautiful town perched on the sloping hills and banks of San Francisco Bay. In the spring, fields of wildflowers illuminate the hillsides; ferns line the cascading streams; redwoods, live oaks, Douglas firs, and California buckeyes spread shade under blue skies and sun; winter rains are problematic, but summer fog from the ocean pours down through the gaps in the hills keeping the greenery fresh. The earliest humans lived comfortably here on the wild game, fish, shellfish, and acorns that provided a cornucopia for life. Sailors stopped for fresh water that streamed down from the verdant hills and lay in deep groundwater wells. Priests founded missions. Mexican cattle ranches spread over the hills. Anglo settlers came to harvest the lumber. Portuguese fishermen and farmers found the land and climate similar to the landscape from which they had emigrated. Fields were planted, gardens tilled. Cabins were built and then houses. The railroad arrived and ferryboats and before long a town was incorporated. Boats were built, bootleggers found refuge, gamblers arrived, then came libraries and schools and churches. Not long ago, the houses were cheap and the rents low enough for artists, writers, reporters, civic employees, nurses, and boat builders to settle here. Even cheaper rents and sales were to be found in the colonies of houseboats that sprang up in the mudflats and along piers out into Richardson Bay. Vast stretches of protected wilderness coastlands stretched for miles northwards, easily available to intrepid hikers and cyclists and nature enthusiasts. You could say that until the turn of the twenty-first century, we lived in Arcadia.

I

But even in our Arcadia, the miseries of life and of death lurked. On a somewhat dilapidated houseboat moored at Easterbury Dock, Waldo Point Harbor, Samuel Smithey lay dying of cancer in the main cabin/living-room where a rented hospital bed had been installed. His first and second wives, his son, and oldest grandson hovered about the narrow space, bumping into one another as they attempted to make him comfortable. Samuel's second wife, Berenice, who owned the houseboat, had been his mistress during the latter years of his forty-year first marriage. He had been stunned when his first wife, Michelle, had asked for a divorce. Even before taking up with his mistress, he had indulged in a number of short-term affairs that seemed acceptable to him given that the marriage had been a tempestuous battle from the beginning.

Samuel, a poet, had been a prodigy, winning the Yale Younger Poets prize in his early twenties. At the time he was considered the leader of the next great generation of American poets. Michelle, a serious translator in German, French, and Russian, had greatly admired Samuel's poems before they met at Iowa, where they were both in the graduate writing program. That first meeting at a party of writers had become a legend of passion in American letters. Michelle's brilliantly perceptive admiration of Samuel's work that she had expressed immediately upon being introduced to him aroused Samuel to such a pitch that he had dragged her into a closet off the kitchen. When the two emerged a half hour later, his ear and her neck were bleeding and they both looked as if they had been struck by lightning. They were married within a month, after which the battles commenced. She claimed he did not take his great gift seriously; he claimed she was compulsively organized and tried to enclose him in a muse-strangling regime. The struggle went on for forty years, the birth of three children, Samuel's loss of five jobs, his deteriorating career, and his many affairs with students, while Michelle supported the family through distinguished translations, editing, and part-time teaching. When Michelle divorced him after forty years, he was stunned. She asserted that while she still believed in his talent more than he or the critics, she could no longer put up with his willful behavior. She had patiently endured the affairs and his senseless rebellion against authority that had cost him jobs and had sent the family from one university town to another less distinguished; but his laundry on the floor, his beer cans over the entire house, his awakening the children at all hours of the night with his sudden squalling of folk songs accompanied by his clumsy strumming on his out of tune guitar, had become intolerable. Worse still was his inability to keep a schedule, so that he was often late to dinner and forgot engagements that she had made with their friends. Samuel was a passionate athlete and outdoorsman—mainly a hiker, fisherman, sailor, and a kayak paddler, all of which he did very well; also he played tennis with passion, but not very well, admonishing himself so soundly in a loud voice that he annoyed other players at the courts. When on the water, the tennis court, or pursuing his gallant dalliances, he tended to lose track of time and of his marital responsibilities.

On the whole, though, Samuel was very good-natured, which was why, even after the divorce, in which he quite generously allotted everything Michelle desired without a quibble, he considered her still an integral part of his family. He ran errands for her, took her to the airport bus and picked her up on her cross-country trips to her new partner. Before she had announced her intention to leave Samuel, Michelle had emailed three of the suitors of her youth, announcing her intentions. All three declared themselves willing to unite with her. She chose the most attractive proposition and had been quite happy in her new situation for some years, returning to the West Coast on a regular basis to maintain contact with her children and her medical plan.

Now Samuel lay dying and somewhat uncomfortable. The cancer had metastasized from the prostate to the liver, the lungs, and the bones. Nevertheless, he maintained his sense of humor as he watched his wives, his son, and his grandson bustling about the cramped space out of concern for his comfort. He loved them all and enjoyed the nautical arrangement of the cabin, complete with the elegance of the antique oriental rugs and period furniture his first wife had acquired over the years at barn sales, country shows, and in the many foreign countries she had visited when he had gone off to catch fish and be inspired in the wilderness. Michelle had retained enough of these valuable objects to enhance her pied-à-terre in town. Through the aft-window of the houseboat lay the bay on which he had sailed and paddled over the years. A light wind ruffled the water as flocks of ducks, seagulls, cormorants, and pelicans landed and took off. He knew that the feeding was very good at this hour because the sea flood tide was meeting the fresh water pouring from the delta into the bay, thus causing an upwelling of bottom morsels. He would dearly love to be out on that water where he had spent so much time, but he was resigned to his illness and death.

The doctor had offered extraordinary procedures to prolong his life for a week or two, even for a month, but he had preferred simply to accept fate and to die peacefully on this occasionally buoyant wooden wreck. He did have one desire that he had put off until he was certain the end was almost achieved.

"Call Monty Wolfe," he demanded, his lungs so clogged and his voice so low that no one heard him the first time. He reached for his cane, suspended from the bedstead and pounded it on the deck. "Call Monty Wolfe! I want him to write my obituary."

* * *

Monty Wolfe had lived in town with his wife Talia and children for fifty years. He earned a meager living as a freelance writer and a small investor in the stock market. For five years he co-partnered a company that created early-learning materials for eastern publishers, an enterprise that yielded small royalties for a while. He also wrote novels and plays that earned nothing. They had moved to town and bought a decaying house on mortgage with a down payment from the insurance on the life of his wife's father. When the call came from Samuel Smithey's son, Matt, Monty had been writing copy for an environmental museum south of the airport, detailing the threat to the earth by fossil fuels, industrial pollution, and the expanding population of wasteful humans. Just yesterday, a reliable scientific report had established a record-breaking melt of the Arctic ice that would threaten the existence of low-lying islands and coastlines throughout the world.

"Mr. Wolfe," said Matt on the phone in his dry methodical tone, "Dad is dying and wants you to come down as soon as possible to write his obituary. You're the only one he trusts."

Monty sighed. Samuel was not alone in his dying. Many other of his friends and relatives were on their way out, if not already departed. According to scientists, the earth, as Monty had enjoyed it, was in a similar condition. Although Monty felt that Samuel's wives, Michelle and Berenice, and even his son were capable of writing Samuel's obituary, he didn't argue with Matt. If one of them had tried, he knew, there would be an inevitable deadlock. Michelle and Berenice got along well enough in order to deal with the kids and grandkids, and with Samuel, but they barely understood one another. Michelle thought Berenice on the edge of insanity. Berenice, who had grown up in the wilds of Alaska, had never understood the cosmopolitan New York scene in which Samuel and Michelle had been born. She confided in Monty's wife that she thought Samuel's marriage to Michelle had broken up because Samuel was a Polish Jew from the Lower East Side of New York and Michelle, a French-German Catholic from Morningside Heights. She found it strange that friendship or marriage between such diverse groups was normal in the "Lower 48." In Alaska, the Inuit, the Indians, the Anglos, and the few Blacks had very little to do with one another. Even among the Anglos, the Irish Catholics, the German Lutherans, the English Episcopalians, and the Quakers had remained separate. To be sure, Berenice's mind-set had little to do with such ordinary sociological distinctions. From childhood, Berenice had lived in an odd realm of fantasy, paranoia, and sensual gratification. Added to this curious pottage were the years of Jungian therapy she had undergone, from which she had adopted a mix of archetypical deities. During the few conversations Monty had had with Berenice, she had explained to him that from her earliest years mysterious tundra spirits had protected her and still guided her during her sojourn in the lower states. She had been quite drunk at the time of this confidence, but Monty suspected this was actually her deep belief. He was mystified as to how these tundra spirits found an acceptance in Jungian therapy or how all of this was digested by a psyche formed in Berenice's peculiar Alaskan childhood.

As Monty set off on his mission, he declared to his wife, "Everyone is dying, dead, or succumbing to Alzheimer's."

"I'll wager you've already composed poor Samuel's obituary," Talia replied, laughing, although she grieved deeply for all the dead and dying in their lives. Samuel had spent a lot of time at their house, bemoaning his career, his marriage, and the fate of poetry in America. He always brought flowers and gifts and greatly appreciated her design. She was very sad that he was dying and glad that he would have a lot of company at the end, including her husband to commemorate him. It seemed to her that death had declared war upon them from the beginning. Talia's mother had died when she was a small child; Monty's father had died before he was twenty, and his first wife had died in childbirth; then her father died in a boating accident just after she met Monty.

Monty had been the youngest son and prodigal in the eyes of his Midwestern family, because of his desire to write fiction, his peculiar profession as an exhibit writer, his eccentric second marriage to the daughter of a Belize fisherman, and, even worse, his choice to live in California. He was also the most articulate in the local community of friends and was often called upon to deliver eulogies at memorials. His wife was correct in accusing him of casting up premature memorial speeches, even though he hadn't thought he would be asked for Samuel's. First his mother and then his oldest brother had suffered serious illnesses. Long before they died, on his morning hikes Monty had searched his soul for his true feelings for these dear family members. He felt guilty about the premature speeches he had concocted, almost as if he were wishing Death to arrive and provide him once again the role of chief mourner. Death always appeared in his mind with a capital letter. Monty's father had died when Monty was in the midst of a rebellion. In the years that followed that death, he had been stricken with the permanent role of guilt-ridden mourner. Death had become a familiar presence in his life, a conveyor of distinction. He considered this one of his principal faults and sought to atone for it by redoubling his penchant for caretaking. Perhaps that was why he had become the village spokesman at memorials.

And now he had been called upon to write his good friend's obituary. As he walked up Easterbury Dock to the Smitheys' houseboat, he felt he was showing Death the way. The tide was out and the houseboat sunk down in the mud, separating the steps on the deck to the front door from the dock gangway. Monty paused a moment contemplating the possibility that he might break his neck on the way to writing an obituary. As he jumped down, through his mind came a funny opening to his own obituary; he landed on the top step with his good leg barely able to support his weight. He reached out to the door with both hands to keep from falling. The knee of his other leg had no cushion in the socket between the bones. Monty was only three years younger than his dying friend. His own death was not improbable. He had just celebrated his seventy-fifth birthday and five years ago had suffered a heart attack requiring five stents and three balloons. In his lifetime, he had become so familiar with Death that the heart event had bothered his wife and children a good deal more than it had him. After all, he had lived almost twice as long as his father and felt he had already enjoyed a happier life than he deserved.

Samuel's wives and son greeted him with a reserved, slightly hostile gratitude, almost as if he wore a black hood and carried a scythe. Still they let him know they understood Samuel was asking a peculiar favor of a friend and they were grateful. By rights, the obituary should be family responsibility.

Samuel's first wife Michelle introduced him to their grandson, Sean, a sullen twenty-two-year-old, with a day's growth of beard, an earring, and a piercing in one eyebrow. Monty put his hand out, but the young man merely waved his hand and turned away to open a beer.

Michelle, a tall, handsome woman in her seventies, grinned apologetically and shrugged her shoulders, nodding at her grandson. "He's been a great help." She had told Monty that she didn't understand the young man, although she thought he had a good heart.

"Monty, old boy," called Samuel hoarsely from the bed where Berenice and Matt were propping him up for the interview, "great that you could come." His appearance shocked Monty, who hadn't seen him in a month. Samuel had been a jaunty, athletic six-foot-two, with broad shoulders, a slight beer belly and a square bronzed face, with a full head of curly white hair. He had always been handsome. Today he looked like a pale, shrunken dummy of his former self. Only his bushy white eyebrows had retained their vigor.

"He's lost a lot of weight," said Michelle, her hand on Monty's forearm, as if to steady him. She understood his anguish. He and Michelle were friends, closer than he and Samuel.

"I wish I were bringing my tennis racket, Smithey."

"You should start, Mr. Wolfe," said Matt, with concern. "He gets tired easily."

Matt was a worrier. He had grown up with Monty's children, starting with nursery school and all through high school. In the early days, the Smitheys had lived down the block. Monty had often driven Matt with his kids to school events. Although he had always been polite during those early years, Matt had been reluctant to get in the car. Once the car started up, Matt so feared being in a wreck that he had gripped the seat back until his knuckles turned white.

Michelle had informed Monty that Smithey drove so carelessly and had been in so many accidents when Matt was in the car, that their son distrusted any driver except his mother. After college he became an actuary. Monty always felt his gaze on him to be calculating, as if to discern his possible life span.

Monty sat down next to Samuel with a legal pad and pen. The women and Matt hovered on the other side of the bed. Samuel clasped Monty's hand, gave it an affectionate squeeze, and declared, "I want my full position on the demise of American poetry, lax modern education, and Israel in the piece." He stared up at his family in defiance as he began to dictate.

"It's your obituary, Smithey," Monty murmured, scribbling.

They had obviously been arguing the matter already. When Matt began to object to one of his father's lengthy diatribes about the absence of rhyme and meter, Monty put up a placating hand, "Let me do a draft first, then we can discuss it."

Berenice murmured, "Just remember, the papers charge by the line, and we want a photo, too."

Monty knew which photo she would choose; the one where Samuel had posed with Inuit fisherman on the upper Noatak River in Alaska. It stood prominently on the kitchen counter. Samuel had been a handsome twenty-year-old and in magnificent shape, with that beautiful smile declaring him the best friend humanity ever spawned for the natives with whom he posed.

He was Monty's good friend, too, despite Samuel's deplorable behavior on the tennis court, his ridiculous slurs on generation of younger poets and even the more celebrated of his contemporaries, along with a current of racism in his dumb jokes about Arabs, Muslims, Blacks, Latinos, and feminists. Monty could not understand why a man of such intelligence should delight in offending the innocent liberal ethos of the local community. His behavior almost made Monty believe in a strain of racism within Polish Jewish genes. Over the years, to emphasize his point of view to Monty, Samuel bragged repetitively about his cousins in the Israel Defense Forces who gleefully shot protestors who approached the barbed wire fences of Gaza and made Palestinians wait long hours for no reason at Israeli checkpoints.

As Monty took notes for the obituary, his dying friend's wives and son slipped in additions and murmured objections. He wondered how one could compose a brief column of words to render a life so full of ambivalent impulses. When Monty first met him, Samuel, a true son of his immigrant father who ran a pawn shop on the Lower East Side, had proudly announced that he revered Roosevelt and the New Deal and had voted for Adlai Stevenson. A subtle change in Samuel's politics occurred when they started playing tennis together on the old South Park court. Samuel had been thrilled by Kennedy's inaugural speech touting American exceptionalism, international activism, and his intention of continuing bomb testing. This was a very different sort of liberalism—much more aggressive, militaristic, and dominating. In fact, he understood Samuel's stance. His friend had seen limited combat as a Marine in the Korean War and was an ardent believer in "service" and "discipline" in defense of the democracy in which his parents had found refuge.

Samuel's tennis resembled his new politics: booming serves, forehands that blasted down the sidelines, flailing overheads as if the ball were a vicious insect. He had such a passionate desire to win that he contested every close call. The problem was that the booming serves, the terrific overheads, and blasting forehands landed mostly in the net or out of bounds. Monty's calm, steady classic tennis, clever placement, and gentle lobs triumphed every time. Samuel, generous though he was off the court, never credited

Monty's play. Instead, he carried on a loud angry quarrel with himself for his errors.

Once Kennedy had been assassinated, the Viet Nam War heated up, and the 60s youth revolution blossomed, Samuel's politics, dress, and behavior swung to the left. He took to wearing faded army fatigues, smoking marijuana, and growing his hair and beard to such lengths one could scarcely identify him. He put up posters of Che Guevara in his office and urged his students to burn their draft cards; his classroom schedule became erratic due to his compulsive attendance at protest marches. Although his early successful poetry had been wedded to classic form, meter, and rhyme, he suddenly espoused free verse, the wilder the better. Before long, he had lost prestigious positions at Stanford and then at UC Berkeley and finally at San Francisco State University.

Michelle, who had been teaching all these years at Mills College, a relatively proper private institution in Oakland, decided, for the sake of the family, to take charge of Samuel's career. Armed with a promise by Samuel to tone down his behavior, she was able to persuade Mills to hire him on a probationary basis. After all, he was still one of the leading younger poets in the country.

In fact, he had begun to tire of free verse, his beard, and his fatigues.

As the years passed, Monty was sad to witness Samuel's steady march to the right, especially once the youthful rebellion of the sixties against authority took hold. During their tennis matches, Samuel ranted about the Black, Latino, lesbian, and gay students who disrupted his lectures or walked out in protest against the traditional values of western civilization that he taught. He was full of rage at his fellow professors who weakly tolerated unsatisfactory achievement of deviant students out of a mistaken liberal myth that the students had been hampered by the culture's prejudices. Samuel declared at the beginning of a set, in the middle of a set, at the end of a set, whenever his bile rose, or when he lost a point, "The culture has given the fucking students everything. If students cannot perform, they should be failed. Professors who don't understand that must not be hired or receive tenure. The lower the standard, the worse the education."

The complexities of the human condition, tribal atavism, and economic privation that had remained submerged by a common belief in the American myth had now emerged with blatant exuberance. Monty could hardly blame his friend's consternation when the Tea Party howled, the radical anarchists' broke windows, the KKK marched, and women donned pink armbands. He understood why Samuel Smithey had little patience to face such chaos, especially when it entered his classroom, breaking down all the rules of civility.

"I may not be enough of a celebrity for an official obituary in the *Times*," said Samuel, "but if you talk about my teaching, I want my position made clear. After all, we'll probably be paying for the column."

Berenice nodded her head vigorously in agreement. Michelle rolled her eyes.

Matt snorted in exasperation. "For Christ's sake, Dad, this isn't an op-ed!"

"It will be in the *Times*, by God," Samuel sat up from the pillows, waving a fist, "and I'm fed up with their wishy-washy attitude. They used to stand for something in this country, and they should stand firm now." He sank back, exhausted.

Monty chuckled, waving his left fist in the air as he scribbled. For Samuel and Michelle and their New York peers, the *Times* had always been the arbiter of reality, the conveyor of value. They both still subscribed to the print edition, daily and Sunday. "Maybe they'll do you up free and save us the effort," Monty said. In his opinion, this might be possible given Samuel's prominent position in poetry. But whether or not Samuel's widows shared the expense of an elaborate obituary, it was essential that Samuel's life be validated in some way on the pages of that august newspaper.

II

When Monty Wolfe left the houseboat, Berenice collapsed upstairs on the bed she had shared with Samuel long before his divorce from Michelle. After their years-long hit-and-run affair, her marriage to Samuel had been a miracle of stability in her life. Before his divorce, she had understood that he would never leave Michelle. Then, to her amazement, Michelle, forty years into her marriage, had finally decided to leave Samuel. Michelle had made it clear that she didn't blame Berenice, a generosity that had confused Berenice ever since. Tonight, she lay in bed, rigid in terror at Samuel's impending death. Until Samuel appeared, her life in the so-called "real world" had been a disaster.

She had been born in a small village fifty miles southwest of Fairbanks. The only blessing Berenice had received from her alcoholic parents had been that they had never physically or even mentally assaulted her. Mainly, they ignored her, so much so that if she hadn't been a resourceful child, she might have starved or frozen to death at an early age. There was also the matter of bears, wolves, and wild dogs, all of whom would have made short work of a small girl scooting along, gathering wood for the fireplace, scraps of food for her stomach, or spare clothing to keep her warm during the frequent

Alaskan blizzards. As she lay in the houseboat bedroom above her dying husband Samuel, she tried to return to that village, once more a small abandoned child trudging through the mud and snow gathering the essentials she needed to survive. The villagers treated her like a feral cat, leaving her food and clothing on their porches and door sills. Although many disapproved of her parents for having abandoned her, it was considered pushy to interfere with someone else's family. But tonight, as she bewailed Samuel's imminent departure, she realized, with surprise that in that village, she had never felt as abandoned as she did tonight. From the very beginning of her memory, she had been accompanied by magical companions who took the place of her non-existent family, spirits who somehow protected her and comforted her as she wandered about surviving. Her father raised dogs; her mother raised fighting cocks and hens for eggs; both were busy all day long and drank at the local bar late into the night. Berenice felt they had forgotten they had a daughter, which would have made her doubt her existence, if it hadn't been for her spirits. Then one day the schoolmaster arrived at the door with a truancy notice. That was the first time Berenice understood that she had a place in the world of ice and snow and mud and crude cabins. After all, if she was expected to go to school, she must have some importance. Her schoolmates shocked her. They were nothing like her imaginary protectors and friends. They were much smaller and not at all friendly at first. But her energy and imagination captured their alliance. Just as wild animals did not harm her, because she exhibited no fear, her classmates accepted her. They thought her odd but interesting. *Interesting* was important in that drab village where nothing much happened except for the weather, wild animals, and brutal brawling adults. At first, she made the mistake of mentioning her spirits, the way a child would mention her parents. Of course, the children at school asked her what they looked like, her "spirits." Dumfounded by the question, she had run off and hid in the forest behind her house. For some hours she pondered the question. She had no idea what her "spirits" looked like. They just were always there beside her, protecting her, leading her to food, clothing, shelter, and the love that the wild beauty of the Alaskan countryside lavished on her.

The next time her classmates demanded a description of her "spirits," she replied, "They just simply are there." She spoke with such assurance that the questions ceased.

In middle school, the math teacher, a serious Quaker who taught extracurricular art classes, discovered Berenice's essential parentlessness. The teacher took the child to Quaker meetings, presided by her husband, a Unitarian minister by training. While Berenice was in the eleventh grade, her parents succumbed to alcoholism in quick succession. The childless teacher and her husband adopted her. At first, she attempted to explain to her new parents about her mentors and friends in the spirit world. Their immediate reaction was a mild horror that they attempted to mask. She understood their fear that she might be crazy, which some people in the village had always suspected. Immediately, and to the great relief of her new parents, she pretended to substitute the guidance of a single benevolent God for her alien spirits. Tonight, when she needed the support of her spirits most, she realized that this first radical compromise had sapped the energy of her spirits, even though she made it clear that she meant them when she prayed fervently to God. Still they had faded back a bit, and were less helpful in her current predicament.

With her adoptive parents' support, she attended the new progressive Evergreen College in the State of Washington where she felt completely lost in the foreign landscape. However, after a few months, she found her "New Age" classmates themselves had sought the comfort and power of spirits through all sorts of practices. At Evergreen, her own spirits began to revive somewhat from the temporary invasion of a Christian God and the eastern Washington terrain. She majored in art and graphic design and obtained an MA in computer science that led to a comfortable career. Somehow, she felt her spiritual protectors now inhabited the computers, making it comparatively easy for her to wend her way through complex computer techniques. When people termed her "intuitively skillful," she did not protest. Her spiritual world remained protected against prying doctors and her fellow computer scientists by the clever discretion she had learned early in life.

But, alas, she had to leave Evergreen for the "real world," where the men proved to be a disappointment. Although she led an active and satisfying sexual life, once she explained to her various partners that her spiritual mentors accompanied her physical joys with them, the men proved to be less enthusiastic, fearful even. Very soon after her confessions, the relationships came to an end. Once more she began to compromise, losing crucial support as she faced life in the lower states. The move from Alaska had been traumatic, and each successive change of partner, of location, and, particularly, of weather and landscape left her feeling less and less confident. In her search for a sympathetic emotional climate for her spirits, she moved to Sausalito, where some of her Evergreen friends lived on the houseboats. The time, the late sixties, and the place were propitious. Two docks north was moored the *Vallejo*, a ferryboat owned by the English Buddhist, Alan Watts and the Greek artist Varda.

As she sat on the deck of the *Vallejo*, inhaling the marijuana-laden air, listening to that handsome cadaverous Englishman, a white silk scarf looped around his neck, intoning the wisdom of entering and living within each "moment," she felt her tundra spirits whooping in delight. At the conclusion of Watts' lecture, a cucumber soup laced with LSD was solemnly served to all the worshippers. The effect on Berenice seemed miraculous. For the first time since her adoption by the Quaker couple, she fully re-entered the universe of her spirits, who welcomed her ecstatically. She had to tell someone. Sitting next to her was a lean curly-headed, large-nosed, large-eyed gentleman with horn-rimmed glasses. He had just licked his soup bowl clean. She smiled at him, grinned, laughed. He returned her smile, her grin, her laugh. "The moment!" he exclaimed.

"The moment!" she cried. "My tundra spirits have welcomed me!"

He chortled, "Let me introduce my dybbuk spirits to your tundra spirits!"

They embraced as their drug visions mingled. With gentlemanly grace, he offered her his arm and led her down the dock to a small building labeled with an elegantly lettered sign, "Isaac Koenig, MD, PA, PhD." As their visions had already mingled, their bodies found no difficulty in comingling.

To Berenice's surprise, after a vigorous and joyful orgasm, her partner introduced himself: "Isaac Koenig, a Jungian psychoanalyst."

"Berenice Andresen, an Alaskan orphan."

"My dear Ms Andresen, your *tuurngait*, which is to say, your Alaskan tundra spirits, have embraced me and my dybbuks from the shtetls of the Ukraine and redoubled my sexual prowess that has been dwindling due to my wife's organizational genius."

Berenice stared with amazement at this naked man with his limbs encircling her, his horn-rimmed glasses still perched on his large nose, who not only confessed his intimate marital problems, but had given an elegant name to her hitherto anonymous "friends," who it seemed were to be addressed from now on as *tuurngait*.

Without ceasing to caress Berenice, Doctor Isaac Koenig, launched into a lecture. "It may disappoint you to learn that I am married, but I can tell by your belief in otherworldly companions, that you understand that spiritual journeys, such as ours, cannot be bound by monogamous convention." He insisted that he loved his wife passionately, a remarkable mate and not only mother of two wonderful children, but a PhD in English and a Masters in accounting. However, the infinite complexity of their lives as parents, authors, therapists, and teachers required such a thorough scheduling—his wife Cordelia was a remarkable scheduler and researcher and organizer—that his passion had been seeping away over the years. Tonight, it seemed, he had been seized by the spirit of youth and desire and exaltation and had achieved an orgasm that had been like a divine awakening.

Berenice had never heard anyone speak so eloquently about fucking. She was dazzled.

Doctor Koenig was not through. From the beginning of his marriage, he complained, his wife Cordelia had reduced their sex to just another compartment of daily activity, an accessory to the progress of their service to mankind. Cordelia was extremely progressive. The more Berenice heard about Doctor Koenig's wife, Cordelia, the more Berenice admired her. For the first time in her life, her moist limbs entangled with those of her companion, Berenice felt guilty about sleeping with a married man. It wasn't simply that Doctor Koenig was married, but that she, Berenice, had never done enough for mankind. When she considered the good causes that her lover's wife Cordelia had furthered—the doctor continued to enumerate them as he worked himself and Berenice into another bout of lovemaking—Berenice felt herself a sinful failure. But physically satisfied.

Failure though she was, Berenice continued to visit Doctor Koenig's office for physical and spiritual companionship. When her adopted parents died in a bush-plane accident, she became a therapeutic patient of Isaac's at a vastly reduced rate. Their sex continued, fueled by her enthusiasm for the Jungian theory that he sang out to her during her treatment. Their consuming sexual bouts were now accompanied not only by her alien consorts, but by his own archetypical familiars. In the sandboxes of his analytical office, great trysts and joyous amatory battles took place between her *tuurngait* and his dybbuks, culminating in their own coital climaxes, followed then by his long analytic discourses on her psyche and on his own psyche, which also had its problems.

Isaac's therapeutic treatments were often interrupted by the demands of his family and his many trips around the world to attend psychoanalytic conferences. He was becoming prominent in Jungian circles. During one of his long absences, Berenice bumped into Samuel Smithey on the waters of the bay, which seemed like just another stroke of destiny to her. They were each paddling earnestly in the early morning bay fog when their kayaks collided and both were thrown into the water. When each endeavored to save the other—they were both advanced Red Cross water-safety instructors—they ended up enfolded in one another's arms, laughing so hard that they swallowed a great deal of water. By the time they recovered and warmed up in Berenice's houseboat, they became lovers. Samuel's early routine kayaking exercise made it very convenient to carry on their love affair for some years, during which she gave up her liaison with Isaac Koenig. And then, on the Smithey 40th anniversary, Michelle announced that she was fed up with Samuel's incontinent behavior and opted out of their marriage. At last, after a lifetime of abandonment, Berenice found a permanent home in marriage to her lover, Samuel Smithey.

Unfortunately, nothing is permanent in this life—a prime lesson by Alan Watts, as well as one learned early in Berenice's Alaskan childhood. Now, Samuel was dying and Berenice felt abandoned once more. In her security of marriage to Samuel, she had lost touch with her spirits.

After several hours of raging sorrow in bed, Berenice sought out Isaac Koenig once again, hoping to find some consolation in the sexual union of her Alaskan spirits and Isaac's dybbuks. In the sandbox, to her consternation, a daunting set of short-skirted armed creatures in colorful Magyar costumes led by a black Venus stood between Berenice's spirits and Isaac's archetypes. Isaac confessed to Berenice that his professional duties and obligations made it mandatory that he cease having sex indiscriminately, although he could continue to treat her psyche and her new grief. It seemed that at a Jungian conference in Budapest, he and a female Hungarian colleague took a walk on a moonlight night along the Danube and the Magyar spirits rose from the moon's reflection on the waters and wafted through the mist into their vitals, at which moment he and his colleague plunged into one another on a grassy bank. Now he was on the verge of asking his wife Cordelia if she would join him and his colleague in a tri-body sexual congress.

Berenice responded to Isaac's lengthy confession by volunteering to join Isaac and his Hungarian colleague in a happy conjunction including Isaac's dybbuks, his new partner's Magyar Danubian water sprites, and Berenice's own *tuurngait*. Ruefully, Isaac confessed that his new Hungarian consort, Dorottya, demanded that she would share him only with Cordelia, who, it appeared, was Dorottya's dearest friend.

Unconsoled, and doubly abandoned, Berenice returned to her houseboat. There she found that Samuel's ex-wife Michelle had left for the evening. Samuel's son Matt welcomed her with concern. "I hope you're all right. When you left, I thought you might do something desperate."

"No, no," Berenice turned away. "I'm sorry. Please go home, I'll take care of him for the night."

Matt stared at her, as if trying to read where she had been and what she had been doing all this time. "You're sure you're up to it. Sean can stay."

"No, no." Berenice went to the fridge and took out a meat pie that one of her neighbors had brought over. She put it in the oven. "I'd prefer to be alone with him." She felt weighed down by her guilt at seeking sex in her grief. "I'll get some rest later. The nurse comes at eleven and stays until seven in the morning."

"I know that," said Matt approaching her.

Terrified that Matt might guess where she had been, Berenice hurried to Samuel's side and arranged his pillows. Matt continued to stare at her. "You look worse than before. What happened? Where did you go?

"Please go, I'll eat and make sure he's getting his fluids. Please." She knew she sounded weird, pleading, but she felt so unhappy that she couldn't control herself.

Annoyed, Matt left with his son. Instead of eating, Berenice lay down next to Samuel, who continued in his drugged sleep.

The nurse found Berenice fast asleep in the hospital bed next to the patient. Smoke seeped out of the oven where the pot pie had been cooking for hours. Furious, the nurse rattled about the kitchen.

Samuel came awake, discovering Berenice cuddled next to him and the nurse at the sink. "Good morning, dear Nursie," he called out cheerily.

"It's the middle of the night and your wife is a disgrace. She's a terrible housekeeper and shouldn't be left alone with you. The whole place could have burned up."

Samuel laughed and coughed out a jaunty reply, "Sorry, Nurse Ratched, women just can't keep away from me. Besides, it wouldn't have mattered much to me to die by flames."

"And your wife?"

Berenice woke up and jumped out of bed, jostling Samuel, who groaned out, "You wouldn't mind perishing with me, would you, Berenice, my love? It would only be proper. In India, the widows burn alongside their dead husbands."

"I don't know why I take jobs on the houseboats," growled the nurse. "You're all a bunch of loonies. Look at this mess. And India, too. I'm a fucking nurse, not a housemaid."

"Sorry, sorry," Berenice muttered, attempting to clean up the oven and the counter.

"Just go up to your own bed and leave me to my job," said the nurse, pushing her aside. "It's what you pay me for. And you, Mr. Smithey, go back to sleep."

"Come keep me company, dear Nursie." Samuel held back the covers.

"A lot of good you could do me in your state."

"But I'm your patient and need womanly care."

The nurse snorted and continued to scrub the pie pan.

Berenice kissed Samuel's forehead and went upstairs to bed, where she wept herself to sleep, feeling abandoned in life three times over—first by Samuel who was about to die and have his body cut up for science, now by Isaac, who seemed to be shackled in a tower by his Amazonian Hungarian Princess, and worst of all, by her demon protectors who seemed to have fled back north in confusion.

III

Berenice Smithey's visit so disturbed Isaac Koenig that he was unable to work on his current book. He set off on a walk along the Richardson Bay bike path. The high tide lapped against the rocks and mud bank, threatening to flow onto the crumbling asphalt. As Isaac danced along the margins of the path, the dark water's destructive force seemed appropriate to the emotional chaos of his life. Grieving widows, along with other damaged women, had been a mainstay of his practice. Inevitably, his therapy involved a transference on the part of his patient from the dead husband, a live abuser, or simply an indifferent partner, to Isaac as a healing reincarnation of their youthful dreams—a gentle, loving, understanding mate, able to repair life's injuries. The mantle of Carl Jung hung gracefully over Isaac's shoulders. It was a simple matter of lifting an arm to welcome the suffering maiden into his embrace. Under the Jungian mantle, bodies mingled beneath the benign forces of eternal archetypical gods. Unfortunately, a few days before Berenice's grieving visit, his assurance had been shaken by two soul-shattering events. The beginning of his affair with his Hungarian colleague Dorottya Kodaly, and the death of his wife's parents.

Isaac was prone to find every incident in his life significant, symbolic, universal. His love affair with Cordelia at the age of twenty-seven had been bound up in death, just as his current marital dilemma was entwined with the death of Cordelia's parents in a plane crash on the northernmost island of Japan. Berenice's need for his therapy and sexual comfort had all to do with death. Love and death had been the themes of Isaac Koenig's life. Although his attempts to harmonize the two sometimes resulted in a cacophony of discordant emotions, he managed to accept his practice as a continuing and improving process. Many of his clients recovered, many did not. He had learned early that life was a mixture of success and failure.

As a youth, Isaac had always felt that the early death of his mother had destined him to a fate of mediocrity. He had been only three years old; the sense of abandonment had never left him. Ruefully, he admitted that this chronic injury made him attractive to maternal women. His haughty father, a professor of law, had dismissed him from his attention the moment Isaac's mother died. Isaac still could not understand why his father blamed him for that death—at least, that was Isaac's judgment of his father's behavior.

An errant wave splashed over the path, wetting his trousers. He snarled at the wave, the bay, the night, his father, and at his predicament. Gritting his teeth, he marched resolutely on, ignoring the slap of his wet trouser legs against his flesh and the squish of his foot in his shoe. However, once launched on the symbiosis of past and present, his painful analysis continued. He admitted that there were extenuating circumstances involved in his father's treatment of him. He had not walked until he was four and had not learned to read properly until seven. His father always compared him to his precocious older brother, Gunther, who had walked at nine months and read at three and from the moment he entered school had been a brilliant student. Once Isaac had graduated from "special learning" classes, he had barely managed a B average through laborious study. His brother earned a PhD in law and became the youngest Appellate Court judge in Massachusetts. Only through arduous labor had Isaac managed to become a doctor and then a Jungian psychoanalyst, the choice of which specialty his father disapproved.

As he marched determinedly in the dark around the Mill Valley Middle School playground and the dog park bordering Richardson Bay, he groaned, unable to abandon the defeat of his childhood and youth. Both his father and brother looked down on Jungians as a somewhat inferior brand of medical mystics. When Isaac announced his intention to enter Boston's Jung Institute, his father observed, coolly, that he considered Jungians to be "romantic swindlers, trafficking on vacant universal symbols that could be made to mean almost anything to suit each occasion." Those words remained lurking in Isaac's mind tonight, some twenty-five years later. His father and brother were voracious readers and had studied literature as well as the law. They claimed that Jung's symbolism did not approach the true value of allegory and symbol as practiced by the Greeks and Romans, the great English Renaissance poets as well as the French and Russians in the late 19th and early 20th century, capped off by Joyce and Proust and Virginia Woolf.

It wasn't until the passionate prelude to his first sexual union with his future wife Cordelia that he disclosed to her the discovery of his childhood trauma. His eyes glowed and blood rushed to his face as he revealed the moment of his mother's death and his expulsion by his father. Tonight, as he anguished over the need to confess his new Hungarian alliance to Cordelia, their entire marriage leaped into his mind, from that first moment he told her about his father and his brother. He knew very well that the intensity of the revelation had been the binding moment of their relationship. He sighed once more, admitting how well he used his weakness and vulnerability to seduce.

It had been the middle of the morning, after Cordelia's final analytic session. At the end of the hour, Isaac declared she no longer needed therapy. His thesis had been accepted with honors, he had officially been declared a psychoanalyst by the Boston Jung Institute, and, according to him, Cordelia had been freed of her obsessive guilt for the death of her brother—freed, at least, he said shrugging his shoulders modestly, as much as one can be of early traumas. "Together, dear Cordelia, we have done our best against the Romans."

Cordelia's PhD thesis had been about Antony's and Cleopatra's confused gender identities, the battle between Roman austere manliness and Egyptian luxuriant femininity. At the same time, Cordelia had emphasized the contradictions in the lovers' personalities: Cleopatra's fearlessness, Antony's desperate anxieties and lust for Egyptian luxury and concupiscence that led to the defeat and death of each at the hands of Octavius. Over the course of Isaac's treatment of her, he identified Cordelia's parents as the Romans in her life, just as his father and his brother had been the Romans in his life.

"Therefore, we have both survived the judgment and punishment of the Romans." He invited her to celebrate their mutual graduations at his apartment.

The wind from the bay picked up and Isaac began to shiver as he methodically re-enacted that first seduction of the innocent Cordelia, hoping somehow to calm his fear of the coming confrontation with his increasingly skeptical wife.

Once in his apartment after that final analytic session, they sat together on his couch, drinking champagne. He turned to her, gazing into her eyes. "Dear, dear Cordelia, for more than two years you have revealed the most intimate details of your life. You have become…" He paused and breathed deeply, "become like a daughter, a sister, a wife." His eyes teared. "I feel that I owe you…owe you my own confession." He took up her hand in both of his. "Just as together we have managed to dredge up the details of those minutes when you and your brother took your final flights off Butternut Mountain in the Berkshires, so many years ago, so now I ask you to imagine that buried memory of a three-year-old child, me, still unable to walk, considered by his father to be backward, even defective in some way."

He dropped her hand, leaned forward, and gazed out the window. His voice quavered as he spoke. "I was only five months into my training analysis, when I uncovered the terrible moment. My mother was dying in the master bedroom. At her request the nurse picked me up and placed me in her arms. Suddenly my father strode into the room, snatched me and practically threw me out of the room, slamming the door behind me. Sobbing I crawled to my room, where I managed to haul myself onto the bed, pulling the covers over my head. I wasn't discovered there until the next day. I had wet the bed."

"Appalling," said Cordelia, laying a hand compassionately on his back.

"Not appalling, not appalling!" he exclaimed, turning toward her, his eyes glowing. "It was like discovering a vein of pure gold in a dark, impoverished mine, the devastated waste of years suffering an obscure guilt upon which, suddenly, a light illumined the source of the injury—my father's brutal rejection—not imagined, but in plain sight as if spot-lit on a stage.

"A week later, after Mother's funeral, I discovered the trash bag filled with her clothes that my father had gathered to throw away." Isaac turned again to the window, pausing. "Just imagine, Cordelia, that moment six months into my training analysis when

I stumbled into a fragment of that memory—the dark closet, my mother's aroma emanating from her silks and cottons stuffed willy-nilly into those plastic bags. I can't describe the tingling I felt all through my body at that moment in therapy. And then hour after hour, my training analyst and I reconstructed the memory—horrifying and at the same time deliciously satisfying—of my visits to that closet. It took my father many months to dispose of those trash bags. Before he did, that so-called backward child who still could only crawl, devised a way to retain the spirit, the sacred presence of the one person who loved him without condition. Taking care not to derange the bags, I selected items of clothing and hid them under the mattress of the twin bed in my room—a bed that was meant for playmates. Of course, I had no playmates. I never asked for any child to stay overnight."

He stopped then, breathing heavily, as if moved by the vision of his lonely childhood. Cordelia massaged his heaving back, her own breathing quickening in response. He burst into tears, turned and embraced her in gratitude for her solace. Knowing that he had not finished his confession, she prompted him to continue, which he was more than ready to do.

"Stealing the clothes was only the beginning. You have no idea how terrified a three-year-old thief can be—a child with a stern, morose father who is angry at him for no apparent reason. It took me days before I pulled one garment out from under the mattress. Thank god, we had a slatternly maid, who cleaned only those rooms my father inhabited, and my brother's room that my father visited often. I was so obviously neglected that she hardly bothered with my room. It took me six months before I was brave enough to pull out a blouse and a skirt and another six months, a slip and undies. Finally, by my fourth birthday, after I was certain that my father and brother had left the house for the day, I began to put on my mother's clothes and to murmur all those endearments I seemed to remember she had murmured to me. Of course, I was making it all up: I was my mother, I was me, and we loved one another."

Isaac began to sob now, uncontrollably. Cordelia, astonished and entranced at this account, took him in her arms and soothed him, murmuring endearments. He prompted her with memories he seemed to dredge up of his mother's loving words.

At this moment in his walk along the bay path, he stubbed his foot on a rock, causing him to plunge to his knees, tearing his right trouser leg, and scratching his right shin. He remained down for a moment, the waves lapping over one leg. The fearful thought that he had been avoiding now encompassed him. How would Cordelia take the news of his Hungarian adventure on the banks of the Danube? He shuddered and rose slowly pulling his left shoe out of the tidal mud. He was on his way back to his office now. More than once in the last few years, Cordelia had begun to question how he used his dramatic flair to shape events. Sweat streamed down his forehead as he recalled the sharp tone of her voice as she had warned him to cease his eloquent excuses, his analytic jargon to justify some lapse in judgment, a forgotten engagement, a late-night return to their house after one of his affairs. In fact, he had to admit that there had been an edge to her responses to almost everything he said recently, even during their love-making. "Just get on with it," she had rebuked him the night before he left for Budapest, when he told her at great length how much he would miss her embraces, her lips, her thighs, the curve of her breasts. "Just get on with it."

As he limped into his office, he tried to return to his first seduction of Cordelia, hoping somehow to reawaken her innocent belief in him. From that early moment of love, he had cast her as his mother figure, at the same time calling up an image of him wearing his mother's clothes, confusing their roles. "That childhood experience, emerged as the core of my analytic thesis: *death* and synchronicity, my mother's living presence in my body and soul."

He stood shivering and dripping in the middle of his dark office. He went to the bathroom and examined his throbbing shin. The blood seeped down into his sock. He cleaned the wound, dabbed iodine on it, bandaged it, and sat down on the toilet seat.

Feeling desperately sorry for himself, he dredged up the memory of his tragic childhood and passionate appeal to the young Cordelia, his former patient, wounded herself and entranced. Brokenly, amid sighs and sobs, he had described to Cordelia how, from the age of three to five, when the pain was too intense, he secretly put on his mother's underclothes and blouse and skirt, hugging himself, caressing himself, murmuring to himself, playing mother and child until he was calm.

"I thought it was my secret alone, but my brother Gunther knew. He took his time. I think he relished my secret. I still can hardly understand why Gunther, who had our father's complete trust and love and hope, should hate me so much. Of course, at that age, I thought he loved me. Brothers loved one another, that's what a child should believe, no? But Gunther hated me, at least what he did to me was hateful.

"One afternoon, he came home from school early and found me all decked out in Mothers undies, silk party dress, and high heels, hobbling around my room, cradling a bundle of towels as if it were her darling baby." Isaac paused to make sure the absurd image had full effect. Once more he saw the tears coursing down Cordelia's cheeks, her lips half open as she sighed sympathetically. "Gunther told me that he too missed our beautiful mother and that if he were younger, he might have tried to bring her back, just like me. He begged to let him take a movie of me with the new film equipment our father had bought him for his birthday. I was overjoyed that he had approved, sympathized, admired anything I did, especially my grief and sorrow for our mother. I took the performance seriously, posing and explaining just how much I missed being loved."

At this point in his narrative, he began caressing Cordelia again. She responded passionately, lavishing all that lost mother-love upon him. They made love. Once they had exhausted their desire, to her surprise, he went on with his story as if there had been no pause.

"That very night, Gunther showed the film to our father. Appalled, our father punished me severely with his belt across my bare bottom. While I was still sobbing, he made me gather up all my mother's stolen clothing and burn it, item by item, in a metal barrel in the backyard. I can still smell that scented burning cloth in my dreams.

"From that moment on, my father was convinced that I not only lacked intelligence and motor control, but even a basic moral integrity. I have never ceased trying to justify myself to my father. The image of me on that film at the age of five, prancing about enveloped in Mother's silk dress, her pearls looped around my neck, balancing on her high heels, remains burnt in my memory, along with a rage at my brother's betrayal and Father's brutal lack of compassion."

After his desperate walk along the shore of Richardson Bay, Isaac had to dredge up every ounce of compassion for his benighted childhood so that he would have the courage to tell his wife, suffering from the probable loss of her parents, that she now had to share him with her close friend Dorottya.

IV

Monty sat in the main floor lobby of the Mt. Zion hospital during his wife's radiation in the basement. This was the third week of the treatment that would last for four more weeks. The drive over the bridge to the city three times a week had become the landscape of Talia's illness. It seemed to him that once the diagnosis and treatment had become established, he had crossed into another country ruled by medical authorities: a country made up of strangely distorted bits and pieces of once familiar reddish-orange towers of the bridge; the Pacific Ocean sweeping westward to the horizon; the tree-lined streets and steep hills of the city with its freshly painted houses; and finally the latticed-windowed gray medical offices, the sidewalks, parking meters, and street signs, all of which led to the small circular drive and the façade of the hospital. The automatic entrance doors opened to a three-story lobby with a service desk, numerous side-wells, and an assortment of padded chairs and sofas for the relatives and caregivers waiting for the patients to emerge from their diagnosis or treatment. Potted palms and ficus relieved the hard gleam of the chrome, marble, and polished wood of the modernized lobby décor.

Talia had waited until after the lumpectomy to tell their children about the cancer. She wanted to be able to report clear margins and minimal treatments so they would be spared the expense and time of flying home. Their daughter, Louisa, a public defender, lived in Boston with her husband, a musician, and two teenage sons. Monty's son by his first marriage, Jonathan, a pediatrician in Bethesda, had just remarried after a rocky affair with an alcoholic, whom he had heroically attempted to cure. He was in the process of adopting his second wife's two small children. Talia argued that neither Louisa nor Jonathan could afford the time or expense of flying home for what she considered a minor medical event. Monty felt they should have informed their children sooner, but he always allowed Talia to prevail in her own matters. Jonathan, who had lost his mother at birth and, never quite sure of his place in life, was relieved not to have been informed. He loved Talia, who had brought him up, but he found it difficult to face the pain suffered by those close to him. Louisa, a capable, strong-willed woman, was angry to have been deprived of the decision to come home for the operation. Of course, she might not have come, but she felt they should have respected her enough to let her know. Louisa's fiercely guarded principles had astonished Monty ever since her early childhood. She had always seemed to know her "rights."

At the hospital, Monty always chose the well facing the bank of elevators. Today he wrote on a legal pad, attempting to draft the *New York Times* obituary that would satisfy his friend Samuel, his friend's current wife, his former wife, and his son without costing an extravagant amount. From time to time, he glanced up to observe the parade of medical disasters enter and leave the elevators, each a representative of some modern attack on the human organism that hundreds of specialists in offices above and below were attempting to diagnose and treat. The patients came with canes and walkers, splints and bandages, bent in body and spirit. Helpers and relatives, in all the skin colors of the world, wearing a hodge-podge rainbow of costumes, aided the sufferers along. The hospital's patients, regardless of wealth or class, shared one possession: a body in distressful need of aid. Each time he looked up, the occupants of the chairs around him had changed as the relatives and friends, many attending children, parted from their sick charges and greeted them after their visits to doctors and therapists.

And here Monty sat, just another waiting relative, still able to walk upright, breathe deeply, and write clearly, composing death sentences on his good friend, Samuel, whose athletic body during a long life had consumed at least half his energy and interest, either in sport or in sexual exploration, while his exceptional mind had attempted to wield words into song that plumbed the joys and sorrows, the triumphs and defeats of human life. As usual with human beings, that was not the whole story. A writer's job, thought Monty wryly, is to edit, or, perhaps, to censor the tale, not to mention the limiting factor of "cost" to the two prospective widows—if an ex-wife could be called a widow. Michelle had agreed to split the cost of the obituary with Berenice. Monty labored sentence by sentence, excising, interpolating, replacing excisions, and seeking proper qualifiers—neither too excessive nor too modest. Ironically, Samuel, still alive, was directing his own epitaph by Monty aided by a somewhat dissonant chorus of his bereaved.

As he labored, entering his friend's life and character on the page, Monty felt a hand gently clasping his shoulder. Startled, he reared up to defend himself. The hand firmly pushed him back in the seat.

"I'm sorry, dear Monty. I didn't mean to shock you. It's Brooks Gardner, one of Talia's clients. I've brought you pea soup and tuna for your dinner."

Brooks stood beside his chair, handing out a linen bag toward him, a look of deep compassion on her somewhat bloated but still beautiful face. Monty shuddered at this intrusion. He was not fond of this woman who had adopted Talia several years ago—as if Talia needed her patronage. She was from a very wealthy, very old family on the East Coast, had gone to Bryn Mawr, and seemed to know a great many artists and writers—at least that was how she presented herself. By the time she discovered Talia, alcohol had taken its toll on her beauty, and a hard life had dissipated her fortune. But she remained quite handsome and maintained the commanding presence of someone who had once been very beautiful and rich. She had immediately recognized the originality of Talia's design and the work Talia featured in her shop. In fact, she had been very helpful, fostering Talia's creations to the wide range of her friends. But the way she treated Talia as her discovery, her pet, annoyed Monty. Talia found it amusing. In fact, Talia felt sorry for Brooks, who had made so little of what life had given her so that she was reduced to siphoning whatever she could off the people she cultivated. Talia had a hidden talent for taking care of the needs of everyone around her and allowing them the credit.

Monty hefted the bag of food from hand to hand. It was quite heavy—enough, it seemed, for a week of meals. "You really shouldn't have, Brooks. We aren't big eaters, you know."

"I know this is a difficult time for the two of you." The deep whiskeyed and tobaccoed voice almost purred. "A bit of food is little enough. I'm available, night and day, to help."

"We're managing just fine."

"I just want Talia to feel no burdens. State of mind is essential for recovery." Brooks sighed. "You never know with this sort of thing."

The look on Brooks' face was so full of care that Monty suspected she already had sent Talia to her grave. "Thank you, dear Brooks, Talia will be delighted with pea soup and tuna."

Brooks nodded significantly at the legal pad on which Monty had been writing. "Berenice tells me that you are doing up dear Samuel's obituary. When it comes to cancer, it takes the best of us. Samuel was such a beautiful man, such an athlete, and a great intelligence; Talia is so beautiful and kind and such a great designer."

"Talia has not been taken yet."

"Oh no, I didn't mean…I'm sure she will recover. And I brought the food just to help."

"I'd better get back to work on this. There's no need for you to wait. Talia could be another hour or so and she'll be exhausted when she's through with the radiation."

"Of course, of course. I'm leaving. Give her a hug from me. I'm on the way to an important meeting with your friend, Ted Journey. You introduced us and I'm helping him fatten up his list of writers. His Tamalpais Press is going to make waves in the publishing world." Brooks saluted and walked swiftly away. Monty grimaced, thinking that Ted Journey and Brooks deserved one another. He had known they would get along famously.

* * *

Monty had met Ted Journey before the real estate developer founded Tamalpais Press. A friend from an early writer's workshop that Monty had attended introduced Journey as a "rich guy, who loves books and France. Except for the rich part, you two have a lot in common." Journey, who had recently moved to Mill Valley, took the initiative, making a date for coffee, during which the two did indeed talk about literature and about Paris, where both had spent some time. Mostly Journey talked: about his future plans to create a high caliber literary press and about his life. Monty listened.

The cultivated businessman intrigued Monty. He was tall and carried himself with a nonchalant ease that displayed more self-satisfaction than grace. When Monty complimented him on his tweed jacket, he thanked him, tossing off the remark that it should look good, considering what he had paid his Saville Road tailor. "Look Monty," he continued, "I know I've been lucky, which is why I want to share my good fortune." He went on to explain his luck. He had grown up wealthy on the Connecticut shore, gone to Choate and Princeton, and always had that cushion of birth and inheritance to ward off any uneasiness about the future. He spoke so openly about his personal life on this first meeting that Monty got the impression that Journey thought of himself as some sort of nobleman undressing in front of a servant.

After a while, Journey seemed to become aware that Monty had hardly spoken at all. He interrupted his autobiography by saying, "Oh, I read two of your stories in *Abalone*. Pretty good I thought, for ethnic tales."

Monty flinched. The stories were about Monty's Jewish childhood and family. Before Monty could challenge this denigrating remark, Journey continued, "I am interested, however, in the other *Abalone* writers, whom, I would guess you know. Writers whose work might be appropriate for the kind of literary press that I'm about to establish."

"There are some very good writers in the magazine, who have also published in *The New Yorker* and *Partisan* and *The Atlantic*."

"Friends of yours?"

"Some of them. They don't work for free."

"Money isn't a problem. I'll pay advances. I'd like to meet the better writers."

Monty appreciated Journey's candor. Journey wasn't looking for a friend, and he wasn't someone Monty wanted for a friend. For Journey, this was a business meeting and Monty was simply a local literary database. This cold transaction intrigued Monty. If he had thought Journey might eventually publish him, he probably would have found the meeting nerve-wracking. But Journey was obviously not interested in Monty's "ethnic tales." Monty guarded his own writing carefully. His literary ambition was a frail treasure too easily manhandled and shattered; he had written novels. Early on, the books had received a bit of interest, encouragement even, along with rejections. He had ceased sending them out but continued writing.

He was only too happy to recommend writers he admired and promised to introduce Journey. He found Journey interesting as a type: an entitled man, born to wealth, and of immense ambition, who judged most others as not quite worthy, especially if their ethnic identification happened to be Jewish. They began to talk about books. Every author Journey mentioned had been praised in the *New York Review of Books*, the *London Review of Books*, or *The New Yorker*. If Journey took exception to an author, he or she had received praise in the Sunday *New York Times Book Review*, a mark of middle-brow taste.

As for their shared experience in France, Journey showed no curiosity about Monty's. Of course, Monty made little effort to display himself. When Journey asked, casually, about Monty's travels, Monty made light of his French experience; he had taken his junior year at Michigan in Paris and then a year during his graduate study at UC Berkeley, studying existentialism and French literature as part of his major interest in philosophy and literature. "Although my French was perfectly accurate, I never mastered the song of the language, the rhythm and pitch. I'd ask for *beurre* and the waiter would look at me thinking, *Il parle comme une vache espagnole* and slap down a baguette. I loved walking the streets."

Monty was ready to discuss Camus, or Sartre, or Simone de Beauvoir or *La Revue des Deux Mondes*, which he still read, but

Journey merely nodded and launched into a narration of his own experience. He had gone to Paris after college, intent upon becoming a writer. In two years, he had written ten stories and three novels, while living a Bohemian life on the left bank. He had met many of the French celebrities, whom he named as personal friends, but he felt the French were narrowly in love with their own culture. As for his own writing, he discovered that he would never achieve the literary fame he admired most.

"Frankly, I found Paris disappointing. It wasn't the Paris of the twenties with Gertrude Stein, Hemingway, Fitzgerald, Picasso, Les Deux Magots, or the crowd that inhabited the Left Bank. I discovered that the French were overwhelmingly materialistic. I had gone there in search of high culture. They preferred to talk about *refrigerateurs, supermarchés,* and *chauffage centrale.* Frankly, I wasn't inspired.

"I wasn't interested in becoming just an ordinary writer," he said, pausing significantly. Monty felt that he had cut short the phrase "an ordinary writer like you." He continued, "I went home with the plan to leverage family money into my own fortune. California was the obvious locale and real estate the obvious industry. So now I've made my fortune and have decided to return to literature, but this time, in the driver's seat. I will pick and choose, and perhaps you can assist me in the interest of getting writers published, the truly good ones you know and admire. Authentic writers." Once again there was the missing phrase, "But not you."

When Talia asked Monty to describe Journey, he said that he was a cold, somewhat unhappy man, disappointed in his own mediocre talent, but convinced of his own good taste, and profoundly suspicious that the taste of others was somewhat inferior.

"Are you going to see him again?"

"He wants to use me for my connections."

"But not for your writing?"

"He made that clear."

"I'm sure you didn't flog your novels very vigorously."

"What's the point? He rather liked my stories for their 'ethnic' flavor, which he declared wrinkling his long straight nose as if he could smell the gefilte fish in my work."

Talia sighed and ran her hand over his cheek. "Drawers full of wonderful novels and I can never get you to peek out from under the bushel basket, can I?"

"It's comfortable in the shade."

"So what's the point of meeting someone you dislike again."

"He's like a character in one of those French novels. The surprise is how he invents new ways of accomplishing the impossible. Besides, I can help my talented friends as I watch a successful businessman trying to make literature pay."

One morning he and Journey were having coffee outside at the Trieste on Bridgeway when Brooks walked by. "Monty, why aren't you home creating great works?" She stood in front of their table, eyeing Journey as if she were a bird of prey.

Wearily, Monty introduced her and said, "Ted and I were just discussing business." He hoped she would take the hint.

"Journey...Journey..." Brooks purred out the name. "Were you at Choate in the fifties? My late husband's cousin, Alec Gardner, Isabella's grandnephew, was there, on the crew."

"As a matter of fact, I knew Alec quite well."

Monty saw a look of self-satisfied recognition pass between them, like members of a tribe that had been dispersed by time, but still know the most intimate details of one another's early life. There was a difference, however. Brooks' beamed eagerly; Journey's lips barely parted in a wary smile, and yet he invited her to join them. Soon it was established that Brooks lived with Millard Wile, a writer published in *The New Yorker*, who was also on the board of *Abalone*. Journey did not hesitate to fill her in on his publishing plans, nor did she hesitate to promise him her aid in helping to fill in his roster—starting with her lover.

Monty sat back smiling happily: Brooks and Journey, it was a match between leverage experts. They both came from wealthy eastern seaboard families and were educated at privileged institutions. In their youth, they had literary ambitions. They had both gone to Paris and cultivated celebrities.

"When I returned, I went into real estate," said Journey, "and then began buying art."

"And I came back to open an art gallery, which was where I met my former husband, a descendant from Isabella Gardner's adopted nephew."

"The Isabella Gardner of the museum?" asked Journey, his eyes eager.

"The same. My husband..."

"Raoul Gardner, the figurative artist? I have an interesting piece by him."

"The same. I'm glad you're one of the few who still values him. I now work part time with my dear friend, Yvonne Latelier, the agent."

"What a coincidence. I've heard a great deal about her for years from several of my dealers. I've been meaning to contact her."

"She's no longer agenting, but I've been helping her scout out the possibility of a gallery. She knows many of the fine local artists. Would you like to meet her?"

"Of course."

Before Brooks left the table, they made a date when she would introduce him to Yvonne.

When they were alone, Journey smiled almost affectionately at

Monty. "I knew you would be of great help."

"I think Brooks will be even greater help: art, authors, doctors, whatever. She does that sort of thing."

"You're not fond of her?"

"She's a friend of my wife, as is Yvonne."

"Is your wife an artist?"

"A designer. She has a paper shop on Caledonia, but she does specialty clothes for a few clients—Yvonne Latelier, for one, who admires her remarkable design."

"I don't know about women's clothes, except to admire them, but I am going to need stationery and business cards."

"We welcome business."

"About Brooks. She looks like she's been around the block."

"We've all been around the block, Ted." Monty was not about to gossip about Brooks. He had already said too much and she had been helpful to Talia.

Monty took out his credit card to pay for the coffee. He was willing to pay for the unraveling of future developments between Journey and Brooks. Journey waved his hand gracefully dismissing the card. "I've already taken care of it."

Monty did not argue.

Within a year, Journey married Yvonne Latelier, financed her new gallery, and started The Tamalpais Press. Brooks took credit for it all. But that was all in the future.

V

Brooks left Monty in the hospital lobby, on her way to meet Ted Journey and set him off on his literary and perhaps his marital journey. Relieved, Monty tried to return to the obituary for Samuel Smithey. He lay down the pen, shaking his head. The threat of his wife's illness welled up. In fact, the cancer had dominated his thoughts ever since the lump first appeared on her left breast. Although she had been diagnosed with Stage Two breast cancer, the size of the growth was almost at the limit of five centimeters, which would put it into Stage Three. Monty had learned that statistics played a large part in medical science. The oncologist did not label the cancer aggressive, yet it could become so in a moment. Luckily, the lymph node ducts had not yet been affected. The surgery had been successful, leaving a clear margin around the excised lump. Talia was downstairs in the building undergoing radiation as a follow-up, hopefully ensuring a complete recovery without recurrence. But there was no assurance of total success; she would not be considered out of danger, statistically, for five years. Only then free, perhaps.

To his dismay, Brooks reappeared, looking even more dismal. She spoke breathlessly, "Are you going to the Nursery School reunion tonight?"

"Yes, I think so."

"Well, dear Monty, if you see Sylvia Ellenberg there, please treat her gently. She's been under great strain since the split with her daughter. The marriage was difficult enough, but now that she's joined the Special Forces and has been posted to Afghanistan, anyone would be upset. That's all I can say. I promise I won't bother you again." She waved her hand to forestall any response and trotted away.

Monty sighed. Brooks carried about her a dark cloud that cast its shade on everyone she approached. She was always the first to announce bad news, the servant of misfortune. The heavy bag of food felt like a warning of a dire outcome to Talia's treatment. He wondered what threat poor Ted Journey and his press was facing to deserve a visit from the mistress of misfortune.

My dilemma, thought Monty, was not singular. From birth on, death was a culminating reality; it could happen at any time through accident, disease, or disaster. Talia's life illustrated life's accidents. Her father had been born into a prosperous fishing family in Belize. Her mother, an American artist, had vacationed there. Her father had captained a snorkeling expedition her mother took along the barrier reefs. Their love blossomed on the water. Her father followed her mother to the Bay Area, where they married. He took a position at the Point Richmond Yacht Club as an all-purpose boat repairman, keeper of the docks, safety supervisor, and rescue boat operator. When Talia was three, her mother died in a freak auto accident, when a trailer truck jackknifed over the barrier of a freeway. Talia grew up as a favorite of the yacht families. She went through college and design school on scholarships and fellowships, working in restaurants, along with help from her father and the families of his employers. Just before meeting Monty, her father died attempting to salvage two boats that had slipped their mooring during a storm. The mast of one of the boats fell, knocking him into the water, where he was crushed between the boats. The insurance from her father's death, helped in the down payment for their Sausalito house and for Talia's Sausalito shop on Caledonia Street.

If one lived long enough, thought Monty, death would certainly appear, with unforeseen consequences. His first wife, Emma, had died giving birth to their son, Jonathan. Apparently, she was suffering from a never-diagnosed congenital heart defect; the birth trauma had triggered a massive heart attack at the moment of what was generally felt to be one of life's crowning moments. At a group grief therapy session, he met Talia, who was mourning her father's death. They both lived in rentals in Berkeley. Talia took an interest in his baby son, Jonathan. She sat for Monty when he had meetings or had to travel. Within a year they became lovers. When she became pregnant with Louisa, they married and bought the house in Sausalito, where they had lived for fifty years. Their lives had been united by death. Now, at seventy-five, he was definitely on the downslope toward that culmination to all lives. Talia was ten years younger; he had never expected her to be in danger. The lump had been a sudden and immediate warning sign, as if the enemy army had breached the border. The successful operation and radiation had been vigorous defensive actions, repelling the deadly forces. Now one waited, fearing a second invasion. One never knew what swam through the bloodstream and the tissues of the body, or what defenses the body could martial. As he sat in the lobby imagining the worst, he wrote his friend Samuel's obituary, leaving out his infidelity, his bad jokes, and his inherited racism. Samuel was a loving family man, an impressive intelligence, a talented poet, an inspiring teacher, and an affectionate friend. He deserved a significant tribute to mark his death. Monty smiled as he plied his craft.

He was very good at discovering virtues and crediting them; he had to admit, he gave praise with subtle grace. In this, he was willing to give himself credit.

At the back of his mind still lurked that lump in Talia's left breast. It had appeared out of nowhere—at least that was how it seemed, like a suicide bomber without cause in a peaceful market full of life's delicacies. He had known his wife's body since their first romantic exploration of the north coast. It had taken him more than a year to ask her out. He was surprised that she was more than willing and found a friend to baby-sit Jonathan. They drove north along the coast from Berkeley to The Little River Inn, just short of Mendocino. It had been a long weekend in the spring—a weekend of discovery, not only of wildflowers on the bluffs and birds on the beach, but of one another's mind and body in a rustic cabin behind the old-fashioned inn. They made love and hiked on a trail through a forest of redwoods, with fern-banked streams—a trail climaxing in a waterfall, up the sides of which hopped a water ouzel singing the joy Monty felt at his discovery of a new love. Talia and he meandered along a beach enclosed by sandstone cliffs and perched on driftwood logs to watch willets, curlews, dunlins, and marbled godwits feed on the sea's leavings. His late wife, Emma, had been too impatient to perch on beach logs and watch birds. His heart leaped with Talia's delighted laughter at the birds' comically dainty skittering steps, their abrupt pauses to dip their beaks, and their swift resumption in pursuit of the delicacies left by the waves' edges in and out along the shore. They both exclaimed in wonder at the flowing flight of sandpiper and plover flocks, abruptly displaying their white bellies and then dark backs and wings as they swerved and banked and suddenly returned to land in a mass of small plump bodies encased by folded wings, as nondescript as stones on the beach.

From that weekend on, Talia's mind and body, her joyful wonder at the world had taken him into a new world. He had left the anxious landscape of his youth, the turbulent battle of his former marriage; he had abandoned grief on a voyage of discovery, debarking on a continent of contentment. He had loved his first wife, but she had viewed him and life with a critical eye, weighing doubtfully what each of them brought to the marriage, wondering whether he had brought enough to justify her pregnancy. Emma too had been a writer and wasn't certain that she should bind her life in marriage to someone she considered not as ambitious, not as tough-minded, nor as talented as she—until the fatal pregnancy. The responsibility for the pregnancy was never clear. Had she deliberately forgotten to take the pill, or had his demands been so passionate that the error occurred? Of course, there would have been no pregnancy without him. And he was always too willing to take blame, for whatever. Monty had vowed to devote himself to Emma's work more than to his own. Reluctantly, Emma had accepted him in marriage, only, she said, because he could dance so well. She told him quite frankly when he proposed that she did not admire his writing. They had married. He never had the opportunity to prove his faith or his talent.

Only after he met Talia did he discover the possibility of a truly shared love. Talia accepted him; she accepted life; she accepted whatever happened—even the lump that had turned out to be malignant. Over the years, they had returned often to that blessed site of their romance on the Mendocino coast that, like their marriage, had never lost its glow of joyful discovery.

He sat in the lobby of the hospital, unable to fend off his fear for the health and life of the beautiful woman he loved, the woman who believed in him as well as in herself. To divert his thoughts, he conjured up that Mendocino landscape, but all that came to his mind's eye was Brooks Gardner's shadow and the Little River Cemetery on the bluff over the ocean facing the Inn, with its leaning gravestones marking 19th and early 20th-century deaths, the worn engravings of angels and cherubs and the eroded, barely readable, antique lettering that described blessed souls ascending to heavenly peace. He wondered whether Emma would have ever found peace in this life or the next. Strange, he thought, that he should be conjuring up Emma so many years later, as he waited in unnerving doubt about the future of his second marriage. But, of course, Emma had never left him. As he said so often in his memorial talks: the dead remain with us as long as we remain.

At this moment, Talia appeared from the elevators, like a happy exotic sprite among the somber cancer patients streaming toward the exit, their shoulders hunched, their eyes downcast. Marveling at her slim body springing toward him, he thought she could have been dancing in the joyous ballet to the music of Bizet's Symphony in C. She was wearing one of her own creations, a tight-fitting, turquoise pantsuit, with a lavender cape. It was her face, though, that arrested everyone's attention: a narrow oval, with sharp chiseled features. He thought of her as a survival of the lost Toltec nation that had thrived in Mexico before the Aztecs. She always carried her head at a slight angle like an exotic bird, so that she seemed to be peering curiously sideways, with wonder, at the peripheral world through which she danced. When people passed her, they smiled as they might have at an unexpected natural wonder.

He rose to greet her. Settling into his arms, she exclaimed, "You should have seen what Doctor Wentworth was wearing today under her smock—a Balenciaga fringed skirt with a fluid Vareuse top with floral high heels! And those copper earrings with moonstones from an Afghan shop in Oakland. She could have been going to an opening at the opera, but, in fact, she was hurrying to get back to her poor, sick, sad husband stuck in their Napa cottage." Talia's charming curiosity inspired such confidences that only after a few visits, her oncologist and the radiation technologists all became warmly attached to her and spoke freely to her about their private lives. "The radiology assistant wants me to design his business cards and a web site when he retires next month. He and his wife are going into an electronic repair business on the Peninsula. I promised to do their daughter's bridesmaid dresses."

"For next to nothing," said Monty, kissing her on each cheek.

"Next to," she laughed, "but more than nothing," she kissed him on the lips and did a little curtsy.

Talia designed and sewed her own clothes, as well as her clients'. She explained to Monty that her oncologist dressed so beautifully in order to animate a life she and her husband found so dismal—his chronic illness, the medical bureaucracy, her work with the deadly growths that threatened the lives of her patients. "She dresses for herself and for her patients—especially the women. Her husband, it seems, doesn't notice. I fear she wonders why she married him."

And Monty wondered joyfully that Talia had married him.

VI

Prior to attending the 75th Anniversary of the Nursery School, three couples ate dinner at a restaurant located at the foot of Harbor Drive, near the berths of sailing vessels and houseboats. Monty sat next to Sylvia Ellenberg, whose mental health Brooks Gardner had warned him about at the hospital in the city. Sylvia was the mother of their daughter's best friend from nursery school until the eighth grade. In high school, the girls had drifted apart and hadn't seen one another for many years. Monty and Talia had remained close to Sylvia and her husband, Rob, a gruff but sentimental man. Sylvia loved design and admired Talia's work. She knew all the best bargains in the Bay Area; she and Talia loved to shop together—they had the same taste and would only buy "on sale." Lately Talia, too, had been worrying about Sylvia, who was a woman of great enthusiasms and deep depressions. She had been diagnosed "bi-polar," and was under intermittent treatment, which she resisted. Immensely sensitive to the dangers of life, she had been devastated when her daughter married a right-wing fanatic, enlisted in the army, and joined the Special Forces.

The Nursery School, a cooperative, had been the Wolfes' introduction to most of their local acquaintances. Talia and Monty worked with the other parents repairing the facilities, catering events, and providing teacher assistance on a weekly basis. In a curious way, Monty considered their town friends, mostly parents of their children's schoolmates, in a different category from their friends from the past and those with whom they had worked. The division, he had decided, consisted of how little of their inner lives he and Talia shared with their local friends, who viewed the world from vastly different perspectives. It seemed to Monty almost as if the locals had the status of distant cousins to whom one was polite and friendly, somewhat affectionate, but nothing more. And yet, now and then accidents occurred and one was forced to plunge more deeply into the attachments. The Smitheys and the Ellenbergs were such exceptions.

On the night of the reunion, Monty noticed that Sylvia was paying no attention to the lively reminiscences of the others at the table about the "old days" at the Nursery School and the gossip about all the divorces and remarriages. He was struck by the ghostly pallor of Sylvia's face. It seemed as if the skin had died. The hollows under the cheekbones had deepened. She stared at the food on her plate as if it were sending her painful messages. Monty reached out and patted her hand that was clenched on the table beside her plate. She looked up startled and when she realized it was Monty, a wan smile appeared momentarily, and then faded.

Sylvia leaned toward him, speaking privately in a low, halting voice.

"You and Talia have always been Cassie's favorites and mine. I can't bear to think of that beautiful young woman in a uniform shooting people halfway around the world, and I'll never know why she married that cold-blooded monster. I'm sure she joined just to get away from him. I tried to stop her and only drove her away from me. And we were so close." She paused to take a couple of deep breaths, as if she hadn't been breathing before. "For Christ's sake, she's only thirty and smart as a whip. She could have been anything—lawyer, doctor, author, she had all the talents. And now she's in Afghanistan on special missions. I can't sleep at night."

Monty pressed Sylvia's hand, but said nothing.

She went on. "It feels as if one of my limbs had been chopped off and was still suffering agony."

"I know, I know," he said. Sylvia covered his hand with her other hand and smiled, sadly. "You understand, Monty, I know. You always do. Rob tries, but...Rob is Rob."

Monty laughed. Rob, her husband, found it difficult to express the love and the compassion he felt. "I do know Rob. He feels deeply, but..." Monty shrugged. Sylvia smiled.

"He claims I'm depressed, as usual, but who wouldn't be depressed. Pills or therapy is not going to bring her back."

Monty searched for a response. "People don't understand that depression is pain, physical pain! Unbearable, like you're being tortured. I've been depressed like that. We should talk. Can I come over tomorrow?"

Sylvia's smile faded again. Monty could see that she didn't believe she could be helped by any amount of his understanding. This marvelously joyous woman, who took such pleasure in the flowering hillsides of the mountain and the incredible sales of "Black Friday" after Thanksgiving, had given up hope for any future happiness now that she had lost her daughter—an accident that she had feared and awaited. Monty was determined to visit her the next day and try to talk her through her suffering, even though he doubted his ability. He often suspected his attempts at caretaking were more for himself than for those he tried to help. Her depression had reawakened his own lurking despair.

They all left the dinner intending to attend the reunion. Monty was alarmed to see that Sylvia and Rob never arrived. The next morning, he called Sylvia, but there was no answer. All through the day, he called when his work permitted. Finally, at four in the afternoon, the phone was answered by Brooks Gardner, who informed him in a mournful voice that Sylvia had been hurrying across Bridgeway in the middle of the block and had been hit by a bus. She died in the hospital. "The family wishes to be undisturbed," said Brooks. "I know it was an accident, but," she paused to give emphasis, "but, I told you she was in bad shape. I'm here to help Rob and their kids cope. I'll let you know when you can talk to Rob. He'll need you, I know."

Monty could not forgive himself for neglecting to go to Sylvia's house that morning when she didn't answer his first call. Whether the accident had been the result of carelessness or not, he might have been able to help. And Brooks had arrived at the site of the doom she always seemed to project.

Two weeks later, Talia came home from her shop to find Monty in the living room staring out the window at the darkening bay, low clouds blanketing the tops of the city's buildings.

"Are you all right?" she asked, stroking his forehead. "You seem a little down."

"Oh, Cassie flew back from Afghanistan. She and Rob want me to speak at Sylvia's memorial."

"I guess that's your profession, along with your secret novels."

"The only way I'd make a living out of either of them is to write 'how to' books."

"Oh, my dear Monty, you'll never show your true work to anyone." Talia kissed him and went into the kitchen to prepare supper.

The Ellenberg request troubled Monty. He did not know why he should be chosen to speak for the dead. He had already done a eulogy of sorts for his mother, and his oldest brother. He hadn't requested the honors—they simply had been requested, like Smithey's obituary, and now the Ellenberg speech. Monty had never yearned to be an actor, politician, cleric, or a public speaker of any sort. He was a writer. And yet, when standing in front of an audience, he was able to project himself, his seriousness and his humor, without anxiety. It was a little like dancing. He had never learned to dance; he just picked it up, with his mother's help, and managed to stay in rhythm with the music, leading his partner with confidence. From the beginning of their courtship, he and Talia danced together with such ease that they both had the feeling that their bodies had been made to fit together. With Emma it had been a different dance, more complicated, but still very much together.

Perhaps, he thought, as he began to deliberate what to say about Sylvia, his talent was simply being aware of another human being. No, it was more. His father's early death had been his first lesson. Over the years, he had learned to dance with death. In the novels he wrote, it was a matter of getting to know the characters, being aware of them as separate human beings until they spoke to him. Essential, though, was his knowledge that they too, easily enough, could die on the next page. So here he was with Sylvia as he had known her. She loved her daughter; she loved her house; she loved her garden; she loved to read, to hike, to shop. She was a romantic. How did she feel about her irascible husband, Rob? He often exasperated her, but he did many things to please her. He built her a garden window for her kitchen—exactly the garden window she coveted. He took her and Cassie to gorgeous wildernesses and made them comfortable with campfires and tents and the proper gear for hiking or diving for abalone or picking berries. He did his best to treat her wild mood swings. He had been heroic, in fact, changing meds and doctors again and again, hoping to settle her into some comfortable level with which the family could feel at peace. But every slow movement of her moods was often followed by a frenetic scherzo that had everyone grinding teeth and poor dear Sylvia a nervous wreck.

Monty sat staring out at the bay, lost in the mystery of Sylvia's character and her final desperate dash across the street. Sylvia understood it all so well and yet could not find a home, a resting place in the world. When Monty imagined the deaths to which he had been summoned to sing finale, it almost seemed as if Death were a random serial murderer.

Gazing out at the bay, lit by the fading rays of the setting sun that streamed through the Golden Gate, he thought of the glorious dinners Sylvia cooked for her guests.

The memorial took place in the Sausalito Episcopal Church, a small structure of dark brown shingle, with stained glass windows on the side walls and a gold cross on the peak of the roof. "Too picturesque," thought Monty as he mounted the brick steps to the high wooden doors, clad in wrought-iron bindings. It was the sort of structure a child might draw if asked to picture a village church.

The minister, Jim Craig, stood by the door, his white robe cinched with a braided rope. Monty, raised as a Jew, had abandoned all observance early in his life. Now, in his drafted role as eulogy speaker for the village dead, he found himself an integral part of all sorts of services. Craig, a tall, rosy-cheeked, fair young man in his thirties, looked like he had stepped out of an English Public School into the ministry. He welcomed Monty familiarly with a firm handshake, a clasp across the shoulder, and an understanding smile as if to include him in this pleasant Episcopalian ministry of death. Craig kept brushing his tousled blond hair off his forehead as he warmly greeted Talia and the mourners who arrived. Monty left Talia outside and entered. The interior of the church was narrow and dark, the window-light, colored by the stained glass, in shades of violet, pinks, mauve, and bluish gray, rested on the wood walls and benches like erratic faint brush strokes of a mild palette. The first two rows were ribboned off for family. Monty walked tentatively forward and sat at the far left of the third row. The church filled quickly. Rob and Cassie, in full Green Beret uniform, came in toward the last. As Rob sat down, he turned and smiled grimly at Monty.

Craig began the service with a standing hymn to God in Three Persons and a prayer to Jesus. His short sermon dedicated to his friend Sylvia made it clear that her caring life had fully earned God's grace. Sylvia had certainly earned "grace" in her lifetime, despite her unearned suffering.

Monty was listed as the first speaker. As he mounted the pulpit, the words of the opening hymn kept circling in his mind. "God in three persons, blessed Trinity?" How odd, he thought, as he faced the solemn audience, looking up at him expectantly. Did they really think that the God he had prayed to every night during his childhood at the side of his bed was three? Did the "three" act as "one"? Did their God act? If he did, he certainly should have relieved Sylvia's suffering. He stared out at the expectant faces of the audience. He had completely forgotten why he was standing there gripping the pulpit. Fortunately, he had typed his address out. There it was in front of him on the pulpit in 14-point bold letters.

"Sylvia was our dear friend almost from the moment we moved into our house in Old Town, above the South Playground and Tennis Court. The Ellenbergs lived just down the block, and Cassie became our daughter's first friend in town. At Louisa's third birthday party, Sylvia had to pull Cassie into our house she was crying so hard, her heels dragging. In her hand she held a plastic bag full of water in which a goldfish swam. Cassie was certain the goldfish would die in that plastic bag.

"Never had we been blessed by such warm and generous neighbors. Oh, the dinners to which Sylvia invited us: the table set in elegantly simple taste, each glass, candlestick, knife, fork, and spoon chosen with care, the napkins crisp and folded before each place, the sideboards arranged as if for still-life paintings with piled fruits and goblets, and crystal vases resting upon antique Japanese obis. Most significantly, Sylvia never bought anything new or retail. My wife Talia, Sylvia's accomplice, can attest to that. Every beautiful object in her house, she had found at estate sales, in junkyards, at country auctions, and she cited with pride the provenance and amazingly bargain price of each one. Sylvia had been one of the greatest shoppers I had ever known. No hunter on safari had ever equaled her unerring nose for value and her cunning quest for a bargain.

"I want to read you a bit from M.F.K. Fisher's book of banquets, *Here Let Us Feast*. Fisher was one of Sylvia's favorite authors. Fisher's introduction expressed eloquently the spirit in which Sylvia cooked and served her dinners, the way Sylvia expressed her gratitude to the world.

> *Men have always feasted, in huts and palaces and temples, in an instinctive gesture of gratitude to their gods for the good things that have come to them, and it is symbolical of their basic trust and artlessness that bread and wine, the good things themselves, is what they offer back.*

"Sylvia cooked simply, with extreme care, and her guests left her table perfectly nourished in body and soul. There was always a sense of family and fellowship, and a love of humanity and life shared by her guests. One of her favorite passages in Virginia Woolf, an author she prized above all, described a dinner by the Hebrides island shore across from a lighthouse.

"A young couple, entering the dining room late in great excitement, made their excuses. Mrs. Ramsay, the hostess, guessed that the young man had finally proposed to the young woman, and her own anxiety was calmed. The maid, a Swiss girl, brought in the main dish in a huge brown pot, a *Boeuf en Daube*, which she set in front of Mrs. Ramsay, who

> *peered into the dish, with its shiny walls and its confusion of savoury brown and yellow meats and its bay leaves and its wine, and thought, 'This will celebrate the occasion'—a curious sense rising in her, at once freakish and tender, of celebrating a festival, as if two emotions were called up in her, one profound—for what could be more serious than the love of man for woman, what more commanding, more impressive, bearing in its bosom the seeds of death; at the same time these lovers, these people entering into illusion glittering eyed, must be danced round with mockery, decorated with garlands.*

"In honor of Virginia Woolf, Sylvia often cooked that *Boeuf en Daube* for her guests. As I say the name, I can taste the exquisite blend of tastes Sylvia managed to combine for our delight, along with what Virginia Woolf labeled "thought." To be in Sylvia's presence, to taste her dishes, to enjoy her furnishings was literally to be in Sylvia's thought, as we are at this moment in this church with her dear husband and children."

Almost without a pause, Monty called out the name of the next speaker and stepped off the podium. He had wanted to avoid the moment when the audience might feel compelled to make some response. Silence followed his speech as one of Sylvia's brothers-in-laws mounted the podium. When Monty sat down, his gaze sought Talia's and he received a nourishing glance of complete approval

VII

Cordelia received news of the accident by phone from Japanese Airlines, followed a day later by email, and finally by express mail. The airplane had been flying from New York to Tokyo via the polar route. Cordelia's mother had finally been pursuing her lifelong dream of international travel, dragging her reluctant husband along, when an errant storm stalled over the mountains of Hokkaido, Japan's northernmost island. Apparently struck by lightning, the plane went down. Authorities were searching for the wreckage. It was feared that no one had survived.

The day before the phone call came, Isaac had departed on a two-week journey to Budapest for an international psychoanalytic conference. Every day, while Cordelia waited for more definite news, she rose and drove up Mount Tamalpais to Pan Toll, where she hiked along the Matt Davis Trail, and remembered the sad history of her estrangement from her family. When her brother Clem had died on another mountain near Great Barrington, Massachusetts, where Cordelia had grown up, her parents had blamed her. They claimed that he would never have been on Butternut Hill on that fateful afternoon if it had not been for Cordelia and the rich friends she had made while working for the town tourist bureau.

Clem had been the hope of her parents' life; his success was to have given worth to their arduous labors.

Standing on a bluff high over Stinson Beach, where the waves broke in endless columns below, she rehearsed the events of that late summer afternoon, attempting to reverse its inevitable climax. For years since, she had gone over the scenario thousands of times. At every moment in the weeks before the accident, fate could have taken a different turn. Or could it? Looking out at the vast landscape of the California coast and the Pacific Ocean, Cordelia struggled with the confused conclusion that it had all happened as a result of her grandmother's life and character, her mother's life and character, her father's, her brother's, and her own. She could not have acted differently. Or could she? Had Clem's death been her fault? Somewhere she had read that "Character determines fate." Certainly, what happened that afternoon might be traced to the character of everyone involved, especially hers and Clem's, their parents', and their grandmother's.

Cordelia's defensive tale began with her feisty maternal grandmother, tiny Eloise, a Czech immigrant and a single mother. After years of hard labor at the Lawrence, Massachusetts woolen mills, she had helped the I.W.W. organize her fellow immigrant women workers in the Bread and Roses Strike that had paralyzed the textile industry. Their battle cry came from the James Oppenheim poem:

> As we come marching, marching, we battle too for men,
> For they are women's children, and we mother them again.
> Our lives shall not be sweated from birth until life closes;
> Hearts starve as well as bodies; give us bread,
> but give us roses!

Cordelia had heard it often during her childhood and the words became an odd litany that lasted. Cordelia had been brought up as a woman to labor, to battle not only for herself, but for other women, and, especially, for the men in her life; she had been brought up to dream, not only of bread, but of roses too, which led, she was convinced, to the disaster on Butternut Hill.

To avoid retaliation for her rebellion at the Lawrence strike, Cordelia's grandmother had changed her name and moved with her daughter, Dominika, to Pittsfield, where she went to work for the Stanley Woolen Mill. As a teenager, Dominika worked at the mill until she met her husband, Tim Bridges, a veteran of the Second World War, employed as a mechanic in the Great Barrington Public Works Department. They had two children, Clem and Cordelia. By the time Cordelia was born, her father had become manager of the Public Works Department, and her mother was promoted to head the Woolen Arts Department of the Stanley Mill, where she studied the weaving of foreign countries. When Cordelia started school, her mother left the factory, rented a store on the Great Barrington main street, and went into business selling art knitting and expensive bedding to wealthy clientele who summered in Great Barrington and came for winter sports and weekend classical music and literary readings at the cultural center.

As newly minted middle-class Great Barrington town-children, Clem and Cordelia grew up under great pressure. Their parents, born working-poor, had arrived at their status through great effort. They believed that Clem and Cordelia would succeed only through the same sort of hard labor they had endured. Although the children were intelligent and good students, their studies were treated as work and monitored carefully. From the first grade on, every evening at supper, they were required to report accurately and in detail, what they had done at school—tests taken, homework assigned, praise or criticism given. At parent-teacher night, their parents quizzed the teachers to make sure their children had not been lying. When each child arrived at the age of twelve, they were set to work, part-time during school and full-time during the summer. Clem labored in the crew of his father's Public Works Department; Cordelia found work in the shops, the theaters, and sports complexes catering to the wealthy visitors. The children's earnings were secured carefully in separate bank accounts for the future to help pay for their college education. In the Bridges family, life was labor and the struggle to rise; at every moment Cordelia's parents feared their position was at risk.

It was only during her breakdown and analysis that Cordelia realized what a prison had enclosed the four members of her family and what a toll it had taken on their affections. From her earliest years, she had adored her brother as had their parents. He was handsome, smart, conscientious, and the kind protector of his sister. He maintained a quiet reserve that attracted everyone. Although he played all the sports, competition did not appeal to him. He preferred hiking alone and from his earliest years took joy in a careful observation of the natural world. In his studies and the manual labor his father encouraged, he considered each new challenge carefully before he undertook it, but then he worked at it with concentrated energy. Cordelia was his closest friend until he entered high school. He took great pleasure in teaching her everything he learned and undertook to restrain her impulsive and exuberant spirit that often got her into trouble. She expressed her affection with disconcerting warmth that caused people to draw back, at which her brother had to console her. She was a quick learner, too quick, a natural athlete and fearless, often requiring her brother's rescue and medical care from countless falls and scrapes and bruises.

When Clem entered high school, their relationship changed. For the first time, he began to make new friends, boys who shared his interests in nature, science, and history. Cordelia read the same books and tagged along on the hikes he took with his friends. He found his sister's enthusiastic presence and demands an embarrassment. Quietly, he discouraged her, making it clear he didn't want her butting in. At first his treatment bewildered her. When she finally understood, she didn't insist, but his treatment hurt her feelings. She sulked and wouldn't talk to him at home. Then he felt guilty, for which he resented her. Her unhappiness was such a reproach that he began to retaliate with taunts and criticisms—but never in front of their parents, for whom he remained the favorite, the hope of the family. She became depressed and sullen. Her grades fell off. Her father reprimanded her for her attitude. Her mother remained kindly, but dismissive.

Early in Cordelia's analysis with Isaac, when reliving her youth, she wailed, "Why is everything about love and acceptance? Who loves whom more or less? It was only after Clem entered high school that we fought. And even then, it was only because we loved one another. I didn't want to be the favorite, I just wanted him to accept me, but I was a wild child, not very pretty, and I hadn't yet learned how to win people over. I only wanted to be Clem's favorite friend, but when he got to high school, he wanted only to go his own way."

The timing was all wrong. Her brother's rejection had turned her waspish, and she wasn't popular with the local girls and boys. During the year she turned sixteen, though, she blossomed. The summer and winter visitors had expensive sports and toys. They owned sailboats, speedboats, and small airplanes and gliders. Their children played tennis, water-skied, and sailed. Some of the boys even played around with hang-gliders, the latest fad at the Butternut Hill ski resort, where many of them skied in the winter. Cordelia outdid all the visitors in their sports.

While working at the Butternut Hill ski resort, she became

friendly with the wealthy boys and girls, who admired her athletic ability, especially her fearlessness, inherited from her feisty grandmother. In the winter, her snow-boarding and ski-jumping impressed them. Her brother did heavy labor in public works, repairing the sewer lines. One of the visitors, Rosalind Story, a wealthy girl from Marblehead, was almost as good an athlete as Cordelia. She confided that she was bored with the other rich visitors and admired Cordelia and the other town kids who had to work. Rosalind was a fine sailor who loved birds and kept a life list. Cordelia, hoping to please her brother, invited Rosalind to dinner at the house—sort of a test, to see whether she might be too snobbish. The girl passed with flying colors. impressing Cordelia's parents. Clem came home late from work and discovered that Cordelia's new friend was an avid gardener and birder, who loved to hike and sail. She claimed to prefer nature to cities and related droll stories about her mother's pretentious boyfriends whom she likened to her life list of birds.

The romance between Clem and Rosalind led to the tragedy on Butternut Hill in which Clem died. It wasn't until weeks after the funeral that Cordelia realized her parents had ceased to talk to her except for abrupt instructions. Then she remembered that even at the funeral, when she had cried and embraced them, they had seemed stiff and unyielding. Day by day, she grieved alone. Finally, one night at dinner she confronted them. "I loved Clem as much as you."

Her father stared at her malevolently, "If it weren't for you, he wouldn't have been up on that hill with all the rich kids."

Appalled, Cordelia looked at her mother, hoping she would contradict this unfair statement. Her mother had encouraged her friendship with Rosalind. Nevertheless, her mother just shrugged and nodded her head, as if she agreed with her father.

"You just have never known your own place," said her father, getting up and striding out of the room.

Her mother cleared the table without looking at her, even when she accused her mother of approving of Rosalind.

Cordelia slumped in her chair, devastated. She hadn't imagined her parents would blame her. The situation on the hill that late afternoon and early evening had been so complicated. She had tried her best to forestall Clem's foolish flight, but what she did had egged him on. And Rosalind had just stood there, when she could easily have stopped it all.

Standing on the western bluff of Mount Tamalpais, gazing at the horizon of the Pacific, Cordelia could not believe that her life had taken such a turn on that small hill in Massachusetts when she was only seventeen years old. Of course, neither she nor Clem would have attempted the dangerous flight from Butternut Hill if they hadn't descended from strong, battling women, imprisoned in a family desperately climbing out of its class. At least, that was what Cordelia attempted to convince herself, before she knew her parents' fate.

* * *

When Isaac returned from Budapest, he greeted Cordelia with joyous enthusiasm, hugging her and kissing her all about her face. "I can't wait to tell you what happened. It was miraculous. An epiphany on the shores of the Danube in the full moon at midnight. I want to share it with you so that we can delve into its meaning together."

Cordelia stared at him and murmured, "I...can't...It looks like my parents' plane went down in Japan."

Isaac recoiled. "Oh my God. That's terrible. Did...?"

"They don't know yet."

Isaac spread his arms to comfort her, but she ducked away and went up to the bedroom to lie down.

For two days they waited for further news. On the third day after

Isaac's return, Cordelia received an express letter from the Japanese Red Cross, that the downed plane had been found on Mount Tokachi a volcano on Hokkaido, the northernmost island of Japan. There were no survivors. Efforts were being made to recover the bodies of the crash victims from the mountain where the plane had crashed. The wreckage had burned and the bodies were unidentifiable. Because the passengers had been of diverse nations and ethnicities, it was decided that once the remains had been gathered to perform a common Buddhist memorial event to be held at a Pure Land Buddhist monastery on the mountain not far from the crash. Relatives and friends were invited to participate.

"I'm going, Isaac, I have to come to terms with my parents... their death."

"I'll be with you, all the way."

Cordelia stared at him. "Why?"

"We're married...I love you."

"This is something I have to deal with alone. You, of all people, know that."

They stood facing one another in the living room. Outside, the sun was setting behind Wolfback Ridge, its golden light penetrating the bay through the Golden Gate, brilliantly outlining the buildings of the city across the water.

"I'm your husband. It's my job to take care of you at times like this."

"Your job?"

"The wrong choice of words. But after all, I was your analyst."

As the light faded in the room, Cordelia realized that she did not want Isaac's therapy or for him to join her on the trip to the memorial. She almost laughed, thinking, "Talk about an epiphany!" She wasn't even sure she wanted Isaac to be with her at all. This was such a shattering thought that she could only turn away and walk rapidly into the kitchen where she busily began to cook dinner. Neither of them was inclined to discuss the matter of the trip again.

As Cordelia began her research on Pure Land Buddhist funeral functions, Isaac joined in without asking. He glanced casually through the books and pamphlets she had assembled. Without much thought, he delivered an eloquent summary of Buddhist spirituality and ritual.

"Isaac, it's my parents."

"But I lost my mother too. I was too young to understand. Our trip can be a common ritual of observance."

It was only then that she admitted to herself what she had been suspecting for some years: how completely Isaac had invaded her life and incorporated it into his—almost as if he had swallowed her whole, past and present.

Cordelia's initial reluctance to have Isaac accompany her to Japan had led her to a day by day examination of their marriage. She discovered that she had never quite trusted Isaac's facile generalizations, though at the beginning, she had welcomed them. She had been a novice to analytic convention, while he, after all, had a degree. She decided that the only way she could recover her parents would be to completely ignore Isaac's intrusion. She knew now that on this trip to Japan, she might finally come to terms with the horror of Clem's death and her parent's abandonment. Once she had dismissed Isaac from her thoughts, she felt capable of confronting her parents' spirit and of mourning their death. Only if she approached this quest alone could she cast off the crippling terror. To her bemused surprise, somehow, over the years, Isaac had become irrelevant to her deepest concerns.

VIII

Talia enjoyed overhearing the long-distance phone calls between Monty and his older brother Doug in Detroit. Monty always put on the speakerphone because his brother's voice was so low. There was such good will between the brothers that the two of them rivaled one another in revealing self-inflicted disasters, provoking laughter during the length of the calls. One night, while Talia and Monty were cleaning the kitchen after a late dinner party—it was after midnight Detroit time—Doug called, opening with the words, "Monty, boy, you'll never believe what happened. I'm crushed!"

Monty did not hesitate to reply, "You're having an affair and Milly discovered you in bed with your lover."

This provoked the first burst of laughter. Doug and Milly had been married for forty years without a single argument. "No, no, much worse than that."

"You've gone bankrupt, lost your business and your house and you need a loan for bail?"

Doug was a financial advisor and had rock-solid investments and an impeccable reputation.

"Tut, tut, I thought you knew me better than that. This was a failure beyond belief. I was driving Jody and his wife to Charlevoix, it was late at night and we were in a hurry..."

Charlevoix was a resort town on the Lake Michigan coast, three hundred miles northwest of Detroit where Monty and Doug's family had spent their summers for many years—a custom that Doug had continued.

"You've had a crash, totaled your car and killed your son and his wife along with the other driver?"

"Oh Monty, you're a novelist and you lack imagination. I've never had an affair, couldn't lose all my money if I tried, and am such a careful driver that Milly threatens to divorce me every time we take a trip. No, it was much worse than you could imagine. I missed the turn to Charlevoix."

"You missed a turn and that's why you're calling in the middle of the night?"

"You don't understand. It was the first time in sixty years and it took us six hours for a trip that I can make in three if I try."

Doug was a fanatic about driving directions. He had been since boyhood. He knew every shortcut, every police trap, every traffic light for any trip. He took pride in directing his family and friends for all of their trips as if he were an AAA representative. He claimed to have the speed record for the Detroit-Charlevoix trip. For him to miss a turn was a true disaster. The two brothers laughed so hard that they had to hang up and resume the call the next day.

Monty told the story at many dinner parties. Every time he told it, Talia knew he was expressing his deep affection for this brother, who couldn't have been more different in every way, except familial love. Doug never read a book or listened to classical music or voted Democrat or spent a moment in nature, aside from on golf links. He played poker, smoked a cigar, watched the Detroit Tigers and Lions on television, and worshipped the Jewish community in Detroit. He was a very sweet and unassuming man for whose wit and intelligence, in Monty's opinion, his friends and acquaintances never gave enough credit.

Doug's next call in December reported a true disaster, but delivered in the same easy tone as all of his calls. During a routine physical, the doctor had discovered lung cancer that had already spread to the lymph nodes and, worst of all, to the brain. The doctor had given him two to six months, no matter what treatment he received. Monty wanted to fly back to Detroit immediately, but Doug said he preferred that Monty write him a letter and make a suggestion as to how Doug should act in preparation for death.

"Doug, Doug, what can I advise you?" croaked Monty, barely able to respond.

"You've always been the thinker in the family. You know me and you've always been the one to talk about these things, life and death, you know." Doug then spoke a bit about his past, that had been, in his words, uneventful, drab, and without great accomplishments. Still, he maintained that he had few regrets. "Just write your thoughts about the situation."

It took Monty a week and many revisions before he sent the following letter. It felt rather formal to him, but it was the best he could do considering his anguish.

Dear Doug,
On Saturday you asked me to comment upon your plans regarding the next year. I was immensely impressed by the way you accepted the situation in an incredibly matter-of-fact manner. The doctor's prognosis was two months to a year, no matter what intervention occurred. The question you posed was simply: "How much medical treatment should I pursue?"

Then you proceeded to lay out the situation. It wasn't clear to me how painful or how involved, or how successful the painful radiation to the brain would be, but my impression was that the lung mass would determine your survival no matter what the effects would be of the radiation.

Then briefly we talked about what you had accomplished in life and what more you could accomplish. You have always been very modest—no beating on the chest, no proclamations of importance, no boasting. Your concentration has always been about what you can do for others—family, friends, community, and clients. In fact, you have led a life that I would hold up as the model for a truly good man. During the call you were frank about your failings and you didn't dismiss them—yet another admirable trait. But, of course, all of us fail often during a lifetime. If I were your accountant, I'd say your assets far outweighed your liabilities: son, brother, husband, father, grandfather, soldier, agent, and responsible volunteer in countless community and civic duties. On the whole, you've been blessed with a wonderful life despite the losses, the illnesses, and the normal anxious wounds you have suffered and survived.

I've given all this a great deal of thought. Unless I'm mistaken about the facts or the odds on the doctor's prognosis, I would say that you should live out whatever time remains—months, a year, or even longer (doctors don't know everything)—as comfortably and as happily as you can. Reduce medical treatment to a minimum. Take advantage of all the help you can get without burdening people. You've done your service and deserve a decent return on your good works.

Finally, Doug, you've been a wonderful brother. I greatly admire you and all that you have accomplished. Despite my eccentric life, you've never judged me (other than as a cranky hippie) and supported me and my family with your love.

I love you, Doug, and devoutly hope that the doctors are incorrect. Your presence is too important to me.

Monty

Within a week Doug called again, thanking him for his very kind words. "I'm afraid, though, I won't have much time to take your advice. I think you better come pretty soon. I'd love to see you."

Monty flew to Detroit for a last visit with his brother, whose condition had deteriorated. Doug was still able to get up and dress himself, but needed assistance in many normal functions. He had shrunk; the skin on his head and face drooped in folds and looked withered and almost translucent; his dentures seemed abnormally large. His clothes hung loosely on his stooped frame. He greeted Monty joyfully, holding him close, "I'm very glad you came."

"You're my brother and my best friend."

They held the embrace staring into one another's eyes for some time.

The visit had a strange hallucinatory quality, like a frozen dream photograph. It was a very cold late January in Detroit. The sun from a brilliant blue sky reflected off the snow and ice gathered in drifts at the sides of the roads. It was the landscape of Monty's childhood, and yet very different. Doug and his wife lived in a gated community in the rolling suburban hills outside the city limits, an area unfamiliar to Monty, who had grown up with Doug on a row of street houses in the middle of the city. He had to show his license to the gatekeeper. Although the development was built upon rolling hills, with woods and a lake, it appeared to him frighteningly like a perfect, modern, institutional prison camp. Doug's condo, spacious and bright with many windows, felt to Monty like a dead space of arrested life. His brother already seemed a ghost, and Milly appeared barely able to mask her despair.

Doug asked Monty to take him out for breakfast at his favorite morning restaurant on Telegraph Avenue. Monty took hold of Doug's elbow to support him through the uneven, slippery parking lot. Doug threw off his grip with an angry growl, "I can still walk, damn it!"

"Okay, okay, don't get so pissed!"

"Sorry, Monty, boy. Everyone's so fucking supportive, it's unbearable."

At 10 in the morning, the tables were full of aged men in loose, comfortable clothes. They all greeted Doug warmly. It felt to Monty like a club of regulars. He was careful not to help Doug fill his tray from the breakfast buffet.

"The food here is fresh and tasty," said Doug, "unlike most of the restaurants around. And the coffee is strong."

Doug introduced Monty to the men at the two adjacent tables, patting Monty on the back as he spoke, "My brother Monty, an alien from California. He's dressed normally today for my sake."

Monty joined the laughter. "Doug sent me out west years ago to avoid embarrassing the family."

This pleased Doug greatly as well as his friends, and the breakfast turned out to be a success.

Monty stayed only one more day. He had to get back. He could see that his presence was a burden on Milly and even on Doug. It was as if he were reminding his brother of the impending loss of the great affection they shared.

Three weeks later, Monty flew back to Detroit for Doug's funeral. Talia's immune system had been acting up and the doctor advised her to stay home and rest. He sat in the same Jewish funeral home where he had attended his mother's funeral, stunned that he was now the sole survivor of his birth family. His father had died fifty years ago, his mother, twenty years ago, and his oldest brother, fifteen years ago. He alone, now, bore the memories of the family life together: the house into which he had been born, the street and neighbors, the schools they had attended, and their parents' friends. There had been something intimate, personal, individual about the family together—arguments, jokes, tensions, habits, an aura, a resonance of life that belonged only to the five of them together in that house in the center of Detroit. When his father died, that special quality started to tear; when his mother moved them to a new house in a better neighborhood further north, the fraying continued; when his brothers went off to the army and school, the aura of that family wafted away. Now he alone retained the memory and the history of all their relatives, the few of whom that still survived sat behind him in the crowded hall. Before he settled in the front reserved rows, Monty made an effort to seek out his older relatives and greet them affectionately.

Doug and Milly had been very active in the Jewish community, whose representatives filled the seats along with Doug's business colleagues, both Jewish and Gentile. Doug was popular with everyone. Many of Doug's boyhood friends came over to Monty before the service and hugged him, somewhat surprised to see him, as if California was such a far country that it would be impossible to get to the funeral so quickly. A few of Monty's old friends welcomed him, asking news of his distant life. Monty's closest childhood friends had fled Detroit, and he had kept up with them by mail and phone. Sitting there, waiting for the chazan and rabbi to begin, Monty mused at the fact that none of his close friends had stayed in Detroit; they were all strays, rebels, unwilling to tether themselves to the strictures of the community, the careers and marriages that were considered normal here.

The rabbi was a younger man, whom Monty had never known. From his speech about Doug, Monty got the impression that he had not known Doug very well. The rabbi likened Doug to the biblical Joseph, the wise steward of the Pharaoh, who predicted feast and famine and provided refuge for his family. Monty prefaced his own eulogy with the remark that as far as he was concerned, Doug had been more like Joseph's older brothers, who had sold Monty to traders on their way to California, because he was a nuisance. This provoked laughter from the audience. He then went on to summarize the letter he had sent to Doug on hearing of his illness.

The service concluded with the usual Kaddish, the prayer of mourning, that Monty had always found rather odd. The prayer said nothing about mourning or the dead. It merely praised God again and again. Monty rode to the cemetery in the limousine with Milly, his nephew and niece and two of Doug's grown grandchildren. The parade of cars was accompanied by police on motorcycles. The grave was located in the circular plot their father had bought as a young man, with the intention of locating his wife there, their children, children's wives, and grandchildren. A stone in the center announced, "Wolfe." His father, Monty's grandfather, had died young leaving Monty's father the sole support of the family at the age of twelve. The large grave plot was a way of asserting Monty's father the patriarch of the continuing family. As Monty watched his brother's coffin descend slowly, he thought Doug and their parents would be quite lonely in the circle. Monty's oldest brother was buried in Chicago, where he had lived and worked; he and Talia and their children would be cremated and their ashes spread over the cliffs of the California coast.

On the way to the airport and during the flight home, Monty ruefully contemplated his new role as patriarch of the family, now consisting of his brothers' children and grandchildren, a family in which he had been considered something of a black sheep or prodigal son, beloved, but eccentric. Stepping into the San Francisco airport, he was no longer certain of his identity. His brother Doug had been his last living link to the blood family in which he had been born. He felt somehow like a ship that had inadvertently slipped its anchor and was floating aimlessly at sea. He drove swiftly toward home, anxious to step into the familiar front hall of the house where he had lived happily with Talia and raised their children.

He found Talia resting in bed, still suffering from her mysterious bout of chronic fatigue. He lay down next to her, embraced her, and asked her, "Who am I?"

She understood immediately his sense of displacement. "You are Monty Wolfe, my darling, admirable husband, the father of our children, a very good writer, and the memorial spokesperson for our entire community, as well as for your own family."

It turned out that while Monty had been in Detroit, there had been more deaths and requests for Monty's words at the coming memorials.

IX

From the moment Cordelia boarded the plane in San Francisco, until the stopover in Hawaii, she hardly spoke. Isaac remained attentive, as if he were accompanying an invalid. Now and then he attempted a conversation, to which she did not respond. She kept her eyes shut so that he would think she were sleeping,

For Cordelia, the long flight resembled a slide into dream-time, a lapse in reality, almost as if she had stepped out of life itself while still awake. However, she was not alone. Four ghosts accompanied her. Three were dead: Clem and her parents, whose spirits she was traveling to retrieve from the burnt wreckage of their bodies. The fourth ghost sat in the seat beside her, Isaac, whose presence had been slowly fading ever since his return from Hungary—if she were honest, long before that. It was not until that moment in the living room when she realized she did not want Isaac on this trip, that she understood the marriage had settled down to nothing but an almost humdrum rhythm of tasks and responsibilities. Both had muted the inevitable edges of anger and exasperation that marriage and children had produced. In the beginning, at Isaac's urging and her own hopeful imagining, they had committed themselves to a perfect marriage. But after their children had grown into adolescence, they realized they had been leading separate lives, without either of them admitting it. She had not been innocent of Isaac's affairs that had been going on before their marriage, and had continued. A few years after the marriage, she had come to realize that he pursued women out of neediness. In a way, this knowledge freed her from constantly having to coddle him and reassure him. Isaac's philandering was a relief, at least until each affair ended. Then she had to console him and put up with his love-making. In fact, he was a good lover, so it wasn't exactly a burden when they got together again. Needless to say, they were very much together as parents. They loved and admired their children; they were consistent in that. Except, of course, he was always jealous that she was the one who gave birth and suckled them. Once their children had been born, she and Isaac had presented a good face to the world as a loving couple and model parents. She provided maternal common sense and while he garnished their experience with psychological theory and flights of imagery. Over the years, Cordelia had begun to question the wisdom Isaac delivered with such eloquence.

All this time, Isaac had moved steadily upward in the Jungian hierarchy. He knew how to network and to offer acute, precise, and affirmative praise. He traveled incessantly to psychoanalytic conventions where he was in demand as a speaker, a panel member, a judge for grants. In the early days, she had accompanied him, but after a while she noticed that there was no place for her in the events aside from a place setting at dinner tables. Her opinion was never asked, even on general subjects, like restaurants, politics, or books. She was often left in the hotel room when he attended meetings. Finally, she let him go off alone, while she pursued her own separate life that led to writing projects in which she teamed up with other researchers. With a talent for clear exposition, research, and editing, she was in great demand.

Now, on the way to recapture her parents' spirits, she began to think that from the beginning of her therapy, she had been determined to believe in Isaac's elaborate recreation of reality. She had always recognized that Isaac skimmed over details, improvised a tale, and then, through his gift of language and theory, he was able to convince her. She finally admitted that she had deliberately blinded herself to his lack of consistency and the fragile basis of his conclusions. She wanted so much to believe in him and his version of their marriage that she acquiesced. It had been his manner—almost like his all-knowing father. He claimed that he had rebelled against his father's rule, but he mimicked his father's style in a gentler fashion. He always appeared to be a fount of wisdom, and she accepted, seduced like all his women by his bravado, the assurance of his presentation, and his underlying vulnerability. But now that he began equating her grief at her parents' death to his own grief, she allowed herself to understand what a captive she had been.

When the plane took off from Hawaii, Isaac asked whether their dear friend Dorottya had talked to her before they left Sausalito.

"No, why?"

"She was very concerned at your loss and wanted you to know she would be available at any time."

"You told her about my parents?"

"Well yes. We had been together in Budapest and I felt I ought to let her know why I hadn't contacted her after we got back."

"Budapest? Oh yes." Now she remembered his passionate greeting on his return, before she told him about the plane crash. "What happened on the shores of the Danube?"

"No need to go into that now. We have our mothers and your father to mourn."

"You used the word 'epiphany.' I should have asked you about that. You sounded so enthusiastic. Passionate. That was not polite of me. I'm sorry. What happened in Budapest?"

He seemed reluctant, but she insisted. He acceded, enthusiastically, as if, despite his hesitation, he really wanted to tell her.

"Well, it was remarkable and, perhaps, it might help season our sadness."

"Nothing will season mine, but I do want to hear about your epiphany."

As he launched into his narrative, Cordelia regretted her insistence, knowing she was in for one of Isaac's enticing tales.

"Dorottya Kodaly and I had just come out of an enthralling seminar on a revaluation of Jung's theories and practice with women—Toni Wolff in particular. Dorottya had been brilliant in her enthralling account of the complex joys of that triad marriage. You know what a brilliant mind she has. She had convincing evidence that Toni and Emma Rauschenbach, Jung's wife, were just as much in love with one another as either was with Jung. I wished so much that you had been there to hear your dear friend."

"That was your epiphany?"

"It was almost exactly midnight. A full moon above reflected in the murmuring rushing waters, along with the lights of the distant houses and buildings of Pest wavering in the mist."

She feared Isaac would go on and on before revealing what had happened. Impatiently she repeated, "And your epiphany?"

"There was a fruit seller on the streets outside of the convention hall. Dorottya bought a bag of fruit and suggested that we eat the fruit and drink wine on the shores of the river—a sort of rite of passage, she said, for the three of us."

"The three of us?"

"I too was puzzled. But she gave me such a powerful look of sly provocation that I followed her. She held the bag out in front of her as she walked that sinuous walk she has—her slim body wavered from heel to shoulder snakelike. She knew the riverbank well, having played there as a child. Soon we were settled on the grass just above the rushing water. The sound of the river was intoxicating, as was the soft air, the odors of damp earth and clay mixing with the odors of the fruit and the foliage of the willow and black poplar trees shading the bank through which the moonlight filtered down upon us."

"For god's sake, Isaac. I don't have patience for a travelogue."

"As we savored the peaches and melons and drank the wine, she told me the tale of her name."

Cordelia felt imprisoned in the narrow airplane seat, surrounded by hundreds of other prisoners thirty thousand feet above earth in the darkened cabin lit only by the flickering light of a hundred mini television sets and laptop computers. She wanted to scream for Isaac to cease his imitation of the Arabian Nights. Instead, she merely sighed, "I've heard Dorottya's fantasy about her name many times. Please get to the point of your epiphany."

But Isaac, his eyes glowing, was intent upon telling it all again. He leaned over and almost whispered into her ear, in his most seductive tones: "She was named after a Christian saint, Dorothea, Virgin and martyr. Dorothea suffered a terrible death during the persecution of Diocletian, on 6 February 311, at Caesarea in Cappadocia. She was brought before the prefect Sapricius, tried, tortured, and sentenced to death. On her way to the place of execution, the pagan lawyer Theophilus said to her in mockery: 'Bride of Christ, send me some fruits from your bridegroom's garden.' Before she was executed, she sent him, by a six-year-old boy, her headdress which was found to be filled with a heavenly fragrance of roses and fruits. Theophilus at once confessed himself a Christian, was put on the rack, and suffered death."

Cordelia, her eyes closed, her ears almost deafened by the sound of the jet, was about to drift off into sleep, when a turn in Isaac's narrative woke her with a start.

"Dorottya then invited me to suffer, with her, *la petite mort*, that melancholy transcendence that comes after orgasm, a senselessness or total calm-like death that comes after sexual union. You know how much in love with death I have always been. How could I refuse, especially when she dedicated our union to you?"

Cordelia almost shouted: "That was your epiphany?"

"No, my epiphany came when I awoke from our incredible orgasm with the full knowledge of the martyrdom of Dorothea of Cappadocia, the fruits and roses delivered to Theophilus, who instantly became a martyred believer. Staring up into the moonlight through the branches of the riverside trees, I understood that instead of God in three persons, the Blessed Trinity was crowned by Love and Death."

"In three persons?"

"It wasn't simply an idea, my darling wife, it was a fulfillment, an act on the shores of the Danube in full moonlight as we dedicated ourselves to you, whom we both love."

"You fucked my friend Dorottya in devotion to me?"

"Cordelia," he groaned. "Why do you always reduce beautiful ideas to such bare bones? You're very fond of Dorottya and she of you. Why shouldn't my love for you include her, in thought, in desire, and in body?"

She pressed the button on her seat arm and lay back, shutting her eyes again, a grin stealing over her lips. Strangely enough, Isaac's revelation gave her joy. It seemed to be a confirmation of a decision that had been brewing within her for what seemed like years. Evidently, she had been planning to leave Isaac without knowing it. Now, with Isaac's appropriation of her grief and the rationalization of his affair on the banks of the Danube, he had made her choice for her. His bizarre explanation of Dorottya's attraction gave weight to her plan.

"Cordelia!" Isaac called out. "Aren't you going to say anything? The three of us are bonded. She's your best friend. We both love you."

Cordelia let out a small snort of laughter that she hoped sounded like a snore. She didn't open her eyes again until they landed in Tokyo.

X

When Samuel Smithey died, his body went directly to University of California San Francisco Medical Center, where its intact vital parts were used to advance medical research. Fortunately, thought Monty, none of Samuel's flaws accompanied the body parts. At Samuel's insistence, there was no memorial, because such a ceremony would cause unnecessary expense to his relatives on the East Coast. The lengthy obituary by Monty Wolfe, upon which everyone had finally agreed, had cost his widows more than enough.

The void that Samuel's death without ceremony had left in Berenice's life led her to seek the comfort of Isaac Koenig. On the door she found a notice that he had departed the country for a few weeks. Disconsolate, Berenice next wandered over to the *Vallejo*, the converted ferryboat/houseboat/studio where she found Brooks Gardner, who had just taken the job of the vessel's caretaker. Brooks welcomed Berenice with open arms, delighted to provide solace to the recent widow.

In fact, the *Vallejo* turned out to be the perfect refuge not only for the disconsolate Berenice, but for Brooks. The vessel still bore the spirit of its charismatic residents: the English Buddhist and his

Greek artist friend. Both had preached a philosophy of life that drew young and old seekers alike and that was best summarized in one phrase, "Live for the present moment." But there were other pearls of wisdom floating on the decks and passageways such as "Words, ideas, and thought mislead. Feelings are true." Or "Act, do not think." Brooks, who had been a constant visitor to the *Vallejo*, was quick to take advantage of its iconic power. She was not naïve. She understood that both the late wise men talked a great deal, eloquently, and their words, along with a penchant for dramatics, seduced. Both had been consummate actors, and it was difficult to know just how much of what they said they truly believed or whether they simply used their words and their gestures and their appearance to entice followers and, indeed, themselves. Brooks took joy in the theater, the aura they had created, which remained embedded in the warped wood of the ancient ferryboat, a romantic structure that rose and fell with the tides, painted in antic colors and decorated with the Greek's mosaics.

When Berenice appeared, Brooks had been in the midst of her own search to fill a void in her life, which had come to another one of its many violent disruptions. Her long-time lover, Millard Wile, a very good writer and an alcoholic, had recently thrown himself off the cliffs just south of Stinson Beach, and she could not afford the rent for the house they had shared in Old Town Sausalito. When the artist and the Buddhist died in close succession, Brooks had appeared immediately to help create a proper memorial, which put her in position with the estates of both men to become the *Vallejo*'s caretaker. Her pitch was simple: to capitalize on the iconic history of the *Vallejo*'s former inhabitants by renting out the premises for religious, literary, and artistic gatherings. The boat also afforded Brooks a convenient free place to live. When Berenice appeared, she had just moved in and was planning a succession of events to justify her position.

"I'm lost," declared Berenice.

"You've been found," replied Brooks, gathering Berenice into her arms. "I need help in running this vessel's events. I too have been widowed, more or less. We can help one another."

Berenice stared at Brooks as if she hadn't understood her. Brooks knew about Berenice's unruly imagination, her belief in spirits, and her sexual exploits. In her own struggle for existence, Brooks found it necessary to know every bit of Sausalito gossip, whether true, exaggerated, or purely fabricated. She had known about Berenice's affair with Isaac Koenig, her affair and marriage to Samuel Smithey, and, in fact, she herself had enjoyed Smithey's embraces now and then over the years. She had never been tempted by Koenig's eloquence or his serial conquests. Brooks had an intellectual conscience; she wanted her sex straight, without theory. She was also aware of Berenice's talents with organization, editing, and computer databases. If that was due to the tundra spirits with whom Berenice had grown up, Brooks has happy for their assistance.

Brooks led Berenice to the upper deck of the ferryboat, where the two sat, leaning against the pilot house, looking out at Richardson Bay, the waters of which were turning rose and red and turquoise with the reflections of the setting sun and distant sky. The bay was so calm, the anchor-outs looked as if their keels were set in stone. Berenice leaned into Brooks' arms as if she were a child seeking comfort. Now and then she sighed and swallowed.

"I know how hard it is. I'm still recovering myself. When Millard killed himself..."

"What?" Berenice sat up. "Who killed himself?"

"Millard Wile, my lover."

"Your lover killed himself?"

"Didn't you know Millard? Sam Smithey knew him well. They

drank together."

"Your lover killed himself?"

"He was a drunk and feared he had lost his talent. He had been impotent for a long time. We weren't getting along together very well—I'm someone who tries to cure people, and he didn't want to be cured. Still, he left a void."

"Oh my, that's a terrible story." Berenice got up, stared down at Brooks and then strode off down the ladder and off the ferryboat.

Brooks was certain her confession had ended any possibility of employing Berenice. Unfazed, Brooks went into the pilot house, where her computer lay on the map table, and continued to plot her future. The first *Vallejo* event she planned was to be the season's prime literary gathering of the Bay Area: a celebration of the fusion of a renowned local literary journal, *Abalone*, with Ted Journey's Tamalpais Press. Ever since the divorce of Journey from her friend Yvonne, Brooks had been discretely courting Journey. She planned to use the event on the Vallejo to cement her conquest of the elusive petty tycoon.

Brooks' campaign had been a long one. One of the first novels Journey had published was by Brooks' lover. When Brooks' lover committed suicide, Brooks had maintained contact with both Journey and the journal, whose publisher, Justin McCarthy, was a drinking buddy of hers and of her late lover. Then, McCarthy, suffering from advanced emphysema, drove his ancient Cadillac convertible off the same cliff from which Brooks' lover had hurled himself—a sort of a tribute to their friendship, as she liked to put it. Brooks, in mourning, began soliciting Journey to buy the journal. "It will function as a farm team for your Tamalpais Press," she explained. Brooks always acted with more than one goal in mind.

When she had introduced Journey to Yvonne, she had no idea of courting Journey. Matchmaking was simply one of her ways of taking care of people. She had been instrumental in getting Journey to finance a city gallery for Yvonne. But Yvonne's marriage to Journey had been a turbulent one and ended quickly in a bitter divorce. Brooks made a point of supporting both Yvonne and Journey during the break-up. Brooks was, after all, a prime caretaker. As Brooks' own affair unraveled due to her lover's alcoholism, she saw a possible future with Ted Journey. She had arrived at a point in her life when she saw the need for a secure future. She knew she could handle Journey much better than had her friend Yvonne. After the death of Brooks' lover and *Abalone's* owner, like a good general, she planned her courtship of Journey with care and patience, wedding the plan to a strategic business proposition that she knew Journey would find tempting. As she suggested to herself, "one temptation leads to another."

To Brooks' surprise, on the morning after Berenice had walked off the *Vallejo* in stunned response to Brooks confession about her lover's suicide, Berenice arrived at the ferryboat prepared to help run the programs Brooks attracted to the *Vallejo*. Berenice never brought up Brooks' past, and Brooks was not tempted to continue her sad tale. The partnership turned out to be ideal. Brooks was the perfect organizer and hostess for events, a manager knowledgeable in the arts and literature, and a superb networker in these fields. Berenice performed secretarial and accounting with ease. To Brooks' surprise, Berenice, whose wild spiritual life remained mostly hidden, found it easy to translate Brooks' new-age rhetoric into precise and direct promotion for the venue. Her years of computer editorial work had trained her mind. The first event was going to be a great success and, Brooks believed, would help secure her future with Ted Journey.

* * *

Monty and Talia received invitations to the literary celebration on the *Vallejo* from both Ted Journey and Brooks Gardner. The invitation spurred Talia to reopen a discussion about Monty's writing that had been going on for some years. "You could show your books to Journey, at last, you know. You've been a great help to him."

"I told you, he made it clear he considered my writing 'ordinary' and worse than that, 'ethnic.'"

"Well those wonderful books are very sad, just lying together in your drawers. You don't just write for yourself. Your novels are remarkable."

"I write for you and a few friends. I learned very early not to push my luck."

"Come on, my darling, you would love people to read your work. They are very good. I don't know anyone who writes about people and landscape as well as you do. The worst that can happen is one more rejection."

"I know, I know. I think I'd rather just hold out the hope that some day my work will be discovered."

Talia put a finger to her lips and hugged him. She had said her piece and left it at that.

"You're a wonderful wife." He kissed her with passion.

She never pressed the point. Still, every time she brought up the subject, Monty revisited his decision, long ago, not to battle against the windmills of the publishing industry. From his experience with his company's early learning materials, he had seen how little the industry cared about authors or books. It was simply a matter of selling product. He didn't have the time or the energy to earn a living, bring up a family, write his books, and attempt to sell them. What he never told Talia, and hardly ever admitted to himself, was his first wife Emma's harsh judgment of his writing. At the same time, he felt he was betraying his labor, his talent, and, most of all, the books themselves. Once he had completed a work, he believed it had its own life, its own interests, separate from him. Leaving the books in a drawer was rude, as if he didn't respect them. Despite the aching memory of Emma's judgment, Monty respected his writing; he worked hard at it and felt he did it well. He knew he should show it to publishers. Emma's death and the first few rejections had cast a shadow over his work, robbing him of the courage to challenge her ghost, which remained hovering over his life, despite years of happiness with Talia. He tried to console himself with the thought of how well he wrote on the worthwhile projects he undertook for money. In the back of his mind was the idea that maybe, one day...

The Wolfes arrived at the *Vallejo* in the midst of the festive celebration. People sprawled about the decks fore and aft and crowded the pilot house, the studio, and the cabins. Journey had been generous, and Brooks knew how to spend his money. She had hired caterers for the food and drinks, but she had specified the menu for both and supervised. Berenice took care of the details and wandered through the party with a benign and wondering look on her face, picking up used plates and glasses. Now and then she paused to gaze out on the waters of the bay as if it were talking to her; perhaps, thought Monty, it was Samuel Smithey laughing as the two collided on the waters. Journey, who had been busy hosting and connecting with the guests, joined Berenice and, with a friendly arm over her shoulder, looked out, commenting on the various egrets, cormorants, pelicans, herons, and gulls that flitted by seeking out their own sustenance. Berenice exclaimed again and again in wonder at his knowledge. Talia noted to Monty how comfortable the pair seemed together.

Monty looked surprised. "And I thought he would settle on Brooks."

"I think he's had his share of strong women."

"Speaking of whom," said Monty, gesturing toward Cordelia who was approaching them.

"She's never come down to the waterfront before. She looks high."

"Of course, she does. She's a free woman, who has settled her past and is ready to face the future."

Cordelia had come to dinner at the Wolfes' on her return from Japan. Exuberant, she had declared herself ready to celebrate her freedom from Isaac and from her past. Monty had opened a bottle of champagne, and Cordelia had launched into the tale of her Buddhist adventure, joyously detailing Isaac's absurd proposal for a ménage à trois on the trip and her decision to leave the marriage.

Cordelia threw her arms around the two of them. "Thank god," she exclaimed, "human beings. I really don't like parties."

"I thought you didn't like the houseboat-hippie-life." Monty wanted to explore her new mood.

"I've been closed off too long, bringing up the kids, thinking too much, writing, reading, working. I was always afraid of meeting too many of my husband's lovers if I came down here. Now I think they're probably more interesting than he was. Ted Journey certainly throws a bash. Who made the food? I've never seen such an array."

"It's all Brooks Gardner," said Talia, "Yvonne Latelier's friend. When someone can foot the bill, she throws the best of all parties. Yvonne always uses her for her openings."

"Isaac and I never went to Yvonne's openings—too many people clogging the art. We'd always go the next week or saw the work at her house. She had the best work of her artists at home, where they sold best."

"There's Brooks now," said Talia, "coming up the ladder. Would you like to meet her?"

"Why not? It's a new life, a new world."

Talia beckoned Brooks who approached. "Brooks, I'd like you to meet our dear friend, Cordelia Koenig."

Brooks came to a sudden halt, staring at Cordelia with astonishment. "Koenig?"

Cordelia looking just as shocked, gasped, "Rosalind?"

The faces of both women had turned white. They looked as if they were about to faint. Monty didn't know what to do. But Talia came to everyone's rescue. "Monty and I will leave the two of you to talk. It seems there's a lot to say." She took Monty's arm and led him away. When they were out of hearing, she whispered, "I'm sure we'll hear all about it later. They obviously knew one another in a different life."

XI

Weeks before the *Vallejo* party, Cordelia had called Talia. She had just returned from Japan and asked to be invited to dinner, alone. "I have a tale to tell you and Monty."

She arrived at exactly the hour proposed. After the three had hugged, Talia murmured, "It must have been difficult."

"No, no. It was exhilarating, beautiful, joyful. I felt that at last my mother and even my father were willing to talk to me. Isaac was the only difficulty, but Isaac is past history. He's found a Hungarian vampire to suck his blood and I'm free at last." She began immediately to narrate Isaac's confession on the plane. "He fucked my best friend and called it an epiphany. Those Jungians are nuts. Dorottya is as bad as he is. They claimed their orgasm on the banks of the Danube was a tribute to me."

Monty laughed, almost in disbelief. Isaac's absurd excuse for his adultery confirmed Monty's judgment that Isaac was not very smart. He could understand Cordelia's joy. He had never liked Isaac, who seemed to suck the vitality out of everything around him with his eloquent theories and elaborate language.

Talia prompted Cordelia, "You said your parents were willing to talk to you?"

"Yes, yes. Isaac is irrelevant. He shouldn't have been on the trip at all. It was all about me and my parents. I went to Japan to retrieve their spirits, to launch them into a better life, along with Clem—that was what the entire Pure Land Buddhist celebration was about."

"A better life?" asked Monty, who regretted his question immediately.

Cordelia flushed in embarrassment. "I know, I know. It took a lot to convince me about rebirth after death. I don't expect you…"

"Please go on," said Talia, rescuing the moment. "It's your parents. Tell us what happened." She spoke with such warmth that Cordelia continued.

"I know, it sounds 'new agey,' but I have parts of their ashes, or at least someone's ashes from the accident, next to my bed in a jar of ashes. I know, not even necessarily their ashes, any one of the victims' ashes, seem to work, mixed with mud, and water from pure mountain springs and exotic mountain ferns. It's a mixture the abbot of the monastery recommended. I light candles next to them or whomever they died with—every night and we speak, my parents and I, as if I were a beloved child again. We've worked everything out—so to speak. At least, I have. It was a wonderful trip. Japan is a holy land." She paused and looked at each of them, quizzically. "Am I crazy?"

"If it helps you," said Talia in a soft voice, "it's a good thing to do. You've suffered long enough from their anger."

Monty, marveling at his wife's discreet and gentle affirmation, opened the champagne. They toasted Cordelia's voyage and her parents. And then Cordelia began to talk. Her narration took the entire evening.

At the Tokyo airport, they were met by the Red Cross representative, a beautiful young Japanese woman, who took them to a private lounge, where other grieving relatives had been assembled.

Then, quite apologetically, the woman explained in a number of languages the rather difficult situation concerning the victims of the accident. Evidently the crash occurred in the back country of Mount Tokachi not far from an obscure Pure Land Buddhist monastery, presided over by a fanatic abbot. The monastery monks were the first to discover the wreckage and gathered the remains, carrying them to the monastery. By the time the Red Cross, the national, and airline emergency forces arrived at the site, the abbot had already directed the construction of an elaborate funeral pyre of local stone and timber behind the monastery, on a precipice facing west. He claimed that because there was no way to distinguish the individual burnt and mangled remains of many faiths from many countries, it was incumbent upon the Pure Land Buddhists to convey all of their souls and spirits to be reborn in the happy western paradise, the Pure Land of the Amitābha Buddha. This was necessary, because the Amitābha Buddha, the abbot claimed, is the only Buddha who promises all people, no matter their origin, to be reborn in the pure land called *Sukhāvatī*, which in Sanskrit meant "possessing happiness."

"Of course," continued Cordelia, "Isaac's Jungian imagination was intrigued by this happy idea. The young woman went on to inform us all that, unfortunately, the abbot required a thousand dollars for each soul to be reborn in the Pure Land. Isaac, who until that moment, I'm sure, had been contemplating an affair with the representative, had a change of mind. He leaped up to object, claiming the charge was blackmail. He accused the poor young lady of enticing us to make the trip in order to extort money. He insisted on going to the American Embassy. I think the tiring trip and my unresponsiveness had pushed him to his limit. He was practically whining when he claimed the Red Cross had deliberately left out the fee in their letter."

The Red Cross representative was extremely embarrassed. She explained, once again in a number of languages, that the government and the Red Cross had known of the ceremony, but not the fee until this very day they all arrived. She went on to say that the Japanese government and the Red Cross would pay the cost for any of the relatives who had come all this way and could not afford the thousand dollars.

She started to explain further, when Isaac interrupted again, demanding to go to the American Embassy immediately to lodge a complaint. Cordelia pled with him to listen to the rest of the explanation, but he insisted on their rights.

The young woman smiled politely, bowed, and agreed to send him by taxi, at the expense of the Red Cross.

Isaac hefted his suitcase and started off, urging Cordelia to follow. Cordelia, clutching her backpack to her breast, refused to accompany him. He turned back astonished.

"I told him I was unwilling to leave this community from all over the world, who, like me, had gathered to grieve. He began to argue, but the young Japanese representative had already started out the door. Furious, he had no recourse, but to follow, alone. He couldn't bear for anyone to see our disagreements. Still, he was too proud to yield, now that he had made a stand."

When the Red Cross woman returned, she continued the explanation that she had begun before Isaac's interruption. The Pure Land abbot's various observances had become so eccentric that the monastery was in danger of total financial ruin. In Japan Buddhist priests and monasteries subsisted only on the charity of the community, the future of whose souls rested in the hands of the Buddhists. A charitable fee for services was not unusual, even though, she admitted, the difficult abbot's fee for this cremation ceremony was excessive.

At that moment, a Japanese airline employee appeared to say that the plane was ready immediately for takeoff to Sapporo, where a bus would convey them to the mountain where their dead awaited them. The young woman offered to let Cordelia remain to wait for Isaac. Cordelia insisted on accompanying the group. "I told her that he was an adult and could find his way back home to the States. He had no need to go to the mountain. It was my parents who had died. The thousand dollars was my responsibility."

With an understanding smile, the representative nodded and off they flew to Sapporo without Isaac.

Cordelia admitted that once on the airplane, she began to feel guilty at having so brazenly abandoned her husband. But when the bus left the vast suburbs of Sapporo a rush of excitement overcame her: at last, she felt that she had truly embarked on her own adventure.

"It was as if I had entered a different universe from one in which I had been living with Isaac. The air that swept through the bus from the open windows felt clearer, with unfamiliar scents. You can't believe how beautiful it was, with fields of lavender and phlox in all colors on both sides of the road, and magnificent Shinto shrines and Buddhist temples, with their gracefully curved roofs, some rising three or four stories, giving the landscape a feeling of intense worship. And the blue lakes and green rushing rivers."

Cordelia, now, was almost singing in her exhilaration. "All those graceful *torii*, those brilliant red gates in front of the Shinto shrines, gates from the secular world to the sacred. Bird perches is the translation of *torii*. Imagine leaving the world of humans and entering the aerie of birds! And I was alone, at last, to experience all this in my own way, uninterrupted by Isaac's incessant Jungian chatter. And in the distance, spaced out in a wide radius from the route, beautiful volcanic mountains rose, some still active, others with traces of snow, on one of which my parents had met their death."

From time to time, the bus passed through Japanese villages, with both modern houses and shops and thatched cottages, as if the villages had been caught in the midst of passing time. Cordelia felt that she had entered a time warp, a space elevated from the ordinary world, where the spirits of the dead wandered before being reborn.

"I had read that the Tibetan Buddhists called that intermediate space *bardo*. And that's how it seemed from then on. It was such a dislocating and unreal experience, but excruciatingly beautiful, full of sorrow and the possibility of joy—at least for the souls of my parents, who were to be transported to a happy land, where they would be reborn.

"Our family was never very religious, or happy, for that matter. The way my parents dealt with Clem's death seemed very personal, negative, egotistic, a total loss to them for which they blamed me. It was as if his life up until then and their love for him counted for nothing once he had died and could not repay their hard work with his success."

Cordelia sighed, her voice wavered. "As the trip went on, I began to understand the value of Buddhist belief in rebirth for people who have lived pure and loving lives. Despite my parents' attitude toward me, which, in a way, I had provoked, their lives had been irreproachable—prudent, hardworking, and responsible to others. It may sound crazy, but I can only tell you how I felt on that bus. Angry as I was, I never doubted their love for me—or Clem's. For the first time, I really felt I held my family's eternal life in my hands." She fell silent, gazing at them, her body clenched up, as if waiting for an objection.

"That's not crazy at all," said Talia, reaching out to smooth Cordelia's hand. "Our loved ones are part of us when we're alive, and when they die and have lost their own bodies, they depend upon us for their existence."

Monty was stunned at Talia's statement. Never before had she spoken so frankly about her deep beliefs—or any beliefs for that matter.

Cordelia paused to absorb Talia's statement. Slowly her face seemed to relax. She embraced Talia. "You always understand more than other people, dear friend."

The grieving relatives numbered about fifty, of all ages, from a ten-year-old French boy with his young mother, to an aged South African couple, whose daughter and two grandchildren had perished. Everyone seemed to have noticed the conflict between Cordelia and Isaac. As a result, they treated Cordelia with gentle sympathy for having been abandoned. "They didn't realize that I had abandoned him." Two sisters in their forties, from Odessa, whose parents had died on the plane, made a special effort to sit with Cordelia. Despite the language difficulties, the three managed to communicate a good deal. Evidently, this was the first trip the sisters' parents had ever taken after a lifetime of hard labor on Odessa's docks. When Cordelia described her parents' lives of work, the sisters adopted her even more firmly. Both sisters had difficult marriages and were very understanding about Cordelia's problems with Isaac. By the time the bus entered Daisetsuzan National Park, the three women had shared many intimate details, somehow freed from normal inhibitions by their common grief. All three had paid their own way from personal savings and had only managed with great difficulty to make this trip. "I had become like their third sister. They too had issues with their parents, which they were hoping to assuage through this journey of mourning. "You can't imagine how comforting it was to be embraced so freely by those two large, tough, good-natured women, who had spent their lives in a factory, like my mother and grandmother."

At the entrance to the park, the bus stopped to pick up a monk, a thin, tall, severe bald man in his thirties, dressed in a not very clean black, long-sleeved robe that looked a little moth-eaten, with a yellow shawl draped over one shoulder. The Red Cross representative introduced him as the assistant to the abbot of the Pure Land Monastery. When the bus started up again, the monk stood braced between the first two seats and addressed the grieving relatives. To Cordelia's surprise, the monk spoke American English. His face was deeply tanned and heavily lined as if he had spent most of his life outdoors. He spoke in fierce staccato sentences, as if confronting a hostile audience. To Cordelia, his entire aspect seemed utterly unlike what she considered a Buddhist belief would warrant. And yet, the words were Buddhist words, gentle, meditative, beckoning the mourners to join their loved ones in accepting whatever had happened, becoming one with destiny in order to aid their loved ones in a graceful journey into the Pure land called *Sukhāvatī*, a land where they would come into possession of happiness.

As he spoke, he began walking up the aisle, keeping his balance like a ballet dancer as the bus swayed. He stopped at each bank of seats and stared intently at each mourner, still fierce, although the meaning of his words was gentle. The young Japanese woman followed closely, holding onto the seat rails, translating into the languages on the name tags she had given to each mourner as they boarded the bus.

"When the monk stopped at the row where I sat with my two Russian sisters, he surveyed the sisters in the same manner as he had the others, but something happened when those startling blue-green eyes met mine—something happened to both of us. A woman knows when a man finds her attractive and she responds. But this was even deeper, shocking, more intimate, and we both felt it immediately. He took hold of his filthy yellow shawl with a fierce grip and seemed to try to withdraw his gaze, but he couldn't, nor could I. My Russian sisters, who understood, began to giggle, which broke the spell. The monk moved on.

"I was dazed, 'out of my mind,' as they used to say in the Berkshires. The name of the national park through which we drove, *Daisetsuzan*, means 'great snowy mountains,' and there were six of them almost seven thousand feet high in the park, towering over a lush landscape. Most of the winter snow was gone into rushing rivers, but I've never been in the midst of such a dramatic landscape. My inner landscape, you can imagine, was just as dramatic. Freed from the shackles of Isaac's sick mind, I was wandering between the life and death of my beloved family, who had been the peaks of my childhood, and on the way to free their souls into rebirth in a nowhere 'pure happiness land,'" she laughed, "at the mere cost of a thousand dollars each."

"Time for more refreshment," said Talia, in order to give Cordelia a pause in her tense narration. She signaled Monty to refill the glasses, while she brought out some sweets.

Breathing more easily, Cordelia continued. The bus took the mourners to the base of Mount Tokachi. A group of rough-clad porters took up the luggage. The tall monk led the group, including the young Red Cross representative, to a tram with polished wooden benches. The rails led along the side of the mountain, slowly ascending, with magnificent views of other mountains, cliffs, and steep green valleys, on the floors of which gleamed colorful fields of phlox and lavender and other flowers that Cordelia couldn't identify. Fleecy cumulus clouds sailed indolently through deep azure skies, which they seemed to slowly approached. The tram came to a stop at a trailhead with a tori gate unlike those at Shinto shrines. This was simple rough timber and somewhat off kilter, but the lintel had the fine sweeping arc that made one feel a sense of entry into yet another world.

New porters appeared, some carrying litters on which the five oldest mourners, along with the child, were seated. The path continued along the western slope of the mountain, narrow and rocky, with steep cliff drops along the outer edge. The monk led them slowly, taking many breaks to accommodate the foreign travelers. "It felt like a funeral caravan," said Cordelia, "toward our own graves. And then, as we rounded an immense granite rock, into our view came a magical stone structure, perched literally on the side of the mountain.

"It was of the same stone and dirt and fiber and color as the mountain itself, as if the mountain had given birth to a spiritual expression of human desire. There on the wild backside of a volcanic upheaval, stood a miniature Buddhist temple with its broad, upward curling roofs, one on top of the other in diminishing sizes, the lowest one overhanging an open terrace with graceful pillars of support, spaced at perfectly equal distances."

For a moment, Cordelia's eyes widened into an astonished gaze, hardly believing that the remnants of her parents had found a home in such a miraculous edifice. When the procession reached a stone bridge that led to the terrace of the monastery, the tall abbot, stopped, picked up a horn hanging from a wooden post, and blew three long, echoing blasts, sounding like the bellows of a wounded beast. An echo came back, three times, slowly fading. Out of the monastery came a very small monk, dressed like the tall monk in black over white, with a crimson shawl. He was followed by a line of monks. The small monk lifted his hand and his followers formed two lines on either side of a lane leading to the entrance of the monastery. The small monk walked halfway over the bridge, stopped, placed his hands together and bowed. The tall monk mounted the bridge and crumpled to his knees, hands together at the foot of the small monk. "I had never seen anyone who looked so old," said Cordelia, in wonder, "his face the color of weathered wood, deeply lined as if eroded by the years, in the midst of which were two penetrating emerald green eyes. We all knew that was the crazy abbot."

The abbot turned, the tall monk rose and gestured to the line of mourners, and the procession proceeded through the lane of monks who pressed their hands together and bowed again and again as the group moved toward the temple and entered. The open interior of the temple was separated by thin moveable partitions, arranged now to accommodate the visitors: men in one compartment, women in another, monks in a third, with an open space for meditation and worship and meals. The first order of business was the arrangement for the paying of fees. The American monk sat cross-legged, behind a low rough wooden desk with ledgers and an abacus and a pile of contracts. The Red Cross representative sat beside him. Each of the mourners approached, presented his or her case for the transport of the souls to the Pure Land of happiness, took an oath, and signed a contract. "It was pure business," said Cordelia, laughing, "the purchase of paradise. Why hasn't Christianity or Judaism or even most of Buddhism made such a practical arrangement?"

Monty thought that most religions had worked out that monetary arrangement, one way or another. Talia, always aware of his impulses gave him a warning glance, and he remained silent.

By the time the business had been concluded, the day was coming to a close. The monastery had sparse accommodation for so many visitors and therefore had scheduled the cremation ceremony immediately as the sun was setting in the west, the direction to which the souls would be launched in the direction of the Pure Land where they would be reborn. The exhausted mourners were ushered through a back exit onto a broader terrace on which the funeral pyre had been erected. They were seated on mats in a semicircle facing the pyre, beyond which spread the vast western backcountry of the mountainous terrain. An immense sun hung just above the horizon.

The Red Cross young woman faced the mourners and apologized for their discomfort, promising tea, dinner, and pure mineral hot-spring baths after the ceremony. "Having the ceremony today will cut short your journey, and you will be able to leave tomorrow morning."

The American abbot then joined her to explain the ceremony. Once again, his delivery was fierce, but his words were gentle and promising. "You are now facing the heavenly sun that casts its rays not only here on earth, but beyond to that western pure land of the Amitābha Buddha, the Buddha of comprehensive love. You have come to this holy place as representatives of your loved ones to perform the last rites they did not have time enough to perform. As I light the pyre, our beloved Roshi will recite the *Shorter Sukhāvatīvyūha Sūtra* that describes what one must do to be reborn there. While our beloved Roshi is reciting, you must imagine the sudden death of your loved ones and chant the name *Amitābha* over and over again as long as he recites, visualizing the souls of your loved ones leaving their bodies through the crown chakra, the tops of their heads, as the smoke rises from the pyre, and sending them to the pure land called *Sukhāvatī*"

"By then," Cordelia said, "we were all in such discomfort from exhaustion, hunger, and cold that we hardly understood the words, longing for the pyre to be lit, simply for the warmth it would provide. The short abbot strode forward, followed by a line of monks carrying torchers. The torch-bearers spread around the pyre. The abbot began to sing the sutra, the tall monk took a torch and lit the pyre in front of the abbot, whereupon all the torch-bearers threw their torches into the pyre. The tall abbot began to chant *Amitābha*, again and again, urgently leading us. The uprush of fire was so fierce that we felt we'd be consumed along with the remains of our loved ones. We began to chant weakly, but as our bodies warmed and the tall monk walked along shouting the Buddha's name at us, we began to fill the air with *Amitābha Amitābha Amitābha*, on and on as the fire burned, hypnotized by the flames and by the sun as it slowly set in the west, becoming larger and larger and turning more and more orange and red as it plunged into the mist of the horizon.

"I had never experienced anything like those hours of the cremation. I truly felt I was sending the wandering spirits of Clem and my parents to a paradise in order to be reborn as bodhisattvas, who may well return to earth to help others achieve a true life. Later, in the amazing hot springs bath that flowed through a huge stone basin carved out of the mountain's side, the two Russian sisters and I compared our experiences. We all felt the same: purified of our anger and capable of understanding the love that we had received."

At dawn the next morning, they were awakened by the tall monk and handed mason jars with ashes from the pyre. He instructed them to go to the hot-springs alcove where they would find mountain ferns. They were to mix the ferns with the ashes and water from the hot springs.

As Cordelia filled the three jars she had been handed, one for each of her loved ones, she began to feel their presences all about her, happily urging her on to take their remains home. "A very strange but immediate sense of my family clustered around me. All the way back to Sapporo, to Tokyo, and finally home, they were with me. I placed the jars in my bedroom—cleared at last from Isaac's malign presence—with candles and flowers. They are with me still, here, as I tell you this strange history."

By the time Cordelia had completed her narration to the Wolfes, it was midnight. The three of them had drunk two bottles of champagne. Laughing and crying, Cordelia thanked them for listening so long and late, and bid them good night.

XII

Rosalind Story's apparition on the *Vallejo* seemed to Cordelia like an infernal sign. Her bloated appearance shocked Cordelia even more than seeing her again for the first time since Clem's death. The beauty of that seventeen-year-old Rosalind still could be seen through the ravages of alcohol and tobacco and sun and weather and, finally, age. The high manner remained, to be sure, and the seemingly casual way Rosalind carried off this spectral collision with dead Clem's sister in the midst of a social spectacle dedicated to literature on a barely floating aged hulk of a ferryboat. Cordelia had come to the event as a reluctant gesture to her freedom from the shackles of her parents' abandonment and her husband's eloquent enslavement of her spirit. This was the first time she had come to Sausalito's waterfront in many years. She came aboard the *Vallejo* alone, feeling like a high school sophomore attending her first senior prom.

She was a new woman, the person she might have become if Clem hadn't died that evening on Butternut Hill. She had explained her "new" self to Talia and Monty at that dinner weeks before. When she saw that warm supportive couple who knew her story, her shy reserve lifted and suddenly she felt light-headed and full of delight.

She embraced them, declaring her freedom. And then the decaying figure of Rosalind appeared like something out of Dickens' *Christmas Carol*, a ghost of "Cordelia's past." At that moment, her parents' condemnation came rushing back. She had been a fool to believe in the redemption of the Buddhist ritual: ashes and mountain hot-springs water, ferns and candles, and her family reborn in some western paradise.

As Talia dragged Monty away, Rosalind laid a hand lightly on Cordelia's shoulder, saying, "I think we have a lot to say to one another, don't you?"

Considering the last time they had seen one another, Rosalind's words and her tone sounded trivial, like a high school counselor. Cordelia could not reply. This meeting just after Cordelia had come to terms with her mother's spirit and Clem's death seemed a punishment for the hubris of an Asian delusion. Confused and stumbling, Cordelia followed Rosalind through the party and down a ladder to Rosalind's cabin in the bow of the boat. Rosalind gestured for Cordelia to sit on the high-backed chair in front of the desk, while she pulled out a bottle of Irish whiskey from a cupboard and poured them both stiff drinks. Rosalind sat on her bunk, silent for some time while she drank slowly and steadily.

"Well, dear Cordelia, here we are, all these years gone by since we lost Clem."

"I didn't lose Clem. He's been tormenting me, all these years."

"And me?"

"I don't know you or how you feel. You've evidently become some Brooks Gardner, who gives magnificent parties."

"And you're evidently the wife of Isaac Koenig, the notorious local Jungian. A wife who never appeared down here on the waterfront, or I would have known that we were living a few miles from one another all these years."

"Did he fuck you too?"

"Wow, right to the bone! You haven't changed."

"I've just started changing. What happened to you?"

"I'm a wreck, aren't I?" Brooks could hardly believe that these words came out of her mouth, although she had thought them for years. Her stance to the world denied any problems, except those dealing with others in their need. Here she was admitting the worst before the conversation began. Still, even as a girl, Cordelia had commanded complete honesty from everyone she confronted and delivered it back at them. Now Brooks added, a little tremulously, "We were good friends, weren't we?"

"We might have become close, with time. That's why I introduced you to Clem." They had been together, on and off, two summers and a short time one winter, but Cordelia was always the "town girl" and Rosalind "the rich visitor." Both of them, though, had been trying to erase those differences until the accident. After that, nothing except a searing memory.

Whatever Cordelia had thought she had settled with her family's spirit became unglued as she sat facing Rosalind. Once more she began to reverse each step that led to Clem launching himself into the dusk from Butternut Hill. Why had she even brought Rosalind home to meet her family and to connect with Clem? To win his favor, obviously. And she did. And her favor too. Clem and Rosalind had almost embraced on first sight. Rosalind already knew all there was to know about Clem from Cordelia and she played the chords impeccably. Rosalind also knew how to woo Cordelia's parents, with her tales about her father's supposed death in war and her mother's boyfriends—much of which, even at that time, Cordelia thought were lies or distortions, at least. The Bridges never forgave Cordelia that fatal introduction to Clem, because it led directly to the tragedy on Butternut Hill, where Rosalind's older brother Jason was hang-gliding with his wild friends. What happened then seemed now to be all sibling rivalry and teasing, trivial, until it ended in death.

"It wasn't anyone's fault," said Rosalind, who knew exactly what was going through Cordelia's mind.

"And when did you become Brooks?"

"Do you really want to know all the truths and lies I told over these many years that I was transformed from Rosalind Story to Brooks Gardner? How many times I prayed to turn time back to that afternoon on Butternut Hill and emerge, a pure spirit? Of course, you knew very well that I wasn't so pure before we met. I had been an arrogant drunk already and...not so pure. And then I met you and got a glimpse of...something better, cleaner, more meaningful. When you brought me home and I met Clem, I had a glimpse of what I could be. On the hill, if I had only stepped forward and..."

Rosalind was tempted once again to rehearse her sad life journey, a tale as full of lies as of truths, but she restrained herself. Cordelia's pain made her want to embrace her as was her practice with all the sufferers who had attracted her over the years. It was one of her few honest impulses. She really did understand people's suffering. She too had suffered. But she was smart enough to know that such an embrace would insult Cordelia, who seemed to understand her faulty character better than anyone else in her life.

"I could tell you when and how I became Brooks Gardner and then the desolate story of Brooks Gardner that transformed me from a seemingly charmed, beautiful, wealthy young girl into this bitter hag that knows how to flatter and steal whatever will keep me afloat on this fetid mud bank of life..."

"Enough language please. I'm married to Isaac, who 'worded' me out of my living soul for years."

"Ah, 'he words me.' Cleopatra telling her handmaidens about Octavius' rhetoric. We were both passionate readers, weren't we?"

Cordelia's heart quickened as she remembered the hours they had shared their love of the characters of the stories, the novels and plays they cherished as girls. "You used everything, didn't you?"

"Who really knows the difference between our wishes and the truth? I can't believe that anyone as honest as you were could have fallen for Isaac."

"Honest and gullible, as you well know."

"And you're free now?"

"Isaac's yours or anyone else's now who wants him. I don't." Cordelia stood up and approached her hostess. "To be honest, Rosalind or Brooks or whoever you are, I'm not at all happy to see you. I've been trying to come to terms with everything that has happened to me since that afternoon on Butternut Hill. So let's shake hands and be done with it all."

"You're angry with me?"

"Why should I be? You did nothing wrong. You and Clem might have led a happy life together. And I would have been an adoring sister-in-law." Cordelia reached down, shook Brooks' hand firmly. "Thanks for the drink." She left the cabin, quickly shutting the door behind her before this ghost of Rosalind could see her tears.

Brooks knew she should go up to the main deck and supervise the rest of the event that was reaching its high point. Instead, she sat until late in the night drinking, long after the noise of the party had ended. She had known that the mockery by Jason and his gang would drive Clem to do something foolish, something dangerous, and she could have stopped Clem. At that moment, he had looked at her and she had telegraphed her own doubt about his careful spirit—as if he were just an ordinary town kid without the guts to do anything daring. Just that afternoon, he had been afraid to make love to her. After all, his sister had proved herself. Why shouldn't he, for her sake? He had claimed to love her. He saw that challenge in her eyes and he had answered it.

Brooks had told her intimate history with death to many psychiatrists. The order and emphasis changed each time, certain events highlighted, others left in the shade. She shaped her tale to the therapist, man or woman, whom she was attempting to seduce. She had more style and dramatic intensity than most patients. Sometimes she thought she had wasted her genius in these sessions. In general, her pitch went like this:

"I was seventeen, my first love was eighteen, the only boy or man I ever truly loved. We hiked together, camped together, loved birds and animal life and wildflowers together. He died out of a mistaken wish to impress me with his reckless bravery. I could have stopped him; instead I dared him to prove himself, just the way the others did. I've never forgiven myself. It was then I began drinking.

"Of course, that was my family's curse. My father was an alcoholic, my mother too and all of her lovers. Later, when I was nineteen, my father tried to rape me. It was the middle of the night. I was sleeping at home. He got in my bed, stark naked; his caresses woke me up. I kicked him onto the floor and he fled. It's a good thing I wasn't drunk that night. I might have made love to him. I thought about it then and many times, before and after. A month later he committed suicide. I think my mother knew about me and Dad. She and I were never very close. Close? She was an enemy—not only to me. My father was the one who really loved me. He raised me. I loved him too, in too many ways, I guess."

Brooks rocked back and forth silently. The story, as she rehearsed it in her mind, bored her and shamed her; it was such a false and revealing tale. It only added to her misery. But once begun on her life tale, Brooks never could stop, even to herself.

"I married an alcoholic, of course. Not at first, though. He was ten years older than I, an esteemed Boston artist. Very original, figurative, against the grain at the time, which was abstract-expressionist. I was running a gallery. And there he was, an offspring of one of Isabella Stewart Gardner's adopted nephews. How could I resist such a prize?"

Brooks wanted to throw up as she thought how flagrantly she had used that distant connection to the famous collector who had founded one of Boston's most famous museums. She filled her glass again, took a belt and continued her troubling thoughts.

"I started out to be an artist or a writer—for both of which I had talent—but, alas, it turned out I was a much better hostess. The openings in my little gallery were a legend. My husband's work sold. His reputation soared for a moment. We led a high life, on my money. He wasn't used to it and his work declined. We had a son, Dennis. It was all too much for my husband, and he began to drink, heavily; after all, I needed company in my cups. I'm sorry to say, I wasn't a very good housekeeper, wife, or mother. When Dennis, only five years old, died of leukemia, my husband committed suicide. Death is no stranger to me.

"So you see, the death of Cordelia's brother began a long history of death in my life. Actually, that's a lie I like to tell myself. The alcoholism and the free-form fucking had begun before I met Clem; I only pretend it was caused by his death. In marriage, I changed my first name along with my last to change my luck. It obviously did no good. I was born under a dark star."

Brooks was very drunk now and suddenly it occurred to her that this unexpected meeting with Cordelia had derailed her plan to bed Ted Journey tonight. She shrugged and fell asleep in her clothes on top of her bunk.

When she awoke, she found the ferryboat neat and clean with no trace of the party. A note was pinned to the gang plank railing announcing that Berenice had gone off with Ted Journey.

XIII

Life continued as a prolonged medical experience for Talia and Monty. Their fear was that if the surgery followed by radiation was not effective, there would be a recurrence, metastasis to different organs; radical chemotherapy might be necessary. At some point, Talia's immune system had been compromised, perhaps genetically. She had been subject to intermittent fatigue for years; doctors diagnosed allergy, but once she began treatment for breast cancer, the oncologist began to talk about her immune system. Certain skin problems she had experienced were now deemed part of systemic immune deficiency. Monty suspected that medical science used the word "immune" as a general category under which it listed all human ills for which there was no known cause yet or cure. In truth, Monty was the one who worried and sought solutions. Talia accepted whatever happened in life as normal and to be endured. She was temperamentally optimistic and found delight in whatever situation she entered: for example, in her oncologist's wardrobe and the radiology technician's ambitions.

The fraught meeting between Cordelia Koenig and Brooks Gardner intrigued her. Both women had adopted her, as an exotic; people generally did. It had to do with her mixed birth and the

Toltec angularity of her face. She didn't mind. She accepted their friendship and their interest in her design talents. She cared for them as friends and wished them well. She had known about the death of Cordelia's brother and Cordelia's long struggle to come to terms with her parents' blame. As for Brooks, on many occasions, she had spoken about the death of her first love. Now Talia discovered the two women were linked. Talia felt privileged to have been present at the first meeting of those two women so many years after that disaster had radically changed their lives. Life presented such gifts to Talia, who savored and pondered their meanings. She had a feeling that such meetings were not accidents. But she never mentioned such thoughts to Monty. They would have made him uncomfortable.

Shortly after the *Vallejo* event, Cordelia visited Talia's shop. At first, she made no mention of Brooks. She spoke again about her voyage to Japan and the cremation ceremony, insisting on it, as if she were beginning to doubt the experience. She confided in Talia that she continued to light candles next to the three glass bottles, the remains of her parents, and one for Clem, who had no time to dedicate his spirit. "After all, I'm only honoring the spirit of my family, which, according to Pure Land Buddhism, I've rescued from a restless wandering through the intermediate world between life and rebirth." She took a deep breath and then looked deeply into Talia's eyes. "Do you think I'm being ridiculous?"

"Rituals are healing," murmured Talia. "Your experience on Hokkaido sounded wonderfully therapeutic."

Cordelia laughed. "More than you can imagine. I was embarrassed to tell about this in front of Monty." She put her hand up to her mouth as if to stop herself, but then she shrugged, grinning. "The night we slept in the monastery before the cremation...well that tall monk woke me, gently, and led me to the hot-springs room.

We stripped and slipped into the baths and slowly cleansed one another. Then we made love. It was like nothing I ever experienced before. He was slow, patient, waiting for my body to come alive, and, my lord, it almost jumped out of its skin. Talk about casting off the past! Remembering that helped me when Rosalind, whom you knew as Brooks, showed up. I began to lose my new life, but then I remembered that fierce and gentle tall monk."

Having dispatched this confession, without pausing for Talia's response, Cordelia then hurried on to speak of her joy at leaving her marriage and the possibilities for the future. The financial arrangements had been amicable, but she had made it clear she wanted no further relationship with Isaac, except matters pertaining to their children. She hoped never to be invited anywhere that Dorottya might be included.

Two days after Cordelia's visit to Talia, Brooks appeared. Her first words referred directly to Cordelia. "She was my closest friend growing up, even though I only saw her during a couple of vacations. Actually, she was the only girlfriend I ever had. An amazing girl. Daring. She skied like a wild creature; dove off of cliffs; dared boys to equal her. I knew she was smart, but had no idea she would end up with a PhD. Losing her was almost as bad as losing her brother. She doesn't want to see me again. I can't blame her."

Talia nodded sympathetically. There was nothing to say and Brooks left no time for a reply. She immediately went on to talk about her bewilderment over Berenice's behavior. "I was like an older sister to Berenice, even before Smithey died. I got her work, introduced her to writers and foundation boards who employed her, and then made the mistake of introducing her to Ted Journey. I mean, Ted and I were close and on the way to being closer. I gave him tons of contacts when he became a publisher. My Millard didn't need Ted's press to publish his novel; three major publishers would have grabbed at it and put his name on their list. I gave Millard to Journey and it helped attract Millard's friends. And now it appears Ted and Berenice are an item. For some reason, neither of them answers my calls." She clasped Talia by the shoulders and continued. "Talia, do you think I've become infectious or something?" Brooks delivered this information as if it were a mysterious joke, laughing nervously.

Talia joined Brooks' laughter. But she could see that Brooks was terribly hurt by Cordelia's response and by the behavior of Ted Journey and Berenice Smithey. Talia spent the rest of Brooks' visit to the shop subtly consoling her.

At home, when Talia told Monty about Brooks, Monty shrugged and smiled. He seemed distracted and did not answer immediately.

"I felt sorry for Brooks," continued Talia. "She tries to be helpful to everyone."

"Maybe that's the problem. There's something toxic to her help. She uses it and uses the people she helps."

"That's way too harsh. She does try and she does help."

"And you are too good and loving and always giving us all more than we deserve."

"You, of course, deserve no credit and all the blame, which is why I love you." She kissed Monty. "Don't forget, tonight we're going to Yvonne's gallery in the city for an opening."

Monty groaned. "Another one of her abstract expressionist jigsaw puzzles."

"Philistine! You know I love her openings and you have no taste in art."

"And I love you."

As always, it was a lavish affair, so crowded that one could barely see the paintings, which Monty didn't mind, because he had little taste for Yvonne's stable of artists. The colors and shapes on the canvases seemed to swim deliriously this way and that without any obvious intention that Monty could see. He only came for Talia's sake and Yvonne's. Talia loved the excitement of an opening and had true feeling for the art. As soon as they arrived, Talia waded into the confusion, eagerly gazing at the paintings and the crowd, assessing both in terms of design and appearance. Yvonne captured her as she went by and introduced her to an imposing couple, so well dressed that Monty was certain they must be collectors. He knew that Yvonne was lavishing praise on Talia's designs and calling attention to her own stunning outfit, an elegantly discreet creation by Talia for this opening, a design that took care not to vie with the paintings. Yvonne and Talia always made sure of that.

Monty edged his way along the wall to the buffet, where he nibbled at a paté sandwich and sipped at a glass of white wine. He always felt uncomfortable at these gatherings of the "high art" social groups—curators, heads of museums, wealthy collectors, and the famous local artists. He knew his discomfort had more to do with vanity than with any judgment of the crowd. If he had been a more successful writer, probably, he would have been able to mix. This lack of recognition haunted him even though he kept all his work locked in his file drawers. Talia valued herself as a person and had no need of credentials to feel equal to anyone she met. He admired her self-esteem, but could not conquer his sense of failure—what he vainly attempted to call a failure of nerve, not of talent. The books were good; the books are good, he murmured to himself.

"Monty Wolfe!"

Stunned, Monty turned and found himself confronted by Brooks Gardner. The gallery was the product of Yvonne's failed marriage to Ted Journey, a marriage for which Brooks took credit, as she did for the gallery. Brooks now catered Yvonne's events. As always, she was a genius at divining tortured inner thoughts. "Why are you hiding in the corner?"

"You put on quite a spread, Brooks; it's your art, I guess. It vies with the art itself."

"And you know how to defend yourself, Monty," said Brooks smiling grimly at the retort. "I thought your speech at Sylvia Ellenberg's memorial was magnificent. You write as well as anyone Journey publishes. You know he admires your stories. Why don't you show him one of your hidden novels?"

"A novel is never finished, at least mine aren't," said Monty brusquely and turned away to fill a plate of hors d'oeuvres. He wasn't about to discuss his work with Brooks. She must have heard about the novels he kept in drawers from Yvonne, with whom Talia was close.

"Sorry, Monty," Brooks laid a hand on Monty's shoulder, "that was rude of me. I really tried to be of help, although, apparently, I'm no longer a source of inspiration for Monsieur Journey. For some reason, he's taken up with dear, mad Berenice, who seems to have dropped me also, probably at his request. He bought the *Vallejo* for his press, and I've been evicted. I give him a month and a half before he drops Berenice. She's a genius at the computer, but, apparently, never learned to think like a normal human being."

"I hope you've found a new home."

"Oh, that's never a problem for me. I have friends."

"You always seem to find new friends."

Brooks turned away, murmuring "Please excuse me, the party seems to be lagging." Off she went, circulating through the crowd as if she were the hostess. Despite his anger at her intrusion in his privacy, he had to agree with Talia. Brooks' situation was a sad one: forever depending on the kindness of strangers, whom she made it a business to obligate. Monty didn't know why Yvonne put up with her. Of course, Brooks was not easy to shed. When Journey and Yvonne broke up, Brooks had been careful to sympathize with both of them. She was like Talleyrand, before, during, and after the Revolution—a friend to power, wherever it was located. Her plans for Journey's future had been frustrated, it seemed, but she still managed to be of use to Yvonne.

Talia had told Monty the whole history she had learned from both Yvonne and from Brooks. Brooks had known Yvonne since her youth in Boston. Yvonne, from a distinguished French provincial family, had been an established international agent for some of the most prominent sculptors and painters in the world. She specialized in placing works with corporations—in the lobbies and courtyards of their lavish headquarters. Brooks traveled in the same art circles: openings, exclusive patron parties, galleries. She had played the ingénue and Yvonne had been only too glad to adopt a beautiful, wealthy young admirer who was married to an offspring of the Isabelle Gardner family. Although Yvonne was a consummate networker—one had to be in the business of agenting expensive art—she was not undiscriminating. She was very smart and honest and had an excellent background and taste in art and in people. She saw qualities in Brooks that needed encouragement. They became friends and managed to be very helpful to one another in terms of connections. They lost touch when Yvonne moved west and began to cultivate California artists. Yvonne was the first person Brooks contacted years later when she too moved west. After Yvonne's marriage to Journey, Brooks began to cater Yvonne's openings. When the marriage to Journey broke up, Brooks managed to hold on to Yvonne.

After repeated visits to the bar, Monty's mood lightened. He leaned against the wall, watching the festivities. After all, he was a novelist, successful or not, and Talia had taught him to take pleasure at least in observation. It was a gala scene, with that wild inconsequential art and the company, a mixture of wealthy collectors, dressed exquisitely, the critics looking like Ivy League professors, and the artists, either in torn jeans with tattoos and piercings, or in works of clothing art that looked to Monty a bit like Halloween costumes that clashed with the paintings on the walls. Of course, there were also the artists who dressed like Wall Street bankers—one had to observe with discrimination. Although Yvonne had always been careful to include the Wolfes and to introduce them to the celebrities, he never remembered any names. Talia did.

Talia, Talia, Talia, he thought, as he watched her dance through the crowd, always managing to spend a great deal of time examining the art. It seemed she was the only one who really looked at the paintings. The more he drank, the more he loved his wife, for him the most perfect form of art.

He also watched Yvonne, whom he respected. Unlike Brooks, whose every gesture was exaggerated, needy, and, in his opinion, acted, Yvonne was always honest and in complete command. Monty and Talia had become friends with Yvonne through their son, who had studied sculpting with Yvonne's son from her first marriage. The Wolfes occupied a private space in Yvonne's life that she kept free from the tensions of the art world and her position as an important gallery owner. They were invited to all the openings and the special dinners at Yvonne's Russian Hill house. Yvonne's professional personality, aloof and critical, but always deferential to her collectors, differed markedly when she was with personal friends. Alone with the Wolfes she revealed a simple, almost naïve enthusiasm and a deep interest in the lives of others. She was very fond of Talia, admired her designs, and bought many of her outfits. At Monty's insistence, they saw Yvonne mostly at small gatherings of her personal friends; Talia insisted, however, that now and then they attend the openings to show their support, especially after the trauma of Yvonne's divorce from Ted Journey.

Slowly, as the wine rose to Monty's head carrying with it his love for his wife, he began to enter her generous imagination as it took joy in each of these elusive characters they had encountered in this Arcadian bayside village: Yvonne Latelier, Ted Journey, Berenice Smithey, Samuel Smithey, Cordelia Koenig, Isaac Koenig, and Brooks Gardner. What an eccentric cast of characters to have slipped into the life of Monty Wolfe, a middle-class Jewish boy from Detroit! He had embarked from home in the opposite direction, eastward, for college in New York; sailed westward on a Navy destroyer, through the Panama Canal, all the way to the coast of China and back to San Diego; drove north to graduate school in Berkeley, where he took a wife, who died bearing his son; found another wife, who bore his daughter in the bayside village across the Golden Gate Bridge where he had finally landed, like Robinson Crusoe, and made a long life surrounded by immigrants from faraway lands.

Quite drunk now, he began to think of his neighbors with love. Over the years, he had come to know these castaways and their stories. Their past wounds and failed hopes gave him sympathy for their current lives: deceptions, betrayals, disappointments, and abandonment. They too had been young and brave, venturing forth into an enticing world. And here, in this supposed "promised land" in the west where they finally landed, they found that as swiftly as they had fled their birth families and the towns in which they had been born, life had nevertheless doomed them to ordinary, difficult existence, with all of its wounds, and pains, and failures. And then they died, with Monty to speak well of them in the end. When he made up their final stories, he had always kept in mind the joys and hopes of their youth.

XIV

Many years before the twenty-first century began and almost three thousand miles to the east of the California coast, in Marblehead, Massachusetts, Brooks Gardner was christened Rosalind Story. From her earliest childhood, Rosalind remembered her mother exclaiming in exasperation, "You are your father's daughter! You both live in a world of your own." There was always a definite slur on the word "father's." When their cook, Beulah, a sharp-tongued black woman, heard her mother, she would lift her eyebrows and mutter that "there was little love lost" between Rosalind's parents. When Rosalind first heard these two statements as a little girl, she had asked Beulah what they meant. Beulah's reply did not begin to make sense for Rosalind until she reached the age of nine. "There are many possible fathers to children in any family," explained Beulah then. "Perhaps Jason is not your father's son. But you are certainly your father's daughter, as far as your mother is concerned. You're always reading books, looking at pictures, peering at birds, drawing, and day-dreaming. Most of all, you're kind and thoughtful like your father. Your mother doesn't have a kind bone in her body. As for love, it's found and lost, and often determines the fathers of each child." Rosalind's father said that Beulah was a woman of decided opinions and could talk a coon out of a tree sooner than his best dog.

Jason was four years older than Rosalind and their mother's favorite child. Rosalind came to believe that her mother thought of Jason as her only child. Jason was a very handsome, black-haired, blue-eyed, sharp-chinned male replica of their mother. Rosalind was blonde, like their father, and met the world with the same musing, speculative gaze of her soft brown eyes. Her mother complained that her father never could make up his mind and found it impossible to complete any project. She accused Rosalind of the same faults, comparing her to Jason, whom she considered the man of the house. Rosalind argued that she couldn't compete with Jason, because he was four years older, a boy, and always away at Choate and then at Princeton. Her mother didn't seem to hear her. Although she day-dreamed, nevertheless, unlike her father, Rosalind came to conclusions quickly and acted with decision. She saw, early on, that it was useless to try to win her mother's affection. She encouraged her father's confidences, complaints, and his embraces. As she grew older, they read the same books, looked at the same art, and wandered around Marblehead and the surrounding countryside, kayaking together, peering at the birds, both lost in thought. Her father taught her how to sail; they spent long silent days on the bay and the ocean in her father's forty-three foot, wooden-hulled sloop, a Marblehead classic. By the time she was fourteen, her father was too busy drinking himself to death to accompany her. By then, she had become an accomplished sailor, often sailing singlehandedly just to be alone. When she entered the Corinthian Club races, she took along one of her many boyfriends as crew. She enjoyed ordering them around, little thinking at the time that she was playing her mother's role.

As far back as she could remember, her mother had a girlfriend living in the house. From year to year, there would be an argument—Rosalind's mother was prone to violent rages—and a new woman would appear. Rosalind noticed that each arrival was greeted with passionate embraces and would share her parents' king-sized bed, the three of them making a great deal of noise during the night. The next phase in these recurring dramas always began with her mother's rage at her father, banishing him from the bedroom, at which he would come to Rosalind's room and ask, in a sad and pleading way, if he could sleep in bed with her. She always welcomed him and comforted him. Sooner or later, her mother would turn on the new woman, invite the father back to bed, and then, a new girlfriend would appear. Rosalind was introduced as "my husband's daughter, in a world of her own" and was instructed to call each of these women "Aunt."

In an odd way, Rosalind felt that she had never lived in the beautiful, historic Story house on Washington Street that had belonged to her father's family for generations. Her mother and her successive "aunts" lived there and Rosalind only visited to eat and sleep. Her mother's taunts and rages made the house a dangerous place. When Jason was home from school, he joined their mother in tormenting Rosalind for her "insufferable" meditative gaze, her love of books, and nature. Rosalind often sought refuge outside the house where she did not always have to be on guard. She considered Marblehead's many beautiful old houses, harbor, parks, and forests her home, presided over by her father and Beulah, whose family had lived in that historical town as long as the Storys. Rosalind's father taught her about proportion in architecture, which was why those square high clapboard and shingle houses with the long windows and dormers placed in just the right place were so beautiful compared to modern houses. He also taught her how to draw and paint. She often ate and slept in one of the houses owned by Beulah's sisters and brothers, all of whom welcomed Rosalind's father as well, especially if he had been drinking late at night and could not make his way home. Rosalind's mother often locked the doors when she and one of the "aunts" went to bed. Brooks' mother's family, the Skeltons, as ancient in New England as her father's family, had been pioneers in Salem. Rosalind suspected that her mother was descended from one of the Salem witches, or the judges who condemned them to fire.

By the time Rosalind was fourteen, her father was no longer available to mediate between his wife and his daughter. Rosalind and her mother lapsed into heated arguments about the way Rosalind dressed, Rosalind's mother's affairs with women and men, the way her mother treated her father, and Rosalind's reputation as a homeless wanderer. Their arguments were loud and violent, resulting in a good deal of breakage of valuable pottery and glassware. The culmination of their war came late one night, when Rosalind returned drunk from a high school party. Her mother had stayed up, prepared to confront her.

"My friends tell me you are known as the town whore."

"I'm only taking after my mother. At least, I only fuck boys." Actually, she had only recently lost her virginity to a local Marblehead boy who worked at the Corinthian Marina. She hadn't found the experience very pleasant or interesting. The boy wasn't much of a reader or even a very good sailor. His job was to keep track of the equipment and she had to coach him on how to use the Corinthian's accounting system.

The result of this final argument was Rosalind's summer exile to the Skelton family estate outside of Great Barrington. As a child, Rosalind had occasionally visited the estate with her parents. There were always a lot of Skelton aunts and uncles and cousins there, along with a full staff. There were even stables, but the horses had been sold long ago. Grandmother Skelton seldom left the master bedroom. James, the butler, a local who had been with the family since he was twenty, ran the house and the grounds.

When Rosalind was able to catch her father sober, she told him about her looming departure. Her father advised her to cultivate James. "James has always disliked your mother because she treated him like a servant. He's very proud. Come on to him like an orphan who needs advice. When he hears whose daughter you are, he will understand." Her father bought for her a box of James' favorite cigars, along with a special Irish whiskey impossible to obtain anywhere except a specialty shop in Marblehead. "James will know who the gifts come from. Put yourself in his hands. He'll get you anything you want and arrange for transportation—a horse, a sailboat, a tennis racket, and he'll tell you how to use it. The family belongs to all the clubs."

Rosalind found her Skelton cousins, even the older ones, inexperienced, ignorant, and entitled. Bored, she took advantage of James' connections and decided to spend as much time as she could away from the Skelton estate. On one of her first outings, James arranged for a kayak on Lake Buel. "Cordelia Bridges is a good egg. She manages the equipment. She'll have a kayak with life-vest waiting for you. Be sure you put on the life vest—if you drown, she gets the blame."

The estate jeep dropped Rosalind off at the northern end of the lake at six-thirty in the morning. The sun was rising over the eastern shore, casting shadows of the willows, the red cedars, and the pines across the waters. The faint morning mist gave the mild rolling Berkshire hills a dim, mysterious aspect, thrilling Rosalind. The lake was calm, enclosed, like some protected clear realm of peace. She marveled at the contrast of this secluded pocket in the mild hills of Berkshire with the wild, rocky Atlantic coast on which

Marblehead perched.

The ramp, boathouse, and equipment shed were deserted. Rosalind walked out on the dock, where, to her surprise, she saw a tanned young girl in shorts and a T-shirt hunched over a book, her bare feet dangling above the water.

"Pardon me," said Rosalind, "I'm looking for Cordelia Bridges. James at the Skelton estate told me she would provide me with a kayak and some information about the lake."

The girl, who had been absorbed in her reading, looked up, somewhat confused. She shuddered irritably, shook her head, and examined Rosalind. "Are you a Skelton?"

"Related. James told me…"

"I know, I know. He called. The kayak's over on the beach." Reluctantly, she rose, tucked the book under her arm and led Rosalind back to the shore.

"Shouldn't I sign in with Cordelia. James told me…"

"Oh, James is full of shoulds and oughts and musts. He's a big nervous bear, but he said you were all right."

Rosalind was pleased at James' recommendation, but still confused by this self-confident young girl. She looked to be about fifteen. "Shouldn't I talk to Cordelia."

Without turning around, the girl said, "I am Cordelia, I'm in charge here."

"What are you reading?"

The girl stopped, turned and once more stared at Rosalind up and down as if she were a strange specimen. "If you're from the estate, it wouldn't make any difference."

Rosalind caught sight of the spine of the book. "Oh, it's *Our Mutual Friend*. I love the Boffins and Boffin's Bower. And Louisa Hexham…"

Cordelia lifted her hand and barked out, "Stop. I don't want to know what's going to happen." She turned and almost ran off the dock to the beach, where a kayak lay with a life vest draped over the cockpit and a paddle propped over the stern. "Do you know how to use these things?" The girl's tone was still gruff.

"I've kayaked a lot," said Rosalind, slipping into the life vest. She removed her binoculars, bird book, and a volume of Chekhov's stories from her backpack. "James said there were some marshes nearby?"

In a somewhat gentler tone, Cordelia responded. "If you're looking for birds, there's an outlet to a stream about a hundred yards to the north. It meanders for a while and arrives at a pond. The current is next to nothing at this time of year. There hasn't been much rain. If you're lucky you'll see some rails hiding in the reeds—they're very shy, so keep quiet—and maybe a sora along with the usual."

Rosalind slung her binoculars around her neck, stowed her light backpack and book in the cockpit, took up the paddle, lifted the stern of the kayak and shoved it in the water, leaping in as it floated free. She hoped she had looked graceful and at home on the water. As she paddled in the direction of the stream, she shouted back, "I've read a lot of Dickens." Within a few minutes she steered the kayak into a stream mouth, paddling against the mild current that emptied into the lake. Her mind now was less on the possibility of birds than on Cordelia, and how such a young girl came to be in charge of a boathouse on the lake and all its equipment. She was undoubtedly a local, her accent "country," like all the Berkshire natives. Her remark about the Skeltons had been dismissive, yet knowledgeable. None of Rosalind aunts or cousins read anything but trash. Cordelia obviously knew the lake, the birds, and the equipment; James had spoken of her with respect, and she had spoken of him with affection and perception about his fussiness. As she guided her kayak upstream, she glanced now and then through the binoculars when she heard a bird and noted it in her notebook. She relaxed, sinking into the landscape. Indeed, as Cordelia had promised, she spotted several gallinules, a clapper rail, and one small sora hunched away amidst the reeds, along with a mother mallard followed by seven chicks, an eastern bluebird, singing its head off beautifully, and a number of familiar waterbirds. After exploring the narrow little pond that fed the stream, she turned around and let the kayak drift back down the stream toward the lake. When she came to the lake, she began a leisurely paddle along the shore away from the boathouse. She pulled into a secluded beach after one o'clock and ate her sandwich.

She opened the Chekhov and began reading "In the Ravine." She burst into laughter as Chekhov introduced the location of the story by saying the place was so dull that people identified it only with the words, "That's the village where the deacon ate all the caviar at the funeral," the only remarkable incident that had ever occurred there. As she read on with delighted horror and compassion about what went on in that obscure village, she found herself wanting to recommend the story to the girl at the boathouse, the girl reading Dickens. The impulse surprised her. She had no friends in Marblehead and none in Great Barrington. Now, out of nowhere, there was this local girl reading Dickens, a girl with what seemed to Rosalind a mind of her own and sprightly opinions about people. Rosalind had seldom met a girl who had interested her more on first meeting, a girl who might become a friend. She had always been too unhappy for friendship—bedeviled by too many dark family secrets. Still, a bit nervous at her resolve, Rosalind did not hurry to return to the boathouse. She read until the middle of the afternoon. James had promised to send the estate jeep back for her around four. By the time she got to the boathouse, a middle-aged man in worn dungarees reclaimed the kayak.

"Where is Cordelia?" asked Rosalind.

"Oh, she's off to her other job at her mother's shop."

"Does she live around here?"

"She's a Bridges, lives at home."

Rosalind decided to ask James for more information. The jeep was waiting. All the way back she kept smiling as she thought of Chekhov's boring town identified only by its caviar-eating deacon. She really longed to show that new girl the story.

XV

It was almost like falling in love at first sight, thought Rosalind, as she lay in bed at her grandmother's estate, thinking of the slim athletic figure of Cordelia. It wasn't sexual, she decided, not like her mother and her "aunts." She couldn't quite find a proper word to fit her desire to engage that town girl who seemed to concentrate such power and self-confidence in her presence. Finally, she decided that this Cordelia possessed the one attribute that Rosalind lacked: she knew she belonged here on this lake, in these hills; she knew who she was. As a native, she obviously despised Rosalind simply because she came from the Skelton estate, another privileged, entitled, rich visitor, a relative of the uncaring Skelton clan, an occasional visitor. But Rosalind herself despised her Skelton blood and could not even take pride in her Story blood, much as she loved her kind, gentle, wreck of a father.

Rosalind did not know who she was; she did not know where she belonged. She had been wandering for as long as she could remember. She loved Marblehead, its houses, its shore, the inlets and rocky countryside, but she hardly felt that Marblehead claimed her—considering her fractured family. She was seized with a desire to explain all this to that attractive, independent girl, who sat on a dock early in the morning, utterly absorbed in the tale of Boffin's Bower.

Rosalind wasted no time. The next day around four in the afternoon, with James' directions, she sought out the Bridges' store on the Great Barrington high street. A discreet sign signified "Design Woolens, Fabrics, Bedding, and Bathroom Linens." The windows displayed an elegant array of sheets, pillows, blankets, towels, highlighted by colorful woven woolens, both imported and locally crafted. The appeal, thought Rosalind with interest, was to wealthy visitors, not to locals. Inside, the expensive merchandise was tastefully arranged, with beautifully printed labels describing the provenance of the design, the country of origin, size, and price.

An attractive woman with short curly hair, a beige suit and maroon vest, measured out material for two elderly women in smart summer outfits. As she efficiently rolled out the material and cut, the clerk carried on a lively conversation with the women whom she addressed by their first names. They were talking about Tuscany and Florence, which the women had visited in the spring. The saleswoman showed a lively interest in all the details of the Italian countryside, the art, the cooking. She noticed Rosalind and called out, "Cordelia, a customer!"

Cordelia appeared from an office in the back of the store. She wore a similar beige dress and maroon vest as the older woman. Her hair was tied back in a neat ponytail. She looked completely respectable, a salesgirl in a high-end shop. "May I assist you?" she addressed Rosalind rather absently.

"I rented a kayak from you yesterday at Lake Buel."

Cordelia focused on her now. "Oh, yeah. Sorry, didn't recognize you in clothes."

"You look different too."

Cordelia smiled, a little uncertainly. "It's my mother's uniform. I'm much more polite in these clothes. You want to buy something here?" She sounded skeptical.

"No, I wanted to see you again and talk about books."

Cordelia recoiled a little, as if to defend herself. "You wanted to see me again?"

Rosalind could see she would have to make a convincing case. "As you said yesterday, the Skeltons are a total loss."

Cordelia blushed and stammered. "I…I didn't exactly…"

"More or less. Nobody out there reads or thinks or is quite human. I'm bored out of my mind."

Cordelia shook her head, obviously disconcerted at this frank avowal. After a moment of silence, she murmured, "Hey, I'm sorry. I don't know what I can do for you."

"Could we have coffee and talk?"

"I'm working. My mother," she nodded toward the vested woman who was now at the cash register, finishing her sale to the two ladies, "she doesn't take kindly to me leaving the shop."

Cordelia's mother approached them with a gracious smile, "Is there a problem, Miss? Cordelia knows the goods as well as I do."

Rosalind returned her smile and put out a hand, "I'm Rosalind Story, staying out at my Grandmother's place. I rented a kayak from Cordelia yesterday and saw that she was reading a Dickens novel, which interested me. I wondered whether we could get to know one another, somehow."

Mrs. Bridges laughed. "You're quite self-possessed, aren't you?"

"It's just that it's so boring out there, aside from James."

Mrs. Bridges regarded her more closely. "Are you a Skelton?"

"My mother is."

"Which daughter is she?"

Reluctantly, Rosalind answered, "Priscilla."

Cordelia's mother nodded and spoke in a musing tone, as if she were remembering the past, with reservations. "She was very beautiful...when she used to come up here."

"Did you know her?"

"Simply by sight. One doesn't get to know the Skeltons. I worked at the factory then with my mother." She smiled and gazed out the front window as if remembering the old days. She shuddered slightly and spoke to her daughter. "Have you entered all the accounts?"

"There are a few left."

"Well, why don't you two have a coffee or a soda or something. Cordelia doesn't know many girls who read Dickens."

"It's working hours, Mother," said Cordelia, tartly.

"Old families in Great Barrington should get to know one another."

"Since when..." began Cordelia, but Mrs. Bridges shooed the two of them toward the door, slipping Cordelia's vest over her head as she ushered them out.

They said nothing to one another until they bought their coffees and sat down at an outside table. Rosalind began, "I'm sorry if I got you in wrong with your mother."

"That would be impossible—I'm always in wrong these days."

"Me too."

"What?" Cordelia looked startled.

"My mother...well, it's a long story."

"I don't understand."

"To make it short: according to my mother, I'm *my father's daughter* and my older brother is her son and *there's no love lost* between my parents, even though, apparently we are both their children."

Cordelia took a sip of her coffee and stared at the table, shaking her head. Finally, she said, "I've never met anyone like you." She couldn't believe that this older girl, dressed beautifully, a Skelton, had taken the trouble to seek her out. She claimed to be a reader too, seemed to know what was going to happen to Lizzie Hexham. She was rich and probably very smart and would find out, very soon, that she, Cordelia, had to work hard just to get into any college and knew next to nothing about the world and that everyone despised her, because she was so nasty and unhappy and hated everyone and everything.

"Have you read any other Dickens novel?" asked Rosalind.

"One or two."

"*David Copperfield*?"

'If this is going to be an exam,' thought Cordelia, 'I'll just get it over with and say what I think.' "I hated *David Copperfield*, except for Peggotty and Barkis."

"Yay, 'Barkis is willing.'" They both laughed and then regarded one another speculating at their immediate and mutual appreciation. "I agree totally," continued Rosalind. "Those two were the best characters in the book. *Our Mutual Friend* is a much better book, isn't it? Or don't you think so?"

Cordelia hesitated. Rosalind seemed completely sincere, wanting to talk, wanting to be friends. Cordelia desperately needed a friend. She was terrified she might fall into a trap. She had spent her childhood running after children she liked, ready to embrace them, but they just turned away. Only her brother had welcomed her affection, had guarded her, had taught her, and then he too had turned against her. And her parents too. And now the only places she found any joy or peace or pleasure was alone on the lake, the river, the mountain, and between the pages of a book.

"So far in *Our Mutual Friend*," Cordelia's voice was low, hardly louder than a whisper, so cautious did she feel, "I'm only halfway through, but there seems to be too many characters, everyone mixed up with everyone else, everything happens by coincidence. I like the Boffins, but they seem almost like comic book characters. You need a map to keep track."

"That makes a lot of sense, I guess. Do you have a favorite Dickens novel?"

Cordelia plunged ahead, ready to be rebuffed: "*Bleak House* is my favorite. It's the most serious and the funniest, about the horrors of the law. Imagine, everyone in court laughing when the case is won, because "Jarndyce and Jarndyce" ends up costing the entire inheritance in fees."

"Yes, yes, Dickens really hated the law."

"And the great love affair between Ada and Richard is so tragic, like love affairs should be. He's such a loser."

Rosalind beamed. They were having a serious discussion. She really liked Cordelia. Maybe, she could finally make a real friend, not like those Marblehead girls who looked at her as if she were some sort of a leper, just because of her parents.

"Well, to be honest, I had as hard time keeping up with all the characters in *Bleak House* as you did in *Our Mutual Friend*, but like you say, it is a more serious book, probably his most. Talk about tragic love affairs, what about *Anna Karenina*? Tolstoy?"

"I read it."

"What a way to end a novel?"

"Oh, after I finished, I kept dreaming about trains coming down the tracks. I think that's what I would have done, poor woman. She should have fallen in love with Levin. He is my hero. He is what he believes, and he carries it out."

"If I had married Levin, he would have bored me. I guess all that farming. I'm just too romantic. I probably would have chosen Vronsky and the train. I love a uniform. And the way my life is going, I'll probably commit suicide one of these days."

"Suicide?" Cordelia stared at Rosalind. "Not me. There's so much to do. Anyway, how could your life be so bad, considering?"

"You mean considering I'm a Story and a Skelton?

Cordelia blushed. "Sorry. That's not for me to say. That was utterly wrong of me." She laid her hand for a moment on Rosalind's arm. "Why are you thinking of...suicide?" She shuddered as she said the word.

"I don't know, that's the problem. My father's a drunk and my mother's a witch. And I just wander."

Cordelia stared down into her coffee.

Rosalind regretted her confession and tried to think of a way to return to books. "Did you have any favorite books growing up? *Wind in the Willows*?"

Cordelia, greatly relieved, beamed at Rosalind. "Oh yes indeed, I loved Mole in his boat and the way he tried to take care of everyone and life on the river—my favorite place."

"Toad was just like my dad, irresponsible, passionate about the wrong little things. I am always having to guard him, but I love him dearly. That was the first book he read to me, before bed."

"My father never read to me." Cordelia's voice dropped again, her face losing all its former animation. "He was always working or dead-tired."

"Your mother?"

"She was too busy. My brother Clem..." Cordelia drew a deep breath as she said the name. "My brother Clem taught me how to read. He taught me everything. Not my parents at all. Clem started with *The Secret Garden*, because he thought I was spoiled and loved nature."

"That's a pretty complicated story to begin to read. I loved it. The mystery of the garden, the boy hidden away up in the house. The unhappy girl, especially."

"I didn't like her at first, to be honest, and then she turned out so goody-goody."

"I think I understood how unhappy and alone she was at

the beginning."

"Really? It was hard for me to imagine being so abandoned. My family has always been on my case, even when they didn't like me."

"My dad was good to me, but I hated the way he and my mom fought and drank and . . . all the rest. You're lucky to have such a kind brother. Mine is evil. I've been on my own a lot. I think I was so unhappy with my parents and my brother that I wanted them to disappear and to find a new brother, like Mary Lennox."

This statement seemed to disturb Cordelia, who did not respond. Rosalind tried to change the subject. "What else did your brother read to you?"

"*Tom Sawyer* and *Huckleberry Finn*. I liked Huck Finn better than Tom Sawyer. He was an adventurer, not a good boy like my brother, who is turning out to be too good and not my friend anymore. He...he...he's just not kind anymore. When things got bad, Huck didn't quit, he took off down the river. That's what I'd like to do these days."

This remark interested Rosalind, but she was wise enough not to pursue it. Mark Twain got them going again and they argued happily until Cordelia had to go home to dinner. Rosalind called the estate and the jeep came to pick her up.

That night at the Bridges, Clem had to work late, repairing a sewer line. When he wasn't home, dinners were often silent to avoid an inevitable argument over Cordelia's general comportment. Her father and mother never discussed their daily work with one another in front of the children. If either addressed Cordelia, they couldn't refrain from criticizing her sullen attitude toward school, her peers, or the family, criticism that provoked an angry, defensive response from her. They had finally found it best to pretend she wasn't present. She acquiesced happily.

Tonight, however, her mother seemed quite pleased with her and immediately asked how her outing with Rosalind Story went.

"Rosalind Story?" said her father in surprise. "Where did she come up with a Story?"

"At Lake Buel. Evidently, Rosalind is visiting her grandmother's estate. James arranged a kayak for her and she discovered that Cordelia was reading a Dickens novel."

"She's always reading something or other instead of paying attention. Look at her, smiling into her dessert."

"Why are you smiling, dear? Have you made a new friend?"

"I was smiling, because the two of you were talking about me as if I weren't sitting here—which you would both prefer."

"Please Cordelia," said her mother, "give me some slack. I started by asking how your outing was. I was pleased that such a very nice young lady was interested in you."

"Pleased and surprised?" Cordelia was not about to offer up that precious few minutes with Rosalind to her parents for their critique. She knew her father would be annoyed. He objected to her having anything to do with the rich young visitors, unless she were providing some service for which she was paid. He didn't mind that his wife's shop catered to the wealthy, but if she became too friendly with her customers, inevitably he would make a sarcastic remark.

"Not in the least surprised," said her mother. "You're a very smart and interesting young woman. I've always hoped you would have a lot of friends." When Cordelia did not respond, she continued, "Are you going to see her again?"

"I doubt it," said Cordelia shortly. "Can I be excused?"

Her mother shrugged her shoulders. As Cordelia left the dining room, her father said, "You see. It's no use. I don't know why you try."

In her room, Cordelia sat at the desk, her hands pressing down on the precious volume of *Our Mutual Friend*, all the muscles of her face pressed close together as she tried not to cry. She loved her parents and desperately wanted them to love her, but since Clem had abandoned her—secretly cut her down—she couldn't unbend even the slightest. It felt like a fire within her. Worse yet, she understood the battle between her parents. Her father hated the rich; her mother found them attractive and catered to them. She had been overjoyed that a granddaughter of old Mrs. Skelton had come to the shop to seek her out. Cordelia exulted in the fact that she had done anything, aside from doing the accounts correctly, to please her mother. She just wanted her mother to open her arms and fold them around her, something she had not done in years—ever since she had opened her shop, an enterprise that had consumed her life as much as her father's life had been consumed since he had finally been appointed head of the public works.

She opened the Dickens and began to read, but soon stopped, realizing she was paying no attention to the words. Instead, she was thinking of Rosalind Story. In a million years, that beautiful, rich girl from the oldest New England families would never become a friend of Cordelia Bridges, the angry, unhappy granddaughter of the Czech woolen worker radical, daughter of a shop-owner and a public works administrator.

If the friendship had been up to Cordelia, that would have been the end of it. But once Rosalind made a decision, she persisted. She remained at the estate the entire summer, even though the plan had been to return earlier. She rented kayaks from Cordelia often and they talked about books and the birds around Lake Buel. What was even better, they laughed together, something neither had done with anyone in a long time. Odd things tickled them: the way a bird would try to scare off another bird; an old man, spitting tobacco accurately into a tin can; and whatever boys their own age did to attract their attention. After all, they were both pretty girls and they admired one another. Then they began to sail together, each appreciating the other's skill. Their sails never luffed.

Rosalind called the shop every few days with suggestions for outings at times Cordelia could take off work. James made the jeep available. Cordelia did not refuse. Her mother encouraged her and let her go as much as possible. She told Rosalind that her closest friend had always been her brother. But that ended when he entered high school. Since then, she had no one with whom she could talk about her reading or anything else. "I guess I've become a little bitch—at least that's what he says, and my folks. I have to agree."

"What happened when he got into high school?"

"He made new friends," said Cordelia, who looked then as though she regretted her answer.

"Your mother said you were an old family in Great Barrington."

Cordelia grimaced. "She was being sarcastic. My grandmother was a slave laborer in the mills—first up in Lawrence and then down here. It took my mother years to get out of the mill. My dad grew up on a farm south of here. He never talked about his family—they probably were sharecroppers or horse thieves or peddlers, I guess. He works for the town now. Old family, that's a laugh."

"Well, my 'old family' is a laugh too. Downhill all the way, degenerates."

For the rest of the summer, embarrassed by this frank talk about their families, the two girls kept their conversation to books and birds and whatever made them laugh. They loved to laugh together at almost anything. They indulged in spirited arguments based on their relative assessment of books they admired. Both had read all of Jane Austen's novels at least twice, but differed in their estimates. Rosalind considered *Pride and Prejudice* the best of all. She identified with Elizabeth Bennet and was thrilled that she and Darcy finally fell in love. Cordelia began by liking Lizzy, especially when she ran through the muddy fields to see her sick sister and appeared in the country house with muddy petticoats and stockings, shocking the proper sisters of Bingley. She was disgusted with Lizzy for her appreciation of Wickham's nauseating flattery and unctuous pursuit and was sure that if he hadn't left her in the lurch in his quest for money, she would have fallen in love with him. She delighted in Lizzy's rejection of Darcy's proposal. But she despised the way her scruples faded away when she visited Darcy's amazing property and house. Finally, she didn't believe Darcy would have changed in character so radically, just because Lizzie accused him of not behaving like a gentleman when he confessed that he was asking her to marry him despite the fact that he despised her family. "Besides, none of Austen's heroines work and they always end up marrying someone with wonderful property, as if that's the proper end of a woman's life. Austen's only image of true love is in *Sense and Sensibility*. Elinor and Edward have a meeting of minds and characters. Her sister Marianne is sickeningly romantic; she believes what she wants to believe about Willoughby and she had to almost die to appreciate the colonel's care, a man she considers ancient. If Elinor had a job, I would have liked her more."

"Oh, come on, Cordelia. Willoughby and Marianne love the same music and poetry. He may not have loved her at the beginning, but before his relative threatened him, he would have married her, despite his need for money."

"Money and property and love, all mixed up, it's disgusting."

"It's England around 1800, and probably us now here. Look at the two of us. Who would have guessed that we would become friends?"

Cordelia blushed to hear that Rosalind felt they were truly friends. Nothing could have pleased her more. To make up for her emotion, she continued the argument. "I still think it was wrong to end every one of those novels with a proper marriage and good property."

"Come on, give Jane Austen some credit. Emma Woodhouse is more discriminating, at least. It takes her the whole novel to appreciate Mr. Knightly."

"You mean to appreciate Mr. Knightly's magnificent property. And why should such a serious man appreciate a twenty-year-old girl with terrible values. The way she talks about Robert Martin, the lowly farmer, too lowly and vulgar for her friend, Harriet Smith. I despised Emma the most of all the heroines. A totally spoiled girl."

Rosalind admitted that, unfortunately, she, herself, was more inclined to fall in love with handsome, romantic scoundrels than with wise, rational men. After some affectionate cajoling, she forced Cordelia to admit that she was not averse to romance. In fact, she was somewhat disappointed that Pierre Bezukhov, a heavy-set, bumbling, serious man, turned out to be the hero of *War and Peace* and ended up with Natasha Rostova, the heroine.

All winter, the two young women carried on their literary appreciation and arguments through correspondence. Their united childhood love for *Heidi*, *The Secret Garden*, *The Wind in the Willows*, and *Winnie-the-Pooh* had cemented their friendship as had their frank disagreement about adult novels, their laughter, and their deep admiration of one another.

Unfortunately, their one reunion during ski-week turned out to be a disappointment for both. Between her winter sports job at the Butternut Hill resort and her mother's store, Cordelia had very little time. She had pleaded with Rosalind to choose another week. Even though she was only a sophomore, Rosalind was overwhelmed taking early SATs and visiting possible colleges with her father, while he was still able to navigate. She could only manage three days, during which she witnessed Cordelia's new-won popularity with the visitors. Her summer friendship with Rosalind had given Cordelia confidence, which was bolstered by her daring athleticism on the slopes. It seemed to Rosalind that her friend was always being mobbed by the visiting boys and girls, everyone striving for her approval. Although she attempted to free herself for Rosalind, all the latter could carry with her was Cordelia's helpless look of apology as she was dragged away—apology and, Rosalind suspected, much more contentment at her popularity than was appropriate. When they bid each other goodbye at the bus station, both felt a desolate hollowness open up as if each had failed the other in some profound way. For the rest of the winter and spring, their letters became strained, as if they were duty-bound to respond. At home, neither received the affection and support they needed to make up for what it seemed they had lost.

XVI

When summer came, Rosalind returned to her grandmother's estate at Great Barrington as soon as school was out, determined to repair the friendship in person. Her first objective, though, was to find a summer job. She had noted Cordelia's contempt for heroines that didn't work. James suggested The Outside Inn drive-in restaurant at the end of Main Street. He let her use his address, a cottage next to the estate and his phone. He knew the manager, who was happy to employ anyone James recommended. She began to work as an anonymous waitress immediately, delaying a call to Cordelia before she was sure the job would work out.

Once she put on the uniform, she surprised herself by immediately stepping into the role: Rosalind Smith, waitress with a name tag, "Roz," on her apron. She became pals with the other waitresses and with the cooks; she joked with the customers, treating them always politely, and when they complained about the orders, she never argued. She took the dishes back with a smile. Her biggest problems were the men and boys who hit on her. They assumed she was a college girl, working for the summer. She was deft at dodging the probing hands. She laughed and put her thumb to her nose. Her sense of humor worked and her patience. It helped that they were grabbing at the waitress not at a Marblehead Story. She wanted the job to work out so that she could become closer to Cordelia. After a week and a half, she called Cordelia. Cordelia's response stunned her.

"A waitress at the Outside Inn? Why?"

"I want to find out who I am."

"That's a joke. You're Rosalind Story, old money from Marblehead, granddaughter of Alicia Skelton, more old money. And you're taking the job from someone who needs it."

Furious, Rosalind lashed out. "You criticize people who don't work, and you don't like me when I work. Well, fuck you. I'll be here all summer, stealing some poor girl's job." She hung up before Cordelia could reply.

The next week was difficult for Rosalind. She felt betrayed. After all, she had confessed her misery at home to Cordelia, her misery at the estate, her misery in life. She had never revealed herself to anyone before. They had talked intimately about books, about love, about everything. They had laughed together. She thought Cordelia had understood, that Cordelia was the friend she had been seeking. Instead, she had been branded "old money." She was tempted to quit the job.

And then what? The estate? Marblehead with her lost father, drinking himself to death? And her witch mother and her mother's lovers—women and men? And then, if she quit, what would Cordelia think of her? Fuck her, she thought. After her first paycheck, she'd find a cheap room with one of the waitresses and stick it out until September. She'd show everybody, no matter how miserable it made her.

Betty Anne White, a single local woman of about forty-five, was only too glad to share her room and save some money for the winter when the trade declined as did the tips, except on ski and skate weekends. She liked Betty Anne and Betty Anne liked her, just as she was, a fellow worker, helpful, friendly, funny. She went bowling with Betty Anne one night when one of the team was sick and delighted everyone with a 207. One morning Rosalind woke up realizing that she liked herself better than ever since she was a little child.

To her surprise, by the third week at Outside Inn, she began to love her job. Serving people seemed to be her vocation; satisfying their hungers; pleasing them. The crankier and more demanding they began, the more delight she experienced when she turned them around. She took an interest in the menu and the ingredients. She had eaten in fine restaurants all her life; her mother and father both had refined palates; Beulah was a great cook, and she had spent many hours in the kitchen, helping out. She began to make suggestions to the manager about improving the menu and its promotion. He was a tired, middle-aged man, harassed at home and picked at by the owners over the telephone. They hardly ever appeared. He listened to her, because she was James' protégé and because she approached him diffidently, deferring to his judgment, unlike anyone before. They discussed the potatoes, the salads, the burgers, all tentatively, subject to the supplies and the timing of the chefs. Soon the menu improved: hand-cut French fries; panini; Tuscan salads; Asian salads; and burgers with various imported cheeses and spices. She suggested labeling the produce "local" and "farm fresh," which made him laugh, but seemed to impress the tourists. After some weeks, she suggested a new shape for the menus, a fancier typeface, and photographs like at Denny's, but photoshopped to give it an up-scale look and feel. The local printer was a friend of James too, so it was all in the Great Barrington family and done at cost. She repainted the counter with impressionistic colors. By the second month, the trade was increasing. Many more visitors showed up. She painted the picnic tables in various colors with images of local wildflowers and plants that she photographed and transferred to the wood, complete with their names. The waitresses and chefs were pleased; they were getting increased tips and receiving compliments from the customers. Everyone liked the way their workplace looked. It made it easier to bear the long, difficult hours. She deferred their compliments to the manager, who accepted the praise, winking at her. She replied with a graceful little curtsey. It had become a working courtship.

And then one night, as she waited at the counter for an order, she felt an arm around her shoulder and a hand on her buttocks. She cocked an elbow and swung around ready to strike, when she came nose-to-nose with her brother Jason's grinning face.

"How's my waitress, uh," grinned down at the name tag, "Sis' Roz?"

She lowered her elbow and levered it into his chest. "I'm working, please back off. People are waiting for their food."

"Okay, okay. I thought you would be glad to see me."

"No gladder than you've ever been to see me."

He laughed. "Okay, Ms Roz. I thought you'd be lonely so I brought up some Princeton friends whom I'd told about my good-looking sister."

He had heard from their father, that she was working in Great Barrington, and brought his buddies to crash at the estate. She felt gripped by all the despair she felt at home. He liked the Skelton cousins no better than she, and obviously only came up to bug her. She had never understood why her brother took such pleasure in tormenting her. Her mother made it clear that she disliked her because she resembled her father. And Jason mirrored their mother's contempt for his father. She understood why their father embarrassed Jason. Still, he had picked at her since she was a little girl. And he was four years older. It was only after he had gone off to school and she had reached adolescence that she began her wild ways.

Betty Anne was kind enough to take Jason's table and Rosalind managed to get through the night avoiding him and his friends. At home, Betty Anne commented on Jason's good manners. "He's damned good looking and tips like a baron or something. Are you sure he's your brother?"

"He comes from a different side of the family—first and second marriages, you know," was all Rosalind could respond. She would have liked to pour out all of her unhappiness, but Betty Anne would not have understood; she was a tough, good-natured woman, who had gone through two marriages with abusive husbands. She knew all about first and second marriages and asked no more questions. She read glamour and movie magazines. She would have found Rosalind's problems incomprehensible. Rosalind missed Cordelia more than ever, but Cordelia had never showed up at the Outside Inn. She was obviously uninterested in the friendship.

For two days, Jason and his friends did not appear at the restaurant. Rosalind was beginning to relax, hoping he had become bored with his cousins and his demanding grandmother and had returned home. On the third night, she was stunned to see him and his friends seat themselves at one of her tables with four girls, one of them Cordelia. Betty Anne was busy on the other side of the lawn. She steeled herself and approached to take their orders. To her relief, Jason seemed too busy with Cordelia to give her any trouble. Cordelia ordered only a black coffee. Rosalind kept her eyes above Cordelia's head as she scribbled it down. The other girls were obviously visitors who had to be prompted about the menu. The orders were elaborate and she had to explain the ingredients. Two of the girls were vegetarians, one was a vegan, all of which made it easier as the menu had very little to satisfy their needs. They were not polite and asked their dates to be taken to another restaurant. Cordelia looked uncomfortable. Jason laughed and insisted that they stay. "You do have a 'local' head of lettuce and a tomato for my friends, don't you, along with your so-called local 'farm fresh' produce, Ms Roz?"

"Whatever satisfies the ladies," she replied.

"I didn't want to come here," said Cordelia, directly to her.

"But I did," said Jason. "After all, one should patronize one's relatives."

Rosalind could not resist replying, "You're an expert at patronizing."

"Chalk one up for the Sis'." Jason made an imaginary checkmark in the air.

Two of Jason's friends complained about their burgers, one because it was too rare, the other too well done. She simply switched the two platters around, "Rare for you and well done for you!" They laughed and copied Jason's check marks.

When they were through, Jason tried to pay with an American Express card. Rosalind pushed the card back at him. "We don't take American Express."

"Everyone else does. What the fuck's wrong with this place?"

"Because Amex fees are too fucking high."

The sister and brother stared at one another. Finally, Jason shrugged and proceeded to collect cash from his friends, spreading it out on the table: bills and quarters and dimes and nickels and pennies. He counted it out slowly to show her they weren't shortchanging her. There was nothing left for tips. Cordelia leaped up and ran out onto the street. Jason threw a kiss at Rosalind and followed Cordelia. His friends, laughing, followed him with their dates.

As Rosalind was gathering up the bills and change, her head down, her cheeks flushed in embarrassment, one of the girls came back. "I'm sorry," she said without looking at Rosalind and deliberately left a twenty-dollar bill on the table. Rosalind returned to the counter, waving the bill at Betty Ann. She stuffed the twenty into the common tip bottle announcing, "Royalty rewards us."

As they were cleaning up, Cordelia appeared next to the table Rosalind was scrubbing. Rosalind ignored her.

"I'm sorry, really sorry. I tried to get them to go somewhere else, but he insisted."

Rosalind continued scrubbing the other tables. Cordelia followed her. "I didn't know he was your brother."

"That's all right. One of your dear friends from the city came back and left me a twenty-buck tip."

"They aren't friends of mine. They rented a couple of sailboats on the lake this morning and your brother asked me out."

"And you were available to 'Old Money.'"

"It wasn't like that. I've been really miserable about...about us. I don't know why I was so pissed that you were working here. It was all about me."

"I'm sorry, Cordelia. I'm too exhausted to go into all this. Last winter...no, no, why don't we just let it go. It hasn't been a waste. I seem to like my job and people here actually like me."

"About last winter, it was the first time anyone noticed me—boys, that is, and even the girls. And then...Oh shit, your brother was quite polite, with me, at the lake. He was...attracted to me. I just wasn't used to that. He was a pretty good sailor and taught his friends—we taught them together, it was fun. Tonight, I thought he was a shit."

"I know my brother's a shit. But he does have good taste in girls and knows how to charm them. Good night, I'm going home to sleep."

Cordelia raised her hands in surrender. "Can we meet sometime. I've been feeling terrible about what I said about your job, but I didn't know how to approach you or whether you would want me to. Everything had been so awkward last winter. I thought you hated me, and I sort of hated myself. I've missed you."

"I'll be here every morning, setting up and at home on the corner of Cottage and Russell Streets, on Thursdays, my day off."

All week, Rosalind waited, morning and night, for Cordelia to show up at the drive-in. It felt like the worst week in her life, although she knew it wasn't. There had been worse at home—much worse. Still, she wished and feared that Cordelia might persist, although she had no idea what she would feel or say or do. By Wednesday, she was certain it was hopeless. At least last winter she had hope and had crafted a plan that would bring the friendship alive. She would get a job and Cordelia would be proud of her and the two of them would be working and thinking together about the future. She wanted to tell Cordelia about all the colleges she had visited and why she had chosen Bryn Mawr and not Mount Holyoke, the only two that had appealed to her. Cordelia was the only human being after her father with whom she felt she could share her desire to write and paint and read great literature and become free of all the misery of her childhood and growing up. But now she had no one. Jason had appeared and destroyed everything. No, no, she corrected herself. Cordelia had destroyed everything last winter, when she had suddenly become popular.

By Wednesday night, when Rosalind fell into bed, exhausted from the day's work and her anxious despair, she decided that she hated Cordelia, the beautiful, the athletic, the interesting Cordelia, who, for a moment, had recognized what was most important within her. With Cordelia, she had just been Rosalind, not a Story or a Skelton, a friend who was at last preparing to flee the horror of Marblehead and Great Barrington and to go out into the world—Paris, London, San Francisco, actually out to a suburb of Philadelphia, which was almost as good. No mother, no brother, no father, and, alas, no Cordelia.

The next morning, her day off, feeling very sorry for herself and angry at the world, she attacked the eggs with a fork, whipping them up to a froth. There was a knock on the front door. She ignored it, not wanting to face a neighbor, who probably wanted to borrow something—sugar, milk, a slab of butter—their neighbors were pretty needy in this part of town and considered everyone a relative of some sort, a relative in poverty, she guessed. The knocking ceased. Pleased, she decided to make herself a grand breakfast—a cheese and mushroom omelet and bacon. Betty Ann had a large appetite and stocked the fridge with all sorts of items, leftovers from the drive-in that Rosalind usually didn't eat. Just as she was about to spread the eggs in the buttered pan, there was a hesitant knock at the back door. She turned angrily and saw there through the door's window, Cordelia, a pleading smile on her face. Rosalind began to cry, to sob; she couldn't stop herself; she couldn't turn away. Through the window, she saw that Cordelia too was crying. Carefully, Rosalind put down the basin of eggs, turned off the gas, and took several deep breaths. She turned and walked slowly to the door. When she opened it, the two girls fell into one another's arms.

They spent the day hiking along the Housatonic and talking. They were friends again, sisters who had been miserable until they had met the summer before, agreeing and disagreeing about Dickens and Jane Austen and Tolstoy. It turned out that Cordelia had missed the friendship just as much. Since last summer, she had been going through difficult changes in her life. Her brother's abandonment had soured her affectionate temperament. Until the summer she met Rosalind, she had almost no friends and was considered by her parents to be not only unattractive but a very difficult child. But in the autumn of last year and through the winter, her situation had improved considerably. Her athletic ability as a skier and snowboarder had attracted the attention of the wealthy visitors, who had asked her out on dates. The local boys looked on with disapproval, as did her parents. Her arrival at the restaurant with Jason the other night had been simply a continuation of her popularity with the visitors and alienation at home. In fact, she confessed to Rosalind that she now no longer knew who she was or where she belonged—very much like Rosalind, she admitted sheepishly. By the day's end, the two young women felt closer than ever. Before they parted, on a sudden impulse, Cordelia invited Rosalind to dinner at her house for the next Thursday.

"I want you to meet my brother. I think you two might very much like one another—you both read, bird, love plants and flowers, and hike. I'm sure you will know how to charm my parents, despite your wealthy family. Mother has asked about you often and was quite pleasantly surprised when I told her you were waitressing at the drive-in. That impressed my father too. My parents believe in independence."

XVII

The dinner at the Bridges turned out to be a much more complicated event than Cordelia had expected. Rosalind charmed Cordelia's parents, as Cordelia knew she would, but in a way that disturbed her. She was taken aback by Rosalind's energetic fabrication of her "old family" failure, along with a dire description of her mother's dissolute behavior. As unhappy as Cordelia was at home, she didn't think she would speak disparagingly about her parents to strangers. She was shocked when she heard Rosalind claiming that her father had died in the Korean War, an outright lie. Watching her friend's performance, she began to wonder just how well she knew her.

When Clem arrived late from work and was introduced, he took on an unfamiliar formality, shaking hands with Rosalind and bowing slightly. Cordelia had to keep herself from laughing. He was obviously very interested in her friend. And then Rosalind began to speak eloquently about the landscape, the birds, the plants, and the river. By the time Rosalind said goodnight, Clem proposed a date for the three of them on the next Thursday. "If it's okay with Dad, I'll trade my day off and we can take Rosalind on our favorite Housatonic trail, right Cordelia?"

This was the first time Clem had spoken with such warmth to Cordelia in what seemed to her years. Her parents, obviously taken with Rosalind, urged the plan. That night, Cordelia tossed and turned in bed, wondering why she had invited her friend to meet the family. After all, she had suspected Clem would be interested, but did she want to trade off her friendship for his approval? Or, for that matter, her parent's approval? Ever since she had begun to be popular with the visitors, her father had sniped at her, as if she were betraying her origins. And this evening, she had to witness his seduction by a very clever, attractive daughter of "old money," who, it seemed, was capable of lying, even about the father she loved.

The rest of the summer turned out to be a torment for Cordelia. Although, her responsible brother and her responsible friend always made a point of including her in their plans, there was little time for Cordelia to spend alone with Rosalind. She could tell that Clem and Rosalind would prefer to be alone together. Often, despite their pleas, she pretended to be busy. And then one Thursday, Rosalind called and begged Cordelia to come by the restaurant at closing time. "I have to talk to you, Cordelia, I really do. I'm desperate."

They sat on one of the picnic tables closest to the river. The rising moon was almost full, casting wavering shadows of the willows and pine across the water making its stately, calm way toward the ocean. Rosalind lay a hand on Cordelia's forearm. "Your brother really loves you, Cordelia."

"That's your desperate message?" Cordelia drew her arm away.

"He's the most honest human being I've ever met. He lives by principle, unlike most of us."

"He had a curious way of showing his love to me."

"He explained it all to me—earnestly, honestly. He felt you were too dependent on him and would never grow up on your own unless he withdrew. It hurt him terribly to cut you off, when he saw how much it hurt you. He admits he was pretty mean to you, but look, you made your own life and he's immensely proud of you. He thinks you're much smarter than he is, much more able. He thinks you're going to be very, very successful at whatever you try to do. He's not someone who would make up something like that."

Cordelia believed that her brother was honest, but she wasn't quite sure that Rosalind was. She had seen how deftly she had dealt with Cordelia's parents and then with Clem and even with her. The summer had been very difficult, watching the way Rosalind took over Clem, even the way she had maneuvered him to be affectionate to her. Still, Cordelia very much wanted to believe her friend. "If only what you say is true," she sighed.

"Oh Cordelia, it is, it is. Clem is...he's wonderfully true. Oh Cordelia, I've wanted to spend more time with you. Our friendship means everything to me. I love you and...and...I've fallen deeply in love with your brother, which makes it all so difficult. The three of us are so busy working and there's so little time."

Cordelia did not reply. She had no idea how to respond. Her affections were so mixed with her resentments. First, she had lost her brother; then, she had found a true friend; then, she had lost her friend to her brother; and now, if she could believe Rosalind, they both loved her and, it seemed, they loved one another. Was she mean enough to wish that they preferred her to each other?

The two girls stared at the river and the moon. An owl hooted, three hoots and then a fourth; three hoots and then a fourth. Rosalind sighed. "I love the Berkshires; I love Great Barrington; I love your parents; I love you; and I love your brother. It's so calm here, so serene. Even the hills are rounded and the fields stretch out gently. You're all so responsible, working your way through life, protecting one another, looking always to the future. It's so unlike the mad seacoast, the waves crashing against those jagged rocks, a cursed coast inhabited by degenerate predators like my mother or wasted failures like my father."

Cordelia was moved by this romantic outburst, in spite of an edge of skepticism at how easily her friend's words seemed to flow. What could she do? Clem was pleased; her parents were pleased; Rosalind was happy. And she was no longer an ugly duckling. The best that she could do was to pretend that she was delighted with the way the summer was turning out and hide her anxiety. She embraced Rosalind and thanked her.

At the end of summer, when Rosalind left for home, she hugged and kissed Cordelia and Clem, promising to write each of them faithfully. As the bus pulled out, Cordelia felt very confused about her place in the world.

* * *

Rosalind faithfully wrote both brother and sister, but the pressure of more college visits, applications, battles with her mother, and efforts to take care of her rapidly failing father made it impossible for her to visit Great Barrington that winter. Summer finally came. Rosalind returned to her job at the Outside Inn and was ardently reunited with Clem. They saw each other every moment they were free from their jobs. They were both grateful and kind to Cordelia, but only up to a point, at which they fled to be alone. Clem's courtship of Rosalind was passionate, but celibate; they made love just to the point of intercourse. Rosalind would have gone further. Clem reasoned clearly that, if they went all the way, they would endanger their futures. He had enlisted in the family doctrine: education first, vocation next, and then the fulfillment of passion and marriage. At first, Rosalind felt completely safe in his hands and in the protection of the Berkshire family she had adopted. There were moments, however, when she was alone at work or waking early in the morning, the dawn sun just edging its way up the walls of her room, that her desire overcame her. Once more, she felt within her the bruised child of drunken, spectral parents, one a vicious scavenger, the other a gentle, passive, self-destructive dreamer. At those moments, the waves of the Atlantic beat upon the rocky coastline, tidelands flooded, lightning shattered oaks, and to survive she donned the armor of sardonic pessimism about all human endeavor. She resented Clem's judicious, country timidity. She wanted, she needed to complete their furtive caresses. The only outer sign of these attacks from her early life and the passion of youth was a sudden rude shake of her entire body, like a wet dog drying his fur, ridding herself of that other terror-stricken, embattled self. Once more she became Rosalind of the Berkshires, safe, happy, beloved, able, striding confidently into a future of careful accomplishment with all desire tamped down.

The summer drew toward the moment when Rosalind and Clem would have to say, what seemed, a final goodbye. They were about to enter college—Clem to MIT, Rosalind to Bryn Mawr—and realized that despite their plans to meet during the winter, either in Cambridge or Philadelphia, their lives might finally diverge. Their embraces became more and more passionate. One afternoon, on a long hike into a wilderness area, they fell into one another's arms in a secluded forest dell. They became so aroused, that Clem had to tear himself away, shuddering and muttering curses, leaving a tearful and angry Rosalind slumped in the grass. As they hiked toward town, they did not speak to one another.

They were just passing the ski lifts of the Butternut Hill Sport Resort, when Cordelia, who was working that summer for the town tourist bureau, appeared with a crowd of visitors.

"I'm taking them up to see the sunset. It should be beautiful tonight. Why don't you two come along?"

"No," said Clem, "We're exhausted."

"Yes," said Rosalind, angrily, staring at him. "It will be the end of a perfect day."

Cordelia, seeing the confrontation and not wanting to alienate her brother, waved the two of them off. "There are already too many. You guys go on home."

"No," said Rosalind, her eyes still locked on Clem, "I want to see the sunset. It may be my last time."

Clem put out his hands, pleading, "Roz?" But Rosalind was too frustrated and angry to give in. Cordelia looked at her brother, hoping he would insist. Instead, he shrugged and the couple joined Cordelia's crowd taking the lift up Butternut Hill.

Once everyone had assembled on the top outside the lift station, Cordelia led them on a trail to a bluff facing west, where the sun was just descending toward a hazy horizon. Further along, a group of young men and women were already assembled, gazing out toward the valley below, where a hang-glider, brightly illuminated by the sun's rays, sailed slowly back and forth, rising and falling in the updrafts of wind.

"What ho," came a call, "Folks, my working sister, Ms Smith, has arrived!"

Rosalind was stunned to recognize her brother Jason, who came toward them. He forcibly embraced her. She pushed him away.

"No affection for your dear brother?"

"What are you doing up here?"

"Hang-gliding, of course." He turned and looked at Clem. "Aren't you going to introduce me to your boyfriend?"

Clem put out his hand, "Clem Bridges."

Jason shook his hand firmly and clasped him around the shoulder, "Jason Story, of the Marblehead Storys." He threw out his arm toward the group he had left, "And those are the Salem Skeltons, my sister's cousins along with some disreputable former Princeton comrades."

Clem made a mock bow toward Jason's group.

Cordelia stepped up to her brother's side, waved, and added, "And I am Cordelia Bridges, of the Great Barrington Bridges and the Great Barrington Tourist Bureau. Please don't let us interrupt your sport. We're simply here to see the sunset."

She turned and shooed her group along the bluff away from the hang-gliders. Clem would have followed them, but Jason detained him and Rosalind. "Sister, dear. You're a great adventurer. Wouldn't you like to take a glide into the sunset? Or you, Mr. Bridges. You look pretty athletic and after all, it's your hill."

The Skelton cousins and Jason's Princeton friends gathered around them with expectant looks.

"I'm afraid it's rather late in the day for any more gliding," said Clem.

"Have you ever hang-glided?"

"No. And I don't intend to start now, nor will Rosalind."

"Does he speak for you, Sis?"

"What is this 'Sis' business. You've never called me 'Sis'. Please stop playing games."

"Hey, I was just being polite, brotherly. If you're afraid it's too late to take a leap, just say so."

Rosalind looked around at the group, who were watching her. She felt she had been thrust back into her Marblehead life. "Fuck you, Jason. You know I'm not afraid of anything."

"Then give it a try. Into the sunset."

Rosalind shook herself violently, attempting to return to the safety of her newfound country life. She looked at Clem, hoping he would command her. He stood motionless, his eyes questioning her, as if to find out just how reckless she was. At least, that was what she thought. She was still furiously frustrated that he hadn't made love to her in the forest, preserving his safety and small-town purity. "Okay, I'll leap into the sunset. Where's the fucking contraption."

Clem stepped forward. "No, that's damned foolishness. It's too late in the day."

At that moment, Cordelia appeared. "What's going on here?"

"Your dear friend, Rosalind, is about to prove her courage by taking a maiden flight on a hang-glider."

"Sorry, that's against the rules. No gliding past four o'clock, and not without a safety guide. You guys shouldn't be doing this anyway. It's all posted at the foot of the lift."

"We signed all the releases and the supervisor okayed it."

"Anyway, it's way too late. I've been doing this all summer and I know what I'm saying."

"You going to cop-out, Rosalind?" challenged Jason, taking his sister by the hand and leading her to the remaining hang-gliders on the cliff.

"For Christ's sake, Rosalind. Use your head," said Clem, taking hold of her arm.

Rosalind threw off Clem's clasp and, with her brother's help, began to step into the harness. Clem pushed Jason away and pulled the harness off Rosalind. "These gliders look jerry-rigged, not safe at all." He bent over and began to examine the gliders, carefully.

"Rosalind," pleaded Cordelia, "Clem knows what he's saying. He's a meticulous mechanic."

"He's never hang-glided," said Jason. "He's just chicken. What do you say, dear sister?"

"I said I'd take a leap," said Rosalind. "Just strap the damned thing on me and tell me how to fly it."

Cordelia leaped ahead, strapped on the free hang-glider and

holding onto the other apparatus, dove off the cliff. She meant to get rid of both gliders so Rosalind wouldn't try the dangerous sport. As she left the ground, however, Jason ripped the last hang-glider from her grasp. She went sailing off, expertly taking advantage of an updraft.

Jason held the glider up in front of Rosalind, who was about to step forward, when Clem thrust her aside.

"Behold," announced Jason, "a knight errant, saving his lady. Sir Clem Bridges, are you willing to brave the summer sunset and fly off Butternut Hill?"

Clem turned and looked at Rosalind, who knew she could stop the charade at that moment.

Rosalind remembered that moment for the rest of her life.

XVIII

Some forty years after that Berkshire Hills sunset and 2,980 miles to the west, Brooks Gardner, née Rosalind Story, perched at Smitty's Bar on Caledonia Street in Sausalito at eleven at night, drinking gin and bitters. She had been drinking steadily for three hours. Tina, the bartender, would have refused any other customer who had put away so much alcohol, but she knew Brooks' capacity seemed to be infinite. Eventually, "the grand dame" would rise, curtsy, and walk steadily to her car. The next night, she would arrive promptly at eight o'clock, order a couple of hardboiled eggs, a pickle, and her first gin and bitters. Now and then, Tina would offer a bit of local gossip, a couple breaking up, a woman with breast cancer, a bankrupt local who had tried to commit suicide, and the two would nod sympathetically. It was Tina's way of making her usual customers feel at home. She never expected much of a conversation from drinkers like Brooks.

For years Brooks had come into Smitty's with her partner, Millard Wiles, and their friend Justin McCarthy, all three steady drinkers, but then, consecutively the two men committed suicide off the same cliff just before Stinson Beach, a tale Tina had to offer other customers as local history befitting Sausalito, a town once famous for its speakeasy past, its suffering artists, and self-destructive geniuses. "They chose the same cliff, just south of Deep Ravine, one of our favorite local landmarks. Very appropriate for two such good friends." In recent years, the town had become almost too respectable for barroom chatter. Tina was happy to serve one of the survivors of that glorious past. Tonight, she was pleased to be serving another old-time drinker, who sat at the other end of the bar. Isaac Koenig sipped his drink of preference, a fifteen-year-old single malt Glenfiddich or Macallan, neither of which Smitty's normally carried. He had been willing to settle for a Chivas Regal Scotch, up, with a glass of soda until Tina ordered his favorites from the suppliers. He drank more sparingly than Brooks, but just as steadily. His capacity was a great deal less than Brooks' and he came in only sporadically. Over the years, he had arrived now and then with different young women, never with his wife, who, he once suggested to Tina, was allergic to Sausalito. Very recently he had begun to come in alone and to stay longer and longer. The marriage, it seemed, had broken up on a trip to Japan. When she offered this bit of news to Brooks, Brooks had rolled her eyes and said that she knew all about it, but had offered no further information, much to Tina's disappointment.

Tonight, Doctor Koenig offered to buy Brooks a drink, "Make it a Tanqueray. She deserves the best. Leave the bottle on the bar."

Brooks waved away the offer. Tina reported, "She likes her gin cheap and sharp."

Isaac picked up his drink and moved down the bar. "Do you mind company?" he asked, politely.

"I don't think I make good company these days," replied Brooks.

"We could make bad company together."

"I know you're suffering too, Isaac. Why double the pain?"

"Maybe we can halve the pain."

"If you insist, but I don't want therapy."

"I wouldn't mind some. I seem to have run out, myself."

This interested Brooks, who could hardly believe that Isaac Koenig, the great Jungian, could have lost his belief in himself, even if Cordelia had left him. Surely, he would have found the language to accept her behavior as a grievous psychic fault explainable only by reference to cosmic archetypes.

"Language, language," said Isaac, as he perched on the stool next to Brooks. "That's what did us in. Words like love, ecstasy, individuation, scapegoat, the shadow of our bright side—language saved me from my family, language provided me a profession, language brought us together. Cordelia loved language as much as I did: Shakespeare, John Donne, Doctor Johnson. We met as abandoned orphans, we bonded in ecstasy, we tried to create love, with a capital L, and parted in disillusionment. I know I wasn't physically faithful, but it wasn't until I met my master in language, my middle-European Magyar Queen, who could seduce a crab, an alligator, a camel, or a mere man with a siren song and sinuous body, that I sinned in spirit and am now enslaved by the harshest mistress ever spawned on the banks of the Danube. I can't go home to her without submitting to a third-degree examination. All I asked of Cordelia was to save me from this fate, in the name of our love. Instead, she abandoned me, just as my mother did in death, and my father and brother did in life."

"That's quite a dirge, dear Isaac. You don't seem to have lost your gift in tongues."

"I told you I was willing to listen, if you want to talk. I promise I won't try to be of help. I'll just listen."

"Well, I've been abandoned too—many times, many, many times."

Thus began an odd barroom friendship between Brooks and Isaac, who had avoided one another, more or less, for years. For a month, they met three or four times a week at Smitty's; drank and talked and played liar's dice, ping-pong, and shuffle-board, never ceasing their conversation. Tina told her other customers that she had never heard two people talk so much. In the beginning, they didn't seem to like one another particularly, but it didn't take them more than a couple of nights to realize how much they shared. From what Tina could make out from all the talk was that they had both spent their lives taking care of people, all of whom left them resenting their care, or simply died before their help took effect. One way or another, each of these two interesting Smitty customers ended up lonely, with a deep sense of injustice in their lives.

"I had talent," said Brooks as she leaned over the pool table, squinted down the cue propped over her long, elegantly arched fingers with nails painted in a subdued mauve. As she continued, she delivered a devastating curl to the cue ball that careened off of two balls and sent a third ball squarely into a pocket. "I have talent. I can write a story as well as any of the so-called geniuses who publish in *Abalone*; I can paint a post-impressionist painting with the best of the avant-garde in Latelier's gallery; but I've been cursed with the need, the compulsion, the addiction of caretaking."

"You think I haven't been cursed too?" replied Isaac. "I've got that same disease of trying to help people survive the failure of their lives. The death of my mother left me with the overwhelming need to weld my father, my brother, and me into a nurturing family, an impossible task when faced with two such perversely sadistic, self-hating monsters, who turned their violence upon me." Awkwardly, resting his cue stick on his wrist, Isaac drew it back and thrust it forward, jettisoning the cue ball into the air and off the table. As he scurried over to retrieve the cue ball, he continued his complaint. "And so the rest of my life was devoted to taking care of others, especially Cordelia, who, it turns out, hated me for my efforts and abandoned me, helplessly entangled with her best friend, the Magyar Satan who holds me in bondage."

Death, death, death, the two agreed had dogged their lives, destroying their best efforts to love and be loved. Each night as Brooks won their many games, they confessed the details of their lives to one another, receiving warm understanding and sympathy. Somehow, their conversations inevitably returned to their love for Cordelia, who remained elusive, out of reach, a mysterious, attractive being who seemed to need no one except herself.

"To be honest," said Brooks, sending the puck down the board with devastating accuracy, scattering Isaac's pucks in all directions as it came to rest gently against its target, "I don't think she even loved her brother, the only man I ever loved. Just herself, alone in the universe, from the beginning."

Isaac disagreed, declaring that Clem was the only person Cordelia ever loved. His death had left Cordelia, at base, a cold, unfeeling narcissist sufficient only to herself. "Our children depended upon me for hugs and kisses and tears and admiration. She fed them with bottles and displayed only approval and disapproval: judgment. And, it appears, she judged me severely, while I, blinded by my passion for her, only discovered her disapproval too late."

Brooks did not hesitate to point out that during the entire marriage, Isaac had given Cordelia a great deal of which to disapprove.

He replied: "She never objected to my affairs. I think she welcomed them. It was a mark of my value to her. She possessed what other women desired. And it left her alone."

"Isaac, Isaac, what sort of Jungian fairy tale are you indulging in?"

Isaac did not reply immediately. But after bungling several forehands, he lay down his paddle, and nodded his head. "You're right, absolutely right. Cordelia had every reason to be angry. If she could only know how miserably Dorottya treats me, she would understand that I am more than paying for my sins."

Brooks laughed. "Well, dear Isaac, I feel sorry for you. I only met Dorottya twice, and I wouldn't wish her on anyone, not even the philandering Jungian of Gate 5."

"After all, Cordelia was not the warmest lover. By the time we married, she simply wanted to get it done so that she could get on with her more important work. Everything in her life is scheduled. When her orgasm didn't occur promptly, she simply got up and took a shower and was off to some committee meeting."

"You don't have to make excuses to me. In the end, each of us lives alone. But we do want our sincere attempts to help, to aid, to perform acts of love to be recognized."

"Cordelia was incapable of expressing gratitude—even when she felt it."

"A common disease. After what I did for Ted Journey, providing a brilliant stable of writers, arranging for the acquisition of *Abalone* as a farm club for his fucking press, and organizing a brilliant, festive celebration on the *Vallejo*, he walked off with my dumb assistant. It turned out, he had bought the *Vallejo* wreck even before the party and was planning all the time to have me evicted."

"So, you're homeless?"

"Oh no, there are some good people left in this world. Yvonne Latelier has been immensely gracious. I'm living at her in-law apartment on Russian Hill and subbing for her gallery manager, who's having a baby."

"You do manage."

"I help people and they reciprocate. I was loyal to Yvonne during the brutal divorce. After all, she wouldn't have that gallery if I hadn't persuaded Journey. I was even loyal to Journey at the time, but he repaid me by hating me, the idiot, and walked off with poor, dumb Berenice, when he could have had me with a finger snap. I love Yvonne, but she had no idea how to be a supportive wife to that very wealthy, very disappointed, very attractive, and somewhat morose literary man. Yvonne was simply too proud to put up with him. I've spent a lifetime hiding my pride. I know books, I know authors, I understand literature better than he, and I understand the art he's collected and where it fits in the modern canon better than even Yvonne. On top of which, I remain connected with collectors and society on both coasts. I could have arranged a very attractive life for such a depressive man, without arousing his silly defensive posture."

"It seems you did just that while doing your generous good deeds for him."

"Alas, you're right. And when I think of how good I was to Berenice, the Alaskan orphan. I arranged editing and computer jobs for her all the while she was married to Smithey and then welcomed her into my arms when she was devastated by his death. And suddenly she won't answer my calls. I'm sure it's that bastard Journey, and he'll dump her in a matter of weeks and she'll be back asking my help. Of course, I'll help, sucker that I am."

* * *

Ted Journey did not dump Berenice Smithey. In fact, he married her and built her a house on the Bolinas mesa over the ocean. Brooks had experienced many setbacks in her ambitious life, but Journey's preference for Berenice had been a blow from which she found it difficult to recover. In the past, she had always relied upon a sort of inexhaustible exuberance, an ability to face the future optimistically, without needless regrets. After all, she had survived her childhood, her mother's hatred, her father's decline, and the death of a number of people she had loved. She wondered whether her current malaise was simply the onset of old age. She had counted upon finally settling down with Ted Journey, the first time that she imagined permanence in her life that had consisted up to now of a constant drifting forward, from man to man, from project to project.

In what she recognized as an arbitrary fit of madness, she linked the couple's departure together that night of the *Vallejo* celebration to the appearance of Cordelia. For months after that encounter, Brooks brooded and drank, contemplating the downward arc of her life. She devoted her time to Yvonne's gallery and cooking, but otherwise she hardly went out.

Of course, she couldn't blame Cordelia, who knew neither Journey or Berenice. Brooks simply felt that the three fates had decreed her failures from the moment Cordelia's brother Clem launched himself from Butternut Hill.

XIX

A year after the literary celebration on the *Vallejo* at which Cordelia met Brooks, née Rosalind, and Ted Journey connected with Berenice Smithey, Monty Wolfe was asked to make another one of his memorial speeches. This one caused him more pain than most, because it was for Rob Ellenberg, with whom Monty had become even closer after Sylvia's death. The memorial took place in Mill Valley's Art Center just across the street from the movie theater. The building had the gracious country look of a lodge, with heavy dark beams, a great stone fireplace, and large framed windows looking out onto carefully groomed gardens. The main hall with twenty rows of seats was full, with standing room all around the side aisles. The Ellenberg daughter had asked Monty to speak last, a summing up. When Monty mounted the stage, he had the spectral image before him of Sylvia's tragic accident and the speech he had made celebrating her special joy and love of life. And now, it was Rob's moment for a celebration. Monty felt he was floating some miles above the rolling hills and mountains and sea coast of Northern California where Rob and Sylvia and their daughter had hiked and biked and fished and camped.

"I'll begin with Rob's voice. I'm going to miss that voice, calling to suggest a walk in the morning with his dog along the Corte Madera salt marsh or a ride up in the foothills of the mountain above his house. His voice had an edge to it and a staccato rhythm. There was an edge too in what he had to say—sort of an irascible, humorous challenge in which, after a moment, one became aware of how much affection it contained. As we walked through his neighborhood and familiar trails, he greeted people and chatted with them in such a natural good-humored manner that one felt part of a community. When it was early in the morning, he threw the newspapers of nearby homes from the front walks to the porches.

"If you were bound to Rob in a serious way, he took on responsibility for you without intruding. He was a fairly early mountain biker and inspired me to buy a bike and to go out with him. I never became proficient in the art, but he was as patient with me as if I were a child. I remember with vividness one moment in particular. We had ascended the streets of Mill Valley on our bikes and crossed Highway 1, eventually reaching Coyote Ridge, up a steep incline that he warned me about, tolerant that I'd probably have to walk the bike up part of it. The Ridge, mildly downhill, was quite a relief, but I ran into trouble descending Fox Trail Fire Road. Rob was far ahead of me on the steep hill. I, of course, somewhat of a competitor, wanted to keep up. To my surprise, halfway down he pulled up suddenly. He dismounted his bike and began waving his arms. Fool and novice that I was, I didn't understand that he was warning me. My bike accelerated faster and faster. I will always remember the look of deep concern on his face as my front wheel hit a deep culvert in the fire road, my hands stupidly applied the brakes. I vaulted off the bike, landing on my head in the chaparral. Luckily, I wore a helmet. I was momentarily knocked unconscious and had dislocated my shoulder.

When I came to, he was bent over me, shaking his head with

amused exasperation at my incompetence. His first words were, "You stupid son-of-a-bitch, I signaled you to be careful!" He tended me until he could see that I was not terminally wounded. And then we proceeded on our ride until we parted at Tam Junction. He made no argument when I said I could get home. He respected my decision.

"Rob was not completely a man of sweetness and light. He could be pretty grouchy as we all can—a bit of a curmudgeon. After all, life does not always live up to our standards, nor do we to life's. I've seen Rob weather some very difficult times. I've known and admired three of the remarkable women in Rob's life: his wife and his two sisters. Exasperated though they became with him from time to time, they recognized his remarkable loving nature and drew strength from him. I can say the same for his daughter. He was a good father, grumpy and demanding though he was, and one of the finest grandfathers I've ever known.

"Rob was a man of great affection and of great loyalty for his family, his friends, his school, his fraternity brothers, his neighbors, his town, the schools of his children, and his favorite local teams—not to mention his dogs. We all loved him."

After warm applause, Monty was greeted by Rob's sisters and daughter with hugs and words of appreciation. As soon as he had stepped away toward the buffet, he was seized by Brooks Gardner, who kissed him on both cheeks as if they were French relatives.

"You were magnificent, Monty, as always. No one speaks or writes as well as you. No one understands grief as well as you and Talia." Tears ran down her cheeks.

Monty tried to disengage himself. After wishing his friend farewell, he needed his wife's embrace. But Brooks would not let go. She urgently needed to talk to him and to Talia, who appeared at that moment and rendered the embrace that she knew Monty would need. Much as they tried to get away from Brooks, they failed. Soon the three of them were sitting in the garden of the Art Center, Monty and Talia expecting Brooks to once more pour out her anger and humiliation at the way she had been treated by Ted Journey and Berenice Smithey.

After the marriage between Journey and Berenice, Brooks had sought out Talia to wail about the magnificent house Journey was building for Berenice on the Bolinas Mesa, looking out on the ocean. Brooks felt that the celebration of that marriage was a deliberate blow against her. By the time of Monty's memorial speech in honor of Rob Ellenberg, the house had been completed and had been the site of a number of lavish parties. Monty and Talia had heard Brooks' fulminations about this already, and they feared they would once more have to offer their profound compassion for the latest failure of Brooks' life.

As they sat in the garden, commandeered to hear the downward spiral of Brooks' life again, Brooks now delivered news for which they were not prepared. The Tamalpais Press and *Abalone Journal* had been for sale for some time, and there were no buyers. Evidently, the combined enterprise was deep in debt. Brooks allowed herself a brief smile as she informed them that perhaps all was not well for the Ted Journeys. But there was more news, for which she could not allow herself any gratification. The day after she heard of the pending end of Journey's literary endeavor, she received a curt handwritten note from Journey informing her that on the day he met with the board of Tamalpais Press to declare the end of the enterprise, for which there had been no buyer, his doctor had discovered the presence of cancer in his pancreas. The note ended with a brief sentence, "Come out to our house in Bolinas. Berenice will need your aid to cope with my illness and death." It was not a graceful request, simply a command. There was more in the note, Brooks told the Wolfes. "He asked me to inform Monty that he wanted him to speak at his memorial."

Monty told Brooks that he had decided to refuse all further requests. "I've done my last memorial."

"Well, I don't blame you. I'd like to tell the bastard to go fuck himself too. But I probably won't. I feel very sorry for Berenice. She can't take another death alone."

* * *

Brooks' drive to Bolinas from Sausalito was arduous: up Mount Tamalpais on the winding Highway 1, then climbing further over Panoramic Highway and slicing back down to Highway 1 at Stinson Beach, and finally following the sinuous shore of Bolinas Lagoon, before climbing again to the bluff above the Pacific, facing Drakes Bay and Chimney Rock. The Journey house, of native stone and weathered redwood, looked as if it had simply grown there; Brooks was annoyed at the good taste it displayed.

Berenice answered the door, clutching at her nervously. "Oh my, Brooks, what will I do?"

"You will survive," Brooks replied coolly, disengaging herself.

She found the interior overdone for such a natural structure: too many mirrors, too much silver and brass, clashing fabrics and colors. She assumed Berenice had been responsible for the furnishings. Journey reclined on a straw chaise longue in the sunroom facing the windows and the ocean view. He did not rise. He simply lifted a hand in greeting. He did not yet look ill and his voice was vigorous. "What do you think of our house?"

"Very appropriate, I guess. The outside, at least. And big." Brooks did not intend to curry favor.

"Appropriate? What does that mean?"

"Local stone and wood, built into the side of the cliff."

"You didn't expect me to put up a plantation manor with columns?"

"I didn't expect you to put up anything. I was sorry to hear about your illness and the end of Tamalpais."

"We're planning a celebration of what we've done, not a lamentation. And I plan to die well, which is why I wrote you. Berenice has already lost one husband. She'll need you when I go."

"How long do you have?"

"The doctor gave me four or five months. I'm asking a very few people to be here when I die."

Brooks stared at him waiting to hear, at the least, that he had asked her because he valued her abilities, because only she could do this final service for him and Berenice. He returned her stare for a long moment before speaking. "You'll be available?"

"I came when you wrote."

Journey nodded his head abruptly as if she had agreed, and then picked up a book and began to read.

That was it. She had been dismissed. It was as if once he had received a death sentence, he had no need to pretend to be gracious. She turned toward Berenice, who simply shrugged and smiled weakly. As Brooks began to leave the room, Journey spoke again. "Please inform Monty Wolfe that I would like him to speak at my memorial."

Brooks raised a hand to indicate she had heard. Without turning, she replied, "I informed him. I don't know whether he will. I would suggest that you call him and make a request—not a command." She proceeded to the door without waiting for a response.

Berenice ran after her, holding out an envelope. "This is the material for Monty Wolfe."

"Material?"

"Ted's suggestions for the memorial speech."

"I told him that Monty wasn't inclined to make any more eulogies."

"Please, Brooks, please."

Brooks took the envelope.

Berenice hugged her convulsively, sighing. "Oh Brooks!"

"Call me if and when you need me," Brooks muttered and walked rapidly down to the car. She fumed all the way home. The troops had been alerted that a battle was on the horizon and then discharged. She ought simply to have responded by phone, but she had wanted to see the house and assess the Journeys at home. She comforted herself at the poor taste of the interior. The man had made his choice, and he had to live and die with it.

He had vaguely referred to the upcoming celebration of the end of Tamalpais Press, but had issued no invitation. She wondered whether Journey's command had perhaps included a backhanded request to attend in order to support Berenice. Journey knew very well that only Brooks could have properly organized that celebration. As she entered the small houseboat she had rented after being evicted from the *Vallejo*, she slammed the door. The frail structure shuddered. She froze for a moment to see if it would sink, a fitting nadir to this moment in her life. Even if she received an invitation, she would not attend.

Three weeks later, on a stormy afternoon, with waves and rain beating on the houseboat, Brooks' telephone rang. It was Berenice, her voice croaking hysterically, "You have to come, I don't know what to do."

"What? I can't hear you."

"He's fallen in the bathroom. He's injured his arm, his leg. He's been failing rapidly. I can't move him. He told me to call you. Tonight's the celebration."

"Where are you."

"Home."

"Bolinas?"

"I need you. We need you."

Rain beat into her face as she fought her way up the dock to the parking lot. She didn't know if she had enough gas. As she wound her way up the mountain to Panoramic Highway, wind whipped the eucalyptus groves. She feared one of the shallow-rooted trees would fall on the highway. As she braked for the switchbacks, her threadbare tires skidded. The downhill through the redwoods and Douglas firs was even more treacherous in the driving rain. When she came out of the forest onto the bluff high above Stinson, she could barely see the foam of the breaking waves below. The gas gauge read almost empty by the time she wound around the wind-whipped Bolinas Lagoon and made it up the Mesa to Journey's house.

Journey lay in the bathroom, wedged between the toilet and the shower. He hadn't been moved since he fell. Shit and vomit soiled him, the walls, and the floor.

"Couldn't you get him up?" she asked Berenice, surveying the scene.

"He wouldn't let me touch him."

"Let's get going," said Journey.

"You're conscious?"

"Of course."

"Is anything broken?"

"Just bruised, badly. My arm, my leg, my back. You have to get me cleaned up so I can dress for the event. The fucking doctor guessed wrong."

Brooks turned to Berenice. "Don't just stand there, take off your shoes and stockings and help me."

The two women walked barefoot through the mess to Journey. Brooks gingerly moved Journey's arms and legs to make sure they weren't broken and then, with Berenice's help, lifted him to his feet and moved him onto a plastic chair in the shower. She ordered

Berenice to lay out Journey's clothes for the event and then to get dressed herself. While Journey was cleaning himself with a couple of wash cloths and a towel, she mopped the floor and walls of the bathroom and then dried them with a half dozen towels. Draping Journey's good arm over her shoulders, she got him into the bedroom and helped him dress.

The storm had abated by the time she drove them toward Belvedere where the celebration was to take place in the Corinthian Yacht Club. When she pulled into a gas station on Highway 101, Journey shouted: "What are you doing?"

"I'm out of gas. You're lucky I got this far."

"Well, make it quick. It's my affair."

"And I'm just your fucking chauffeur."

Not a word passed between the three of them during the rest of the journey. Brooks told Berenice to go in and get two men to help Journey. One of the men who came out was Al Jarrett, Journey's chief editor. "Al," she said, "arrange for someone to take the Journeys home."

"Aren't you coming in?" said Al.

"I wasn't invited."

As soon as Journey was out of the car, she started to drive off. But then she changed her mind and parked.

She edged her way into the Yacht Club Hall that was full of writers and editors and journalists, many of whom she knew. Journey sat enthroned on the dais with Berenice and Al Jarrett. One by one, the writers Journey had published came up to the podium to praise Journey for his patient and passionate nurture of their talent. Then, to her surprise, an equally enthusiastic group of men in suits and ties lined up at the steps to the stage to offer their gratitude to Journey for his generous aid in establishing their fortunes through investment in his properties. To Brooks, it appeared to be a dark ages mead hall reception for the dying King Arthur. She escaped after the third man of wealth had offered his obeisance.

* * *

Ten days after the Tamalpais Press finale celebration, Brooks received another desperate call from Berenice. "He's dying, this time he's really dying. Hospice confirmed it and he sent them away. You have to come. Call Monty."

Brooks called the Wolfes and left a message. She had been drinking heavily since the first rescue mission. She had hardly slept and could barely keep her eyes open for the drive over the dangerous mountain road to Bolinas. When she arrived, she found four cars parked in the drive. The front door was open. A carefully chosen few had been assembled in the sunroom, eating oysters and Beluga caviar on toast and drinking champagne. Journey lay on the straw chaise longue, resplendent in silk pajamas, silk robe, and silk scarf as Berenice fed him. This time, Journey looked as if he were fading quickly. His skin had dried out. He could barely open his mouth to eat and drink. He did manage a salute to Brooks when he caught sight of her. Amy Scheer, a young novelist whose first book Journey had published, served the caviar and the oysters to the guests. Al Jarrett poured the champagne, a solemn expression on his face as if he were giving communion to the favored guests.

"Brooks," Journey waved her to his side, "did you give Monty the material I provided?"

"I dropped it off," she replied, her tone curt. "In any case it should have been you or Berenice, who asked him directly."

"Well, I'm obviously in no condition and Berenice is not up to anything. That's why you're here."

"Don't worry, I'll take care of Berenice and Monty and whatever else needs doing."

YET IN ARCADIA

Journey raised his hand and addressed the room. "Listen up. I would like to let each of you know how grateful I am and my urgent wishes for your future, and how I've directed my advisors to help you achieve what I desire for you."

Everyone turned, their gazes upon the supine figure. To Brooks it seemed as if the film had stopped, arresting not only the voices, but the gestures. Suddenly, Bolinas had become Delphi. The Sybil was about to declare the future.

A clear dawn was breaking on the ocean. Brooks could see a freighter in the distance, making its way slowly toward the Golden Gate. The sunlight just touched the white superstructure. A formation of brown pelicans skimmed the surface of the ocean below on their way north.

Journey's gaze sought his followers out, one by one, as he declared the project his resources would help each accomplish. The details were specific, a command, an investment. He told Al Jarrett where he should apply his editorial expertise next, and who would help him on his way. He advised Amy Scheer which publisher and editor to submit the manuscript of her current novel. And on around the room. After each statement, he waited for a nod of assent before he went on to the next guest. When he had addressed everyone in the room except Brooks, he fell silent and waved his empty glass at Al, who filled it.

Brooks waited for him to take a sip. He gestured for Amy and Al to continue serving. Finally, Brooks stepped in front of him, "Have you nothing to say to me?"

Journey stared up at her, silent for what seemed like minutes. She stared down at him, waiting. Finally, he spoke, "I have nothing to say to you."

The entire room seemed to catch its breath and then freeze. Journey looked around, becoming aware that his brutal response had shocked the room. And then he continued as if he had only stopped in the middle of a sentence, "...because you are perfection itself."

The party went on, more quietly now, as the guests attempted to absorb what had just occurred. Once more Journey raised his hand. His gesture was weaker now and his voice quavered. "Music is now required. I must confess to a guilty frivolous love of Puccini. Berenice, if you please, the first act of *Madame Butterfly*. As Berenice fumbled through the CDs, Brooks felt that the lull in the event needed filling. She stepped into the center of the room and turned to Journey, and began to recite:

'Tis a Fearful Thing, by Yehudah HaLevi

'Tis a fearful thing
to love what death can touch.

A fearful thing
to love, to hope, to dream, to be—
to be,
And oh, to lose.
A thing for fools, this,
And a holy thing,
a holy thing
to love.

For your life has lived in me,
your laugh once lifted me,
your word was gift to me.
To remember this brings painful joy.

'Tis a human thing, love,

*a holy thing, to love
what death has touched.*

Journey clapped, his chapped lips cracking open to a large smile. Berenice slipped the cassette into the stereo and the overture to *Madame Butterfly* filled the room. Without a thought, Brooks knelt at the chaise longue and began to massage Journey's feet. Ted Journey died.

XX

Before Journey's memorial, Monty turned over the materials Journey had prepared for his eulogy to Al Jarrett with the message, "I'm not the right one to say these words, Al. It's up to someone closer to him, someone who can believe all this praise."

The memorial took place in a redwood grove between Bolinas and Point Reyes, on the edge of stream that ran down to the ocean. A band of bagpipers greeted the mourners. The elaborately printed program noted that the bagpipers wore the colors of the proud Armstrong clan, the chief of which was an ancestor of Journey's family. The crest of the clan was embossed on the front of the program in clan colors consisting of an armored shoulder and fisted arm raised high with the motto, *Invictus Maneo*, "I remain unvanquished."

"He speaks from the grave," said Monty, waving the program toward the flowered alter.

Talia place a finger to her lips, murmuring, "We're here to mourn a death."

Al ended by making the eulogy himself, a version he had edited, much briefer than the one Ted Journey had composed. Monty, on good behavior now, remained silent, but he smiled thinking, "No wonder the press did as well as it did, with an editor-in-chief like Al." The Wolfes had attended the memorial, even though Talia had been not well for a month. They were to meet with the oncologist in the city after the memorial.

Monty noticed that Brooks sat with Berenice, who leaned her head on Brooks' shoulder through the ceremony. Evidently, Brooks had moved in to the Journey house to help the grieving widow. As the Wolfes drove across the bridge, Monty guessed that Brooks would remain at the Journey house for quite some time, if not indefinitely. "I don't know," replied Talia. "Berenice may well find another mate. She's one of those all-accepting creatures men seem to adore."

"Perhaps. But now that Brooks has finally out-maneuvered Ted Journey, I'll bet she'll even try to work out a deal with Berenice for the two of them to take over the Tamalpais back-list and open up a sort of 'Tamalpais remainder' small press."

That was the last they speculated about Brooks and Berenice or the late Ted Journey. They were silent for the rest of the trip, fearing the news from the oncologist would not be good; the doctor had asked that Monty be present. They were shown to her office, not to an examining room. She appeared without her white jacket. Her stunning outfit, Talia declared, was a Louis Vuitton original. It was as if the doctor knew that Talia would prefer to receive her "sentence" in high style. She sat them down on a couch and pulled up an armchair, facing them, a medical file spread on her lap. Talia's breast cancer had metastasized through her lymph nodes to her lungs and her back. The doctor showed them the X-rays. "In a very short time, the cancer has leaped from 'Stage Two' to 'Stage Four.'"

"Like skipping a grade," murmured Talia with a smile.

The doctor sighed. "You are most remarkable, Talia." She went on in a calm matter-of-fact tone to predict death within a short time, weeks or months, perhaps a bit more with extreme medical procedures. "With such a case, it's impossible to be accurate. You can decide whether you want to continue treatment."

Monty gazed around the room, unable to believe that he had heard the doctor's words in this bland, ordinary office, with a simple mahogany desk, an oak filing cabinet, three framed medical certificates on the wall, and windows looking down on a parking lot lined with palms.

They stood. Talia hugged the doctor, who held on to her patient a bit longer than necessary, Monty thought, as if she could hold her back from that dire prognosis. Talia thanked the doctor warmly and said she would contact her after she and Monty had discussed how to proceed.

They did not speak all the way home. Once in the house, Monty asked if Talia wanted a drink. "No, Dear Monty, make yourself one, please." She went to the living room and sat on the couch, gazing out at the view. It was a bright afternoon, the bay empty except for an enormous cruise ship, white hull and decks rising five decks high, slowly moving south along the city piers, seeking its berth. The pilot's tug followed off the port stern, waiting to take the pilot off once the ship docked. Monty brought his glass of Scotch and sat next to Talia, their arms touching. They did not speak for some time.

Talia broke the silence, her voice was low and firm. "I don't want any more visits to the doctor, no more medical procedures—operations, radiation, chemotherapy. Prolonging life for a few weeks under such a rude invasion, or even months, does not seem worthwhile. No, I'll stay here with you, in this house with our things, and allow myself to die—that's what my body seems determined to do."

Monty resisted the impulse to cry out, "No! Don't die! I won't let you die!" He sighed and remained silent. Talia was going to die, no matter what he wanted, no matter what excruciating procedures the doctor would offer in the next few months.

"And I don't want a funeral or a memorial."

Monty shuddered. Talia picked up his free hand and kissed the knuckles, one by one. "Sorry. At least you don't have to make up a speech for me."

"I'll do whatever you ask."

"Cremation."

"Okay."

"Ashes wherever."

"On our trail?"

"If that's what you want."

"I don't want anything about it at all. Just you."

"And I, you."

They held hands and sat silently as the light of the sunset faded on the elaborately stacked buildings on the city hills across the bay.

Over the next few weeks, as she weakened, she asked Monty for a hospital bed in the living room so that she could watch light brighten and fade upon the bay waters and then see the lights of the city and the Bay Bridge appear under the stars. She had grown up on the docks of Point Richmond. After she married Monty, they had discovered this shambling house on the hills overlooking the bay and the city. She had always found the empty waters stretching out below their house a calming sight, interrupted only now and then by an occasional sailboat, fishing boat, tug, steamer, or tanker proceeding in from the ocean or out toward a voyage. She liked to imagine where the vessels were going, what they were carrying, or whom. On holidays and special occasions, the white sails and colored spinnakers filled the bay, tacking this way and that as if on a merry chase to nowhere in particular. Otherwise, the bay was always relatively empty compared to the other ocean harbors Talia had seen.

Guests who entered the front door and saw the bay stretching out immediately below, asked, "Do you ever get bored?"

Talia laughed. "It's never the same from moment to moment—the light, the color of the sky and water, the shading of the city skyline, Alcatraz, the Bay Bridge, the East Bay, Angel Island."

Today she murmured, "Yes, Angel Island! How appropriate." She smiled and nodded, satisfied with her decision to end her life here in the living room. A bank of low cumulus clouds had rolled in, covering the upper half of the taller buildings in the city, and turning the bay gray.

Monty folded back the carpet and dragged the sofa over to the fireplace to make room for the hospital bed. He bought a light shower curtain to string up in front of the window to dim the glare of the morning sun without totally obscuring the view. He made up the convertible couch at the window so that he could be with her during the nights.

Day by day, he kept in motion except to sit next to the bed, when he could. He scarcely left Talia's side as she lay dying. Although they had paid for Long Term Care Insurance, he did not want anyone else in the house for their final weeks together. Talia protested, in part for his sake, but also for her own. She had always lived independently. She couldn't bear to be a burden on Monty at the end. She didn't want to see him struggling to clean her, to feed her, and to bandage her scrapes—her skin had become very thin and liable to tear. The doctor had prescribed a whole battery of pills for pain and comfort in these last days. To keep track, Monty had to make a graph with times and days.

He pleaded successfully to let him care for her. "It is for my sake, not for yours. I must be with you, alone, in all ways, before we part. Another person in the house would be unbearable. The kids will come, of course. But they can't stay around and wait—they have their lives. I promise to call hospice at the very last."

Reluctantly, Talia agreed.

Day by day, the physical chores became more difficult. For Talia, the worst was being unable to control her bladder or her bowels. This required Monty to perform the difficult task of slowly turning her to one side, while he rolled up the soiled sheet, cleaning her bottom, and rolling her back onto a clean sheet that he had placed strategically in their own roll along the bed. When the task had been completed and Talia was comfortably propped and tucked in, he sat by the bed and held her hand. They had no need to talk. Both understood each other's misery that their life together had reached this demeaning stage. It was as if their loving intimacy had crested in light and was now receding into the darkness of bodily corruption. But that mood did not last long. There were hours that they spent together treasuring the years of love they had experienced. He cooked their meals and placed her tray on a straw bed-tray. He sat in her wheelchair next to the bed and ate with her, morning, noon, and night. While she napped from time to time during the day, he continued to sit in the wheelchair, writing on his laptop or reading. Now and then he read aloud to her a poem or a paragraph or two from an article or a story, but she had little patience or energy for an extended reading. She listened so intensely that she soon wearied, raising her hand for him to stop.

It was only after their children's visit that they had talked for the first time about death. Both Jonathan and Louisa had asked about the cremation service, the ashes, and the memorial. They had been brought up to speak openly about everything. When Talia asked them what they wanted, both asserted that the decision had to be hers.

"But I don't really care."

"Dad said that you decided no memorial and that we could decide where your ashes went."

"That's true. He suggested the ashes go near our trail, on the bluff looking north along the cliffs toward Muir Beach, Stinson, Bolinas, and Point Reyes. I always liked that view. I won't be seeing it then… after…but you and Dad may, if it matters, once I'm ashes."

"What your mother means…" began Monty, who felt Talia was being rather brutal.

"Don't worry, Dad," said Louisa. "We know that Mom's a realist and you're the sentimental one."

"We grew up with the two of you," said Jonathan. "Mom has always been completely honest about how she feels. We know she loves us—and you too. She really doesn't care what happens after she dies—what happens to her, that is. She worries about us, and you." Jonathan always wanted to make sure that no one felt bad or left out.

"You don't have to explain, Jonathan," said Louisa. "We all know Mom."

At the end of the family visit, the children left it up to Talia and Monty. "Whatever you two decide is fine with us," said Louisa. "Just don't keep us in the dark."

"You've always made good decisions together," said Jonathan.

When the door closed, Monty made himself a stiff drink and sat down next to the bed. "Whew, what a pair!"

Talia was silent for some time. Finally, she spoke, "Do you mind that I don't want a memorial? That I don't care what happens to the ashes?"

After a pause, Monty sighed. "I have to think about that."

"You mean, you have been thinking about it. And so have I."

"Louisa put it pretty succinctly. You've always been a realist. Death is, after all, death, and ashes are just what they are, ashes, with some bones mixed in." He took a long swallow of Scotch.

Talia reached out and took hold of his hand. "I'm sorry."

"I love you for what you are. It's just...just that I'm having a hard time understanding what's happening. I've been the minister of death almost all my life and now it has arrived here, and I don't want to open the door."

At last, they talked about death. Talia explained that she didn't want to die, but she accepted the fact that her life was about to end. "Who was it that said that 'we're born into a dying animal'?"

"Yeats, I think," replied Monty, trying to remember. "In 'Sailing to Byzantium,' he contrasted the permanence of art to the decay of our animal bodies, or something like that."

"Well, that's too high-flown for me. I don't know how long some of the outfits I made will last, but even they fray and tear and eventually end in the ash heap. Yeats' poetry lasted a bit longer, but I imagine there will come a day when even he is not remembered and all those pages will shrivel and decay into dust."

Monty chuckled and shook his head to think that he had been lucky enough to live so many years with such a beautifully practical, matter-of-fact woman. He gazed out at the bay, with the red light of the dredging barge in its midst, the Alcatraz lighthouse flashing intermittently, the draped lightshow of the Bay Bridge beyond, and the lighted buildings, houses, and streets of the city. He tried to imagine what it would be like when Talia would not be able to see all this splendor, to register it, to feel it deeply, as she felt everything she saw. He thought of the last lines of another Yeats poem, "A Dialogue of Self and Soul":

> *When such as I cast out remorse*
> *So great a sweetness flows into the breast*
> *We must laugh and we must sing,*
> *We are blest by everything,*
> *Everything we look upon is blest.*

Talia had scarcely ever felt remorse. She had accepted whatever happened and even when there was failure or injury or the mortal accident to her father, she retained her laughter and her song for life. And now she seemed willing to accept even the loss of that life she loved.

He leaned over and kissed her. "I should have learned more from you by now."

She held his cheeks with both of her hands and in the dim light of the bay and sky and lights through the window, stared up at him. "And you, who talk so well about the dead, what do you feel about your death to come?"

"Me?" Monty felt startled at the question. "What do I feel about my death?" He sat back in the wheelchair and remained silent for some time. "I've always said that ever since my father died, I had learned to accept death. The question is whether I was simply whistling in the dark?"

"I don't think so. You're always too willing to suspect yourself."

"You know, when mother died, my brothers and I admitted to one another that every year that we lasted longer than Dad, we considered a year of grace. And now I've lived almost twice as long as he, and longer even than my brothers."

"So you've been graced 'to high heaven' so to speak."

They laughed together.

"Maybe just to ashes on the cliffs along with yours."

"So, you understand why I don't care what happens to my remains or even to my memory after I die. I do care about your life then and the kids' lives. I hope that you all continue on, with a measure of happiness."

XXI

As her waking hours passed, Talia felt more and more alone, even when Monty sat beside the bed, or, toward the end, when Louisa and Jonathan came to try to express whatever one should express during those last moments together. She loved each of these dear members of her family, but hour by hour as she approached death, she became startlingly aware of the solitary path each human treads in life. This perception was not new to her. It seemed she has always known how separate lives were from one another, even though they shared an existence in the world. She wondered whether this knowledge was the result of the early death of her mother. She gazed out on the empty bay, gray and blue and green, reflecting the sky; a solitary sail passed Alcatraz, the essence of life alone, sequestered, gated. The clouds massed and parted in puffy and striated shapes, transforming the hues of the bay from moment to moment. In the distance, beyond the mirroring water, rose the varied erect and angular shapes of the city buildings, each a different height, breadth, and shade. The triangular spears of St. Peter and Paul on Washington Square were almost invisible in the midst of the more massive recent buildings. All through her youth she had fled Point Richmond, seeking elusive joy and pleasure on the streets, the bistros, and clubs of North Beach surrounding Washington Square. Coit Tower remained clear on its Telegraph Hill promontory, with a background sky unclogged by buildings. However, the former highest and most interesting building in the city, the Transamerica Pyramid had been diminished by the towering Salesforce tube that put even the bulky Bank of America building to shame.

All those buildings, all that activity, she thought, with human beings on each floor of every building, in every room of every house, climbing and descending the city's hills with houses pasteled in grays and greens and roses and cream. She had walked those streets marveling at the sight of squat, tireless Italian women in black from neck to ankle, heavy grocery bags hanging from each hand, backing uphill, talking endlessly to a companion, almost a twin in black, with identical bags; and at the kaleidoscope of colors in neighboring Chinatown that was slowly invading the Italian village. Talia had no need for wine or drugs, so drunk had she been by the shapes and colors of the city and its inhabitants by the time she returned home for dinner with her father. Now, all that vibrant life of images lay distant from her withering self, stretched out in this living room, preparing to enter the dark nothingness of death.

That lone sail now came about, crossing the west wind from the Gate, and proceeding toward Angel Island on a far reach. The shadow of her father reached across the water from that sail beckoning her now to join him. With an effort of will Talia forced herself to ask just how close she had been to him or to any other human being: even Louisa, the daughter who had emerged from her womb, a creature whose every effort had been to wriggle free of embraces, commands, pleas, directives; even her stepson, Jonathan, longing for her maternal embrace, for the love he had lost at birth; and, most of all, her precious husband, whose caring sentiment had pervaded this house. Talia almost cried out to think of those dear separate existences, walking alone through life, like herself. She smiled when her thoughts turned to Monty. He had known all along about the loneliness of each life, although, perhaps he never thought of it as being sad, full of sentiment though he was. He had struggled free of his own family, had pursued his craft alone, and had chosen not to launch it and himself into the world. He had committed himself to her, but from the beginning had respected her space, her independence. That had been the deepest vow they had observed in their marriage.

It was two in the morning, when she finally had let her mind dwell on her husband, who lay sleeping on the couch-bed stretched out before the window. A crescent moon was just rising over the Berkeley Hills, casting a frail silver path across the waters to her eyes. The Bay Bridge, festooned with a discreet shower of tiny lights, opening and closing at intervals on the San Francisco length, and rising in a sweeping pyramid of light on the Berkeley/Oakland side. How thoughtful, she laughed, a "light show" to entertain her at her passing, just the sort of event Monty would have planned: distant, discreet, joyous, but not intrusive. He always celebrated life for her and the children, with a deep affection that accompanied their lives, but never intruded. That was one reason she had fallen in love with him during that first year of mutual grief after they had met. He recognized her need for intense privacy. She supposed that was the requirement of all art: to experience the beauty and wholeness of life without interference. She felt this when designing and sewing; he must feel it when writing. For the first time she recognized the possibility that perhaps he had ceased showing his novels and stories for the same reason: the lack of expectation led to true freedom. With his work safely sheltered in file drawers, he felt no compulsion to please anyone. A contradiction, perhaps? Why create if not for the response of another human being? And yet the anxiety over that response can ruin the impulse to create. And she remembered a Camus short story that very early in their marriage Monty had insisted that she read. The story began with a poor unrecognized artist struggling to create and provide for his family. Gradually, after much suffering and wretched labor, he becomes successful. His studio is flooded with wealthy curators and collectors, but he has disappeared. At the end of the story, he is found on a loft, dead in front of an immense blank mural, with one small word inscribed across the middle, the word *solitaire* (alone), or is it *solidaire* (together), the "t" or the "d" are indistinct, impossible to guess.

And that's the way they had lived together. Their daughter, Louisa, had resented the complexity of her parents' relationship, their devotion to their arts, and the discretion they practiced toward her life. From the beginning, she had wanted to free herself from all restraint and at the same time was angry that her parents had been content to let her go her own way, as long as she was more or less safe. They both felt a little guilty at not having embraced Jonathan as much as he needed. They had demonstrated their love for both children without end, but, at the same time, their love for one another had somewhat excluded the children. And then, of course, both she and Monty needed to be left alone with their work: alas, solidaire and solitaire, the universal contradiction, was not ideal in a family.

Day by day, as she failed, Talia viewed the bay, empty most of the time, but then, unexpectedly, a container ship, or an oiler, or an automobile carrier would appear, crossing the bay on the way from or to Point Richmond or Oakland. Only the cruise ships made their way to dock along the San Francisco Embarcadero. The ships' passages were stately, slow, like 19th-century fashion modélistes, displaying their demure decor, sometimes in simple black, but more often with the waterline displaying a red underskirt, a white hemline, a robin's egg blue or orange or carmine hull, and sparkling white superstructure. Some of the ships had graceful lines, long and low and curving to a sharp bow, carving the water in white foam; others seemed foreshortened, too bulky, as if their bow had been pressed back, blunted toward their stern by the waves; and the autocarriers had no line at all, simply a top-heavy, completely enclosed hulk without a deck, a package full of cars somehow propelled across the water. The indolent tempo of these appearances perfectly suited Talia's mood, utterly patient as she awaited death. There were days when only three of these vessels passed; some days six or seven crossed her view; but always one at a time, slowly, a chubby small tug, in black and white, following like a pet dog, ready to take the bay pilot off and convey him back to his home dock. At night, the dark shapes of the hull were only lit by their green starboard running lights if they were on their way out to sea, or red port running lights if they were headed for the docks.

As the end approached, Talia felt closer and closer to her father, a man of uneasy, often turbulent moods. He had been a rebellious oldest son, unwilling to submit to the role expected of him by the culture of Belize. He had seized upon every possibility of escape, culminating in his marriage to Talia's mother and emigration to the United States. At the same time, he never ceased to love and respect his parents and his siblings, which burdened him with a haunted guilt at his desertion. The early death of Talia's mother seemed to him like a heavenly retribution. It wasn't until she reached adolescence that she understood her father's depressions; nonetheless, even as a small child, she knew he felt he deserved whatever accidents befell him. At home, he displayed a deep maternal sensibility, making up for her lost mother, a tenderness shaded by a deep and grieving sadness and that ever-present guilt.

From infancy, she had sailed with her father past the towering ships that now kept her company, out into the far reaches of the bay and sometimes through the Golden Gate, their boat lurching up and down perilously on the ocean waves thrown up by the shallows of the Potato Patch Shoals. On the water, he was tough and demanding, the captain of the vessel, in charge at all times, with limits and rules and instructions for his crew, of which, often, she was the only one. At the same time, once she cast off the lines and leaped into the boat, she had been thrilled to enter an incandescent region of her father's joy. On the water, except when he needed to "captain," he was a happy, carefree boy. It had been on the water that he had met her mother and fallen in love. Although Talia had been too young to understand, she had been told as she grew older, by the patrons of the yacht club, friends of the family, and even by her father, that the marriage had been a difficult one. It seemed that he never ceased to apologize for his stubborn rebelliousness toward his own family and then toward his beloved wife. Very early during their mourning together, Talia would tell Monty that she had an apologetic father, very much like him. From the beginning Monty had been quite frank about his own pervading guilt toward his own father and then toward his first wife. He too had been a rebellious son, who hadn't lived up to his father's ideals, and he somehow had managed to disappoint the demanding Emma, who had died giving birth to his son. As their love affair developed, Talia had laughed at Monty's confessions, claiming that although she had probably fallen in love with him, because his guilt resembled her father's, in no other way was there a similarity.

Lying in the hospital bed, gazing out on the bay, Talia smiled contentedly to think of what a good and caring man she had married. Monty accepted and valued life, no matter what setbacks he experienced. And then she revised her previous assessment. There was another way in which Monty resembled her father. He too had retained his boyhood joyfulness in each moment, not only on the water, but as they walked on trails, on beaches, taking their children on adventures, cooking campfire meals for the family, making posters and maps to celebrate each of their birthdays, Valentine's Day, or even the first day of spring. Whatever guilt or sadness he felt was always directed inward and hidden. Only she knew about them, because she sensed them and asked him to tell her, which he did reluctantly.

And then Talia died.

XXII

Louisa arrived a week after the cremation. As soon as Jonathan came from the airport, she demanded a family conference. The three of them sat in the living room that had been put back in order after the hospital bed had been removed. Louisa placed the lacquer box containing Talia's ashes on the mantel. Monty was inclined to remark that their mother's ashes, indeed, made it officially a family conference, but Louisa would have objected to his irony. In fact, he thought, Talia would have been dismayed by this ceremonious display of the box. She had disclaimed any identity with these remains of her body. Worse yet, she took offense at any rearrangement of her carefully designed decor, especially in such a prominent location as the mantel. Still, if the ashes could speak now, thought Monty, they would have ruefully submitted to Louisa's impulse at command—submitted with a slight grin of amusement. Almost from birth, Louisa had attempted to command the family and often succeeded. As Monty prepared himself for his daughter's list of grievances and directions, he wondered at the fact that Louisa seemed to have inherited the personality and judgments of Emma, his first wife and Jonathan's mother, rather than of her own mother.

"Dad," said Louisa, pacing back and forth in the middle of the living room, "I know you have a good heart and do your damnedest not to discomfort Jonathan and me, but now, at this climax of all of our lives, you've botched it."

"I don't think..." began Jonathan.

"Exactly, Jonathan, you don't think and you never have very clearly." She stood over her brother, fixing him with a stern gaze. "Please let me continue. It's essential that we bring all this into the open so that we can proceed." She paused now and turned toward the window, gazing out at the bay. When she began again, it seemed to Monty that she was explaining herself to the bay. "Mom died and we weren't here. We could have been here, we should have been here to be with her at the end, but Dad, our dear sweet Dad and even our more matter-of-fact Mom, did not want to inconvenience us." She turned now and stood over Monty, who sat, leaning back on the couch, his legs stretched out, a strong drink in his hand, awaiting his execution. "Or could it be that our dear sweet parents wanted to be alone for the dissolution of their partnership?"

"For Christ's sake, Louisa." Jonathan stood up, "Even the doctor couldn't predict how long Mom would hold on. It's absurd to blame them for sending us home. We could have been waiting here for months."

"In order to be with my mother at the end."

"She was my mother too, from the moment I was born."

"I wasn't accusing you of disloyalty, Jonathan." Louisa turned now and addressed Talia's ashes. "I was accusing our folks. You may have been too dense to understand, but they have been a closed corporation for our entire lives."

"And you've spent your life trying to get free of the family." Jonathan picked up his suitcase and went upstairs to unpack.

Louisa stood still for a moment, braced, as she absorbed her brother's accusation. Then she threw herself on the couch, her head in Monty's lap, and began to sob. He gently patted her back and drew his hand through her hair. "I know, I know. She loved you and Jonathan with a passion. She understood both of you, completely, and thought you were wonderful."

"I wasn't a good daughter."

"You were a perfect daughter. Neither of us ever doubted your love."

"Jonathan was right. I…I kept trying to…to escape."

"You simply wanted to be yourself. That wasn't easy when you loved us so much, and your mother was such an admirable example."

Louisa sat up and wiped her eyes and nose. She began to laugh. "Oh Dad, I can't bear how smart you are. You understand too fucking much." She embraced him and kissed him on both cheeks and the forehead. "I'll go get cleaned up and then we can discuss what we have to do."

Although Louisa disagreed with her mother in the matter of a memorial, she was unwilling to go against her will. Nevertheless, she cleverly found a way to celebrate her mother's life: a show at Talia's shop of all of Talia's designs, her wardrobe, none of which fitted Louisa or suited her taste, and a plea to display some of the outfits Talia had designed for her clients. Talia's friends could come before the show opened and could take whatever they wanted. All Jonathan wanted were a few scarves and one of Talia's favorite necklaces that he had always admired. The remainder, aside from the clients' outfits, would be for sale.

Louisa set out to write a brief biography of her mother's life, demanding the aid of Jonathan and Monty. "All you have to do, Dad, is to be there for everyone who loved Mom. They'll want to express themselves to you. I promise you won't have to give one of your speeches."

In the end, Monty wrote the biography as Louisa knew he would.

Neither she nor her brother wanted to change a word. There it was at the door of the shop, a copy for each mourner, beautifully printed with a lovely photo of Talia at the top, a page and a half in 12-point Algerian bold, a printed version of one of Monty's memorial speeches. Writing it made him wretched. He felt his daughter had made him dig a hole in the ground and force Talia into it, piling dirt upon her, shovelful by shovelful, sentence by sentence. When he handed the pages to Louisa and Jonathan, he managed a smile and a spasmodic hug, before he fled to the bedroom.

On the day of the open-store, he stood at the door to the shop, a maître d' greeting the mourners and receiving their consolation. He felt condemned to be stabbed slowly to death by each kind word. Every one of the visitors had cared for Talia; she had understood and cared for each of them. He did not resent them or even Louisa for punishing him in this fashion. Even though her mother had not wanted a memorial, Louisa needed one, to display the passionate love she had felt for Talia and had spent her life attempting to escape. She had never been as beautiful or as graceful or as joyous or as generous or as understanding as her mother. From her earliest childhood she had been vastly disappointed in herself, mistakenly attributing the same disappointment to her mother. In fact, Talia had marveled at her daughter's competence, logical mind, practical abilities, and courage in striking out into the world alone and conquering each obstacle. It was not in Talia's nature, though, to broadcast pride or approval or even love, no matter how much she felt these emotions. She did not express anger or disapproval, either. Today, she would have been embarrassed at the tribute being paid to her as a friend, an artist, a great beauty, a generous spirit. She preferred merely to accept existence and to be accepted by it with no great fanfare. Monty had understood this from the beginning and she had been grateful. Monty had learned this acceptance from her and so was now willing to stand and nod his appreciation for the crowd's sincere emotions. Jonathan, his devoted son, who felt equally uncomfortable in this outpouring of love for his mother and understood his father's pain, stood loyally by his side, slightly behind him, but touching elbows, as if to prop him up. Every now and then, Monty reached around to gently clasp Jonathan's hand in recognition of his support. Louisa circulated around the shop, showing her mother's creations, arranging her marvelous sketches, and displaying scarves, and bracelets, and jackets that her mother had worn. Louisa made a point that the proceeds of the sales would go to the homeless, a donation her mother would have wanted. Monty felt a great surge of love for their daughter, who had found such an appropriate way to express her admiration and sorrow for her mother.

Just as the last visitor left the shop, a van drove up, and Louisa directed the driver and his helper to take everything that had been left in the shop—clothes, desks, work tables, and sewing machines. To Monty's surprise, without telling him, his daughter had arranged for the store to be cleared. "I knew it would take you months, Dad, or even a year to let go of these remnants of Mom's life. If there's anything you want to keep, tell me now. Otherwise it's all going to people who need it."

Monty and Jonathan watched with wondering admiration as Louisa directed the efficient disposal of Talia's lifetime of work. Louisa retained for herself Talia's patterns, her drawings, and all the images of her mother's creations. When Monty expressed wonder at this sudden interest in style by his daughter, who had always dressed with extreme practicality and, even as a child, had refused her mother's attempts to provide her with more attractive clothing, Louisa replied that she would explain, later.

"I want to take a walk with you, alone, Dad, on the Headlands before I leave." She stood before him, her eyes full of tears. "There's a lot to my life that you and Mom never knew and it's important to me now that you know me better. I'm heartbroken that I never had a chance to tell Mom." She turned away, trying to hide her intense emotion.

Monty was stunned. This was the second time Louisa had broken down since her arrival. Never before had she shown so much emotion, even when she came to say goodbye to her dying mother. And her request for a walk on the Headlands disturbed him. That was one of the adventures on which he had often taken the children, a hike she had claimed to hate the most. She had complained with each step and had regaled her mother with the absurdity of her father's attempt to teach her how to appreciate nature. "Nature's fine for the birds and animals," she declared at the age of five, "I like people." It was a maxim she repeated for the rest of her childhood.

Monty offered to have the conversation in his study. But as soon as they arrived home from Talia's store, Louisa insisted that he and she drive out to the Headlands and take his favorite walk up on the cliffs above the ocean. As they climbed the trail, she moved along quickly ahead of him, not realizing that he could no longer keep up the pace. When she paused at the first overlook, where he had often stopped the children to gaze south along the breakers on the beach, past Bird Rock, down the coast, San Francisco's Headland, Seal Rocks, Ocean Beach, all the way to Devil's Slide. She stood there waiting, looking back as he labored up to her.

"You'll have to be a little patient," he said, puffing. "I've slowed down a bit, these days."

"Sorry, Dad, I wasn't thinking. Too anxious to see these glorious views, I guess."

"Glorious views?" he asked, laughing.

"I was a little bitch, wasn't I?"

"I think I was a bit too enthusiastic a father."

"You were perfect. I really liked your adventures, but I kept wanting to declare my independence. Besides, Jonathan always seemed too full of admiration, for you, for Mom, for nature. It wasn't my style."

"Your mother didn't display her feelings so openly, either. In many ways, you were alike."

Louisa turned to him, her eyes wide in surprise. "Were we, really?"

He hugged her. "Yes, really! In certain ways, in others, not."

They moved on up the trail, more slowly now, Louisa obviously moved by Monty's observation.

They stopped again at a severe cleft in the cliff that created a narrow inlet. Below, the waves rose, collided with the two rocky arms, proceeded up the sides of the cliff and fell over the scattered rocks on the narrow beach below them.

"You always had us stop here to wait for three waves."

Monty almost cried out to hear how precisely his daughter remembered these walks she had resisted with such anger.

"Why three?" she asked after the third wave hit the beach.

"Three has always been my lucky number, or multiples, since I was a little boy. There were three of us brothers and I wanted us to be together—although we weren't, really."

"Why not?"

"Oh, I'm not sure now. For years I thought it was sibling rivalry. I was the youngest and…I don't really know. It started with Jack. He was an only child until Doug came along to rob him of affection, and then I came to rob them both." He sighed. "There was always enough for all three of us. Still, we fought for more until we grew up. And then we became quite fond of one another—Jack distantly, Doug a lot more fond, I guess."

"You never told me that."

"You had your own sibling problems."

"I certainly did. But…" she paused and shook her head. "I didn't ask you much about the family or… about your life, did I? Pretty selfish of me."

"You had your own problems. You weren't selfish, though. You took care of your older brother a lot."

"You mean I tried to boss him around."

"He needed some bossing. Neither Talia nor I were good at bossing."

They stopped now on a mound above a lower bluff along which another trail ran. Tufts of blue-purple bush lupine flowered here and there, scatterings of bright golden coast poppies and pink mallow brightened the hillside, and along the very edge a thick border of brighter pink-red sea fig succulents formed a secure blanket before the steep drop to the breaking waves.

"Your mother loved lupine."

"This is where she finally wanted her ashes, isn't it?"

"She didn't particularly care. I suggested this, because she was fond of the view here. South, all the way to Devil's Slide and north, with the waves breaking against those black stacks, remnants of the eroded cliffs. She said the view reminded her of the immense wave of time in which we were infinitesimal eddies."

"I guess Mom was very poetic, but she didn't talk much about it. We knew it though. Somehow she made our lives richer without trying so hard."

Monty laughed. "Like me?"

Louisa elbowed him good-humoredly. "Like you, Dad." She sighed. "This walk isn't turning out to be what I thought it would be."

XXIII

It wasn't until they had reached the end of the trail north, that Louisa was able to tell the tale she had prepared. They settled themselves on the grassy edge of a bare bluff high above the ocean, from which they could see north past Tennessee Valley, Muir Beach, Bolinas, the Drakes Bay sandstone cliffs at the end of which Chimney Rock stood proudly at the south end of Point Reyes. As soon as they had settled, she launched in:

"You were surprised that I wanted all of Mom's designs and sketches and photos of her creations. I don't blame you. I'm a frump and I've always been one deliberately, in spite of Mom. I'm just the wrong shape to dress up. Anyway, I'm taking Mom's creations to the woman I love." She took a deep breath. "I'm a lesbian, a dyke, gay, and I guess I've always been one, which explains why I was so difficult growing up. We always thought I was just a tomboy, athletic, like some girls, and so on, which I was. Anyway, labels are stupid. Let me just say that I fell in love with Michelle, a twenty-two-year-old French au pair that we hired to take care of the kids while we worked." She paused and took a number of deep breaths, as if her confession had been an enormous effort.

Stunned, Monty stared down at an oblong shoal, a few hundred yards off the shore. The waves broke in white foam around the black rocky outline. Now and then, every sixth or seventh crest submerged it.

Having recovered, Louisa went on, a bit calmer now. "The strange thing—I really didn't think I had a chance—she fell in love with me. You'll like her a lot. She's very much like Mom: slim, graceful, perceptive, a lover of design and beauty. She will delight in Mom's work, and so will I, finally."

Monty had always prided himself in his perception, and yet never had he imagined that Louisa was gay. Talia probably knew all the time, but would have kept her suspicion to herself so as not to trouble him or her daughter. Talia let people make their own discoveries. Of course, it made perfect sense: poor dear Louisa had never been comfortable being a conventional girl, which is why she made everyone around her uncomfortable.

"Well Dad? Aren't you going to say anything? Are you shocked?"

"Only at how dumb I have been, insensitive."

"Does it trouble you that your daughter is a dyke?"

"No, not at all, if you're happy. And Joel? And the kids?"

She had prepared her tale beforehand and she recounted it smoothly. The marriage had never been very successful. She wasn't quite sure why she had accepted Joel's proposal. She hadn't liked the way he played the violin. "Too much schmaltz," she declared. She felt his compositions lacked spine. She couldn't bear his romanticism, not only in music, but in everything. Still, his gentleness appealed, as did his willingness to take directions, which, of course, she was only too willing to give. The sex had never been good for either of them. She probably would have been willing to go on, however, especially once the children were born. He was a good father, "a terrific father, like you, Dad. He really liked taking care of the babies, which I didn't, and he's a born teacher and housekeeper.

"And then Michelle appeared. It was like an epiphany, almost from the moment she danced in the door. I couldn't take my eyes off her and could hardly keep my hands off either. Like you, I never suspected. What blockheads we were! I must have made you and Mom miserable. And poor dear Jonathan, whom I probably hated, because he was lucky enough to have been born a boy.

"For months I was tortured. Finally, I confessed my feelings to Michelle, saying that she could quit if she wanted to. I would pay her enough to get along. To my amazement, she told me that she had fallen in love with me and the children and didn't want to leave, ever."

The two of them went to Joel, full of trepidation. To their joy, he welcomed the news. It turned out that for a year, he had been having an affair with the second violinist in the orchestra of which he was the concert master. He had been terrified to tell her, because he loved the children too much and didn't want to leave them, even if it meant abandoning his violinist. Of course, the practical Louisa found a way to satisfy all of them. She had them buy a larger house in Waltham that would accommodate Louisa and her lover, Joel and his lover, and the two children. The children had their own rooms, the husband and his lover, a self-contained part of the house with its own facilities and she and the au pair had theirs. The second violinist contributed to the purchase. It worked so well and they all liked one another so much, that they often all ate together and relaxed together in one of the units. She didn't know how long it would last, but certainly until the kids went off to college.

When she had finished her story, Monty embraced her. "I'm very happy for you and immensely impressed at how you surmount every obstacle. Your mother would have smiled contentedly, and said nothing, of course."

"She probably understood from the beginning."

"Do you want to help deposit her ashes before you leave?"

"No, Dad, I agree with Mom, the ashes are just ashes. I want to get back to my new life as soon as possible. But from now on, I promise to keep in close touch with you and tell you how it's all working out. I want you to be part of my life, to understand and enjoy my joy, as well as my grief. We're going to be completely honest with one another from now on."

He replied that would make him happy. As he hugged her at the airport, though, he wasn't sure he wanted all the details of that complex household that he knew, before long, would have many of the same problems that all households inevitably had—more, certainly, considering the complex relationships it contained. He would have preferred the simplicity of not quite knowing, but hoping she would find her way through life. He was too old to start worrying about his grandchildren, living with their mother's lover, his son-in-law, and his mistress, and probably four or five animals, not to mentions a couple of violins or more and probably a grand piano.

Monty arrived home to find Jonathan anxiously awaiting him. He had out-stayed his sister, so that he could be alone with Monty. Now, he too suggested a walk, on the Matt Davis Trail, another of Monty's adventures for the children. Monty was not anxious for a second hike along with another confession, but he acquiesced with pretended warmth. They drove up to Pan Toll on Mount Tamalpais and parked. Jonathan eagerly led the way, pointing out the spring flowers: the tall Douglas iris and the small live-oak at the trail head, shooting stars and Brodiaea on the moist grassy downslope before the forest, and then their favorite flower of this hike, the tiny Calypso orchids sprung up from the duff of the forest floor under the high Douglas firs.

By the time they got to the end of the forest, Jonathan was far ahead of his exhausted father. He stopped and waited. "Sorry, Dad,

I lose my head on this trail in the spring. I love every step. Did you see the scarlet larkspur and the mission bells by the dell of live-oaks? I promise we don't have to go beyond the knoll where we always had our picnic. I hope the ground iris are out."

Monty laughed to hear his son's excitement, which revived him a bit. He felt ready to hear Jonathan's confession, or, perhaps, a veiled accusation. It wasn't long before they were settled on the open knoll with its commanding views north past Bolinas to Point Reyes and South to Devil's Slide. This was the landscape, Monty felt, where he was condemned to hear the difficult stories of his children's lives. Jonathan began gently.

"I suppose Louisa told you about her new love? I hope it wasn't too upsetting."

"So, you knew?"

"Of course. We had no secrets with one another. She helped me get through my childhood, you know, and then Mitzi's addiction, our divorce, and… all the rest."

"When did you find out about Louisa?"

"I knew about her always. Mom and I talked about it a lot."

"Your Mom knew… before Louisa…?"

"Dad, Mom knew everything. You and Louisa were the only ones who didn't suspect. Mom told me there was no point in telling you. She said you would only make it an issue."

"Me, making an issue? I was always the one who mediated."

"That's the point, Dad. You would have tried to make Louisa feel better, and Louisa would have hated that. I, of course, welcomed all the help you or Mom could offer. As for Louisa, Mom thought it best that Louisa should find out by herself and work it out, which is what Louisa always wanted to do about everything. She was very happy when she called to surprise me with the news that she had fallen in love with Michelle. I put on a great show. I've always known how to bow down to Louisa's self-importance."

Monty lay back on the grass and stared up at the clouds and blue sky. He was too old to find out just how blind he had been about his children. He could hardly believe that they had worked out such a complex relationship before they had left home and then kept it up after they had established their families. And, of course, his incredible wife had known everything all along and thought it best that he should be protected. He wondered now whether he should be grateful or angry.

Jonathan now explained his life to his father, much of which Monty already knew. "I know I was a pretty needy kid, always asking to be hugged and read to. Funny to think of it, I depended on Louisa, my kid sister, a lot. I didn't exactly know what was wrong until you and Mom told me about Emma's death. I must have been eleven or twelve. I took me a long time to figure out how I was related to my 'blood mother.' Even though I'm a pediatrician, I still have no idea what babies know, but I must have missed mothering that first year. At least, that's what the books I read in medical school said. It couldn't have been easy for you, when you were alone with me, before you married Talia. The books use the word 'abandonment' as a trope for what orphaned kids feel. I don't think I felt abandoned; you and Talia hovered over me all the time. But there must be something in it, must have been difficult for me, even though I wasn't aware that I had been abandoned by my mother. Even after Talia took over, I seemed to need more mothering than she could give me."

"Dear Talia gave you and Louisa a lot of love."

"Loving, but not 'mothering,' I mean, not taking charge of my life, directing me. Talia never directed anyone. Strangely enough, Louisa did, almost before she could talk. And I obeyed her, but resented her bossiness." He paused, picked up a handful of grass and let it float away on a breeze that had started up from the west. "I guess it was my need that I resented more than Louisa."

"Talia and I did our best."

"You both were the best. I learned a lot from the two of you about different ways of caretaking—very different ways. That helped me a lot in practicing medicine. A pediatrician has to listen and wait and only subtly begin to direct the child and his parents. I guess that's what attracted Mitzi. She needed a lot of care. So she married a pediatrician, and the pediatrician thought he could help her. What I discovered was that I was very good with children, but completely unsure of myself with adults, worse even with my alcoholic wife. I burned out after the third commitment. She went on binges, abused me and everyone who tried to help, physically abused, I mean. I probably would have driven myself crazy if Louisa hadn't flown down from Boston and knocked some sense into my head. Called me a co-dependent, a cliché, I guess, but very true. I was no one to cure addiction. Luckily, I was smart enough, or maybe Mitzi was smart enough, not to have children."

Monty sighed, full of wonder at this revelation. He could hardly have imagined that Louisa would be Jonathan's savior from his devastating marriage. He was tempted to ask whether Talia knew about that too, but he restrained himself.

"Joanne was one of our counselors, very maternal, strong-minded, a caretaker, the sort of mother I had always needed. So I married her. Her children were already teenagers and glad to have a male in the house to take the pressure off their mother's command. It isn't exactly an ideal situation, even now. I'm fond of Joanne, and I guess I need her, but it isn't the great love I had hoped for. Still, it's certainly a relief from taking care of an alcoholic. Besides which, Joanne is a great cook and a gardener. A man could do worse. So that's the story, Dad."

"Thank you, Jonathan." Monty had a hard time getting the words out. "I'm grateful that you trusted me."

On the way back to the car, they did not speak until just before they got to the car, when Jonathan stopped. He turned and took Monty by both arms, looking fully into his eyes. "Dad, I've always trusted you, just not myself."

Monty tried to soothe himself by thinking what a wise son they had raised. It didn't help. Once they started driving down the mountain, Jonathan laid his arm over Monty's back. "I hope I didn't depress you. I know it did." Before they got out of the car, he added, "I just want to be more open with you from now on, to let you know how my life is working out."

Monty wished his children would not be so anxious to share all of their lives with him. He felt too old to be able to witness their difficulties.

When Monty did not immediately answer this promise for future confessions, Jonathan continued. "You don't have to worry, Dad. I am really pretty content. I love my profession and am a very good and successful pediatrician. I'm gentle and understanding, as you know, and I let the kids tell me about their illnesses before I say a word. I take them seriously, which they appreciate. As I told you, I learned to listen from you and Mom. It's the greatest skill a diagnostician can possess."

XXIV

As he drove home from the airport, Monty felt weighed down by the details of his children's complex lives. And now they both promised to share their future problems. He hadn't realized how comfortable he had been with only the general outlines of their successes and failures. He had always sympathized and offered any amount of aid. Louisa had wanted no aid or advice, no matter how much she complained in general and blamed them—mostly Monty; Jonathan, who only blamed himself for everything, had asked for a great deal of help and comfort, but had never before offered the details of his misery. Talia asked for nothing. Monty had always valued her independence. She simply wanted to live, to love life and her work, and to love and admire him and the children. She was not fond of elaborate discussions of motives and attitudes. That had been a great relief in the beginning, especially after life with Emma.

Entering the empty house, he closed the door, stood in the foyer and listened. Not a sound, except for the hum of the refrigerator and the occasional start-up of the furnace. He walked around the downstairs, slowly beginning to understand the meaning of solitude. And yet he hadn't lost Talia. She was part of him and part of the house, every object in which they had chosen together: the wrought iron candle-holder they had found in Paris, replete with alternate lab flasks to hold single flowers; the ceramic bowls with vivid raku glazes a friend had tossed for their twenty-fifth anniversary; the two rosewood Chinese chairs they had bought at an estate auction in the city, chairs in which they had sat across from one another to discuss family decisions. He was surrounded by objects and furniture and etchings and wall hangings that marked the years of their marriage. And upstairs, he had placed her ashes, the meaning of which puzzled him. How could that beautiful, lively human being be reduced to ashes that fit into a small lacquer box. For two days he contemplated the box, which he had rested carefully on the other pillow of their queen-sized bed. He ate, drank some wine, stared out of the window, and kept returning to the ashes in the bedroom. He was able to do nothing else. He sat in the bedroom, thinking what an odd man he was to put Talia's ashes on her pillow. Did he believe that when he awoke in the morning, the ashes would have reconstituted themselves, and Talia would be there to greet him?

On the third day after Louisa and Jonathan left, he understood why he had become paralyzed. He descended to his studio and pulled a large leather suitcase out of the space between the furnace and the hot water heater. It was a handsome old rawhide case, resplendent with columns of brass buttons and worn leather straps. Emma must have found it in a pawn shop on the lower East Side of Manhattan, an offering by a starving, much-traveled Greenwich Village poet to secure food for a couple of days, or maybe just for one glorious party. On its side were faded stickers from many European countries and cities. A tag on the end identified the owner as Emma Pinchas, with a street address in Berkeley. She had traveled through Europe with it before she entered graduate school in Berkeley, where she had met him.

He sat for some time at his writing desk staring down at Emma's case. He had packed it with all of Emma's papers and favorite objects after she died. He hadn't dared to open it again. He had carried it with him and the baby Jonathan when he moved to a smaller apartment in Berkeley. After he and Talia married and moved, he brought it to this house in Sausalito and hid it next to the furnace. One of the many criticisms Emma had leveled at him had to do with his superstitious nature. He had responded sharply that he was spiritual, not superstitious, and accused her of misusing a phantom pragmatism to rob life of its beauty. Exasperated, she said that he wasn't perceptive enough to recognize beauty when it stared him in the face. He countered, that she was really a romantic and only used reason as a weapon. He was twenty-six and she was twenty-two; they were in the first flush of love and found their arguments exciting. They shouted, pounded on the table, and slammed doors. Their early fights always came to a climax in bed, with a redeeming mutual orgasm. Now he reflected, sadly, there had never been orgasms like that with Talia. Remembering those passionate arguments of his youth, he chuckled to think he had ever used the word "spiritual." It had been a lifetime since he had dared expose himself like that. Guardedly, he stared at the suitcase. He sighed. Emma had been correct. He was deeply superstitious. He knew that once he opened the suitcase, Emma's spirit would escape and release all of the pain that had attended their love affair, their marriage, and Jonathan's deadly birth.

Stepping carefully over the clasped suitcase, he left the studio and went upstairs to the house. He stood in the kitchen for some time trying to decide how to spend the rest of the day. Finally, he shrugged, poured himself a glass of gin and carried it up to the bedroom. He sat in a chair on Talia's side of the bed, raised his glass in a toast to the box of ashes on the pillow, and took a long slug of gin, shuddering as it went down.

He addressed the lacquer box. "You probably knew I had Emma's stuff in the studio all these years. The kids suspected that you knew everything, even when they were little. They said it again on this trip." He took another swallow and waited. After some time, he continued, as if the ashes had responded. "We were in love, weren't we? In love all these years, full of respect and admiration for one another?" He paused, drank, and then went on, "So why did we leave so much unspoken? Were we afraid?"

He waited. Then, abruptly, he stood up. "Oh shit, what the fuck am I doing? Talking to a box of ashes!" He strode to the bedroom window and stared out at the bay. For days, they had watched the bay together, hardly speaking, while she declined toward death. That's when he should have talked, expressed again all of the love he had demonstrated year after year. Now he wondered whether he also should have explained about the suitcase in the basement, about the ghost of Emma, who had accompanied all those years of their happiness together. Was that a betrayal? Should he have confessed that and so much more about the complexity of his feelings for her. Talia knew. Of course she knew. What good would a confession have done during those last days? It would simply have been redundant. And yet, he felt he had never been completely honest with Talia. This was especially troubling when he thought about their love-making, which had been more than good enough, but never as explosive and inventive as it had been with Emma.

At this point, he turned dejectedly to the stairs, avoiding even a glance at the box of ashes on the pillow, as if he had already revealed too much. He made his way to the kitchen and poured another strong drink. He took his gin out into the living room where Talia had spent her last weeks in a hospital bed. He collapsed by the window. A fully loaded container ship slowly made its way toward the bridge and the ocean. Across the brilliant sapphire-blue hull massive block letters in white spelled out CMA CGM. The white superstructure rose four decks midship. Fore and aft, colored containers were unevenly stacked almost as high as the ship's bridge. The red waterline barely showed through the curling white foam of the water as the bow cut its way forward. He knew very well the feeling of leaving port, leaving a continent behind, entering an endless expanse of water, with currents and shoals and waves and winds and unexpected squalls and storms. He had spent three years in the Navy as an officer on a destroyer in the Far East, a role Emma had derided. How could a man who claimed to be a socialist or even merely a social-democrat have joined the Navy? He had responded by asking how could a woman who claimed to be an anarcho-syndicalist have married a man who had been an officer in the Navy?

"I only married you," she shouted, "because you danced so well and fucked like a demon, and besides," her voice subsided and she grinned, "I was pregnant."

The ship was making less than ten knots on the way to sea, suggesting a hesitancy at embarking on its voyage. A tug followed in its wake, ready to take the cautious pilot off once the ship had cleared the Golden Gate. Talia, in her hospital bed, had confided to Monty that she found solace in the slow progress of those large, laden ships away from the populated continent out to the unmarked wilderness of the ocean. It was, she said, an image of the hesitant progress her body, weighted by a lifetime, as it made its way towards its dissolution into the unknown regions of death. Talia never hesitated when she spoke the word "death."

Monty drew a deep breath and sighed. His second wife was a supreme realist. No aspect of life made her blink—neither joy, nor sickness, nor wealth, nor poverty, and finally not even extinction. He doubted whether Emma, even after a long life, would have accepted death so calmly. She probably would have feigned a resolute stoicism, but he imagined her standing on the ramparts of her life, one breast exposed like that fiery French woman, Liberty, in 1830, painted by Delacroix; Emma, raising high an impotent flag against the attacking black specter of death, his resistless sickle sweeping forward. For Emma, life was a passionate struggle that had begun in the cramped Brooklyn tenement apartment, where her radical widowed mother battled against her four children, a stingy landlord, a tyrannical boss, and American capitalism. Emma's last words to her mother when she left home at sixteen were, "I may be a Trotskyist-anarchist, but you will always be Josef Stalin, who leaves only wreckage and dead lives in your wake."

Monty groaned. Here he was invoking Emma, while he should be mourning the beautiful wife, who had made his life possible. He sat watching the sapphire-blue hull and white superstructure slowly disappear around the green cliff studded with houses of south Sausalito, his soul locked in memories of his two marriages, each one struggling to take precedence. The gin began to take hold, lifting him into a cloud of his past lives shared with Talia and Emma. He accepted them both and carried them down to his studio along with the bottle of gin. He sat determinedly in the chair facing Emma's suitcase, leaned over, unfastened the straps, inserted the hanging key in the lock, and opened the case.

There she was, Emma Pinchas, all that materially remained of her: her most precious objects, scarves, and hats; her essays, her stories, her photographs, and her letters; and the deep maroon lacquer box containing her ashes. The faint odor of lavender rose from the packed case, emanating from sachets of lavender she had placed in the drawers of her dresser. He had forgotten that he had put the sachets in the case before he closed and locked it. Emma had loved lavender, the smell, the color, the flower. When she got drunk or high, she would always launch into an eloquent description of the fields of lavender in the Luberon, east of Avignon, where she had stayed for months working on a farm. "Just the scent of those fields was pure poetry. Just the scent, no words." He could see her declaiming her love for the Luberon lavender fields in a firm quiet tone of conviction unlike any of her passionate, fiery pronouncements on life, class, society, economics, war, capitalism, or gender. He inhaled deeply, taking Emma into his lungs, and sat staring at the box of Emma's ashes.

He had called Emma's two sisters and her brother—they lived in different cities—to tell them of her accidental death. They received the news calmly, offering their sympathy. They were not surprised. Emma had always done everything excessively. Dying in childbirth seemed just like her. No, they didn't want to attend a ceremony or take any of her belongings, especially not her ashes. And the baby? Well, they had children of their own, which was burden enough. The way they spoke, it seemed as if their children were too much of a burden. Their mother had died three years before. When Emma went back for the funeral, the four siblings had gone through the ceremony and parted, each hoping never to see the others again. Emma had never told him the details of that last family meeting. Their mother's angry spirit had pervaded the home from the beginning, dividing them even as children. Meeting for the first time in years invoked that crowded, contentious apartment in Brooklyn from which each of them had fled. When Emma returned to Berkeley, she had celebrated her freedom from the past with two bottles of Veuve Clicqot Champagne, most of which she drank. Emma never did, or felt, or believed moderately. "All engines ahead, full!" as they would say in the Navy.

He began to cry. Emma had always hated his sentimentality—at least, that's what she considered his sensitive feeling toward those whom he loved. "You're not going to carry on, are you?" she would say at one of these moments. Today, he replied, "Yes, I'm fucking going to carry on for you, my wild and fiery Emma. I was too shocked when it happened. Women never died in childbirth anymore. And then I had the baby. How could I break down when I had to take care of a baby? Just think, Emma d'Arc, if you had lived you would have had to be a mother. Could you have handled it, or would you have delegated that role to me along with finding fault with me as a father?"

He drank from the gin bottle now, thinking, "Here I am talking to Emma's ashes too. She would have laughed hysterically to see her sensitive husband, alone in the house, except for the company of the ashes of both of his wives!"

The comedy of his situation dried his tears. All these years he had forgotten that he had placed Emma's ashes in the suitcase along with everything else. He had known it would be dangerous to open the case, but not how dangerous. Their life together came flooding back along with the dizzying effect of all the gin and the scent of lavender. They had met on an Anti-Vietnam War march, or was it a Free Speech march against the university? They marched and protested all the time in those days. They recognized one another across the plaza, because they were both graduate students in the English Department with a major in comparative literature and a minor in creative writing, what the snobbish department called Rhetoric. They had been eyeing one another for weeks, admiring their comments in class and the pieces of writing each had submitted for discussion. In a lingering Indian-summer autumn twilight, the protestors had gathered to begin their march from the university down Telegraph Avenue. Spirits were high. Everyone waved handprinted signs and wore colorful T-shirts, bandanas, long flowing dresses, boots and sandals. Many were accompanied by their children, strings of helium filled, floating balloons painted with protest messages tied to their wrists. There was so much marijuana in the air that one could get high merely by taking a deep breath. He and Emma had entered the plaza from opposite sides and caught sight of each other simultaneously. Monty had felt an instant shock. Her gaze was intense, joyous, welcoming. His must have been the same, because he saw its effect reflected in her response. They were very happy to see one another and hurried through the crowd. In a moment, he had embraced her, lifted her off her feet, and she began to laugh. Blushing he set her down, "Sorry, I was really glad to see you."

"Why sorry? I was glad to see you too. This is where we should be, together."

He didn't know whether she meant here at the march or always together, but he felt a joy that he had never felt before, a quickening of all his senses, and a deep desire for her body. They marched together, talking all the while about what they believed, who they read, how they would spend their lives. After the march, they ended up in a Black nightclub built out of railroad cars in Oakland. They danced together for hours. It seemed as though they knew each other's moves without thinking. He had never danced with a woman who flowed with his body so effortlessly. They ended up in bed at his small cottage behind the house of one of the professors. It was more of a hut than a cottage: a single room with bed and desk and bookshelves and hot plate and sink and a cramped bathroom and shower. With Emma, it wasn't "making love," it was "fucking" without hesitation, fucking powerfully, with passion. Their orgasm seemed volcanic to Monty. He lay back full of wonder. "I've never felt like this before," he said.

"Bullshit. You guys all say that after a piece of ass."

"I've never said that before, and you're not my first."

"Well, I enjoyed it too, but let's not go overboard."

"Whatever," he replied, feeling satisfied that although it hadn't been easy for her to admit, she had given him a lot by merely saying she had enjoyed it. "Are you hungry?"

"Ravenous."

That night had been the beginning. Luckily it was many weeks before Emma learned enough about him to arouse her political fervor. He had not only been a sailor, he had been an officer, and worst of all he had joined. It made no difference to her that he admitted that he had joined out of a deep depression brought on by graduate school at Columbia, that his enlistment had a lot to do with his guilt that his older brother had been drafted and sent to the front in Korea, and even more to do with his guilt toward his patriotic father, whom he had deserted before his father's premature death. Emma considered all his excuses subsidiary, "personal." She lectured him that Lenin called all "personal" motives traitorous to the revolution.

"Then you're a Leninist?"

"No." Her tone became insistently pedantic, teaching Monty a lesson. "Lenin, for your information, mistakenly laid the basis for a repressive, bureaucratic state. I am an anarcho-syndicalist: a consensual government by groups of laborers who work not for the state, but for everyone who labors together."

Their life alternated between angry arguments, satisfying agreements about books and poems they both loved, and happy bouts of hiking, drinking and dancing, and fucking. She was outraged to find that he had grown up in a comfortable, loving middle-class home and had been left a small income. She accused him of deliberately pretending to be poorer than he was. Worse yet, he had learned to dance from his mother and had been elected president of the seventh-grade dance club of his elementary school. "An apparatchik from the beginning," she scolded. It didn't matter that he had rebelled against his loving father and had missed his death and funeral—all personal matters. He was from a degenerate class and would never liberate himself from it. He claimed to be a pacifist socialist, and yet he had joined the Navy as an officer, in a war he didn't believe in, that wasn't even a war. He had eaten in the wardroom, served by Asian stewards. He had no backbone. In her opinion all his writing was careful and class-bound, with a deep hidden sentimentality. He worshipped nature, but was annoyed at sharing park campsites with ordinary people in RVs who played loud music and watched television rather than listening to the birds. When he cooked, he consulted cookbooks and tried to make gourmet meals. She had grown up on canned spaghetti and meatballs, canned chicken soup, and day-old bread in plastic. He pointed out that when she chose a restaurant, it was one that was rated highly by Michelin for its original food and was not always inexpensive. As for wines, she seemed to have a very sensitive palate and was always urging that they go to tasting bars. Luckily, he thought, grimacing, their sex was classless; it was simply and supremely satisfying for both of them. They loved the same books, agreed that the university was no place for someone who wanted to learn how to write, disliked most of their fellow graduate students, and dreamed together of going to live in Paris, or Provence or Tuscany. They were in love. He asked her to marry him, again and again and again. She refused saying that they had been born into different classes and there was no way they could vow to be together always; their class was in their bones. And then she became pregnant. They married and moved to a larger apartment, which they scraped and painted and furnished, working happily together, preparing for the baby.

In the end, it was never clear whether she had deliberately forgotten to take the pill or his desire had been so compelling that she did not have the time or opportunity. The birth killed her. Could one blame faulty genes for the bad wiring of her heart, or did someone have to be guilty? In his love affair with Emma, he was, by class definition, the guilty party. But then, in his life, since his rebellion against his father, Monty had always considered himself guilty.

XXV

When Emma died so unexpectedly in childbirth, Monty had little time to decide what to do with her body. She had been such a complex mix of pragmatic realism and passionate romanticism that he could hardly guess at her wishes in the matter. Although the two of them had profoundly considered, discussed, and argued metaphysical, aesthetic, and philosophic issues, not once had they approached the problem of death and the disposal of their remains. They were too young and had not known one another long enough. Although he had missed his father's funeral and burial, he had attended his mother's and both of his brothers', all of which were traditionally Jewish. Emma had come back from her mother's last rites full of anger and derision. "Do you know," she said, bitterly, "that the Hebrew prayer for mourning, the Kaddish, says nothing about the dead. It speaks only in high praise of the Almighty God of the Jews, who evidently demands nothing but praise! Do you think he deserves praise after what happens in the world he supposedly created?"

For once, Monty was in complete agreement.

In addition to her revolutionary anarchism, Emma was passionate about saving the earth. She decried the waste of nature on graveyards and the cost of maintaining graves; she maintained that the entire American funeral industry was just another example of modern addiction to consumption. After the disastrous childbirth, Monty barely had time to sit in shock for an hour with his dead wife, before he consigned her body to the medical school. As a Marxist, Emma believed in science and the importance of material life. Emma's box of ashes represented not very much of Emma, when he considered the uses that he had allowed science to make of her remains.

This evening, after some hours in the studio, musing about the past and drinking gin, Monty carried the box of Emma's ashes along with the bottle up to the bedroom, where he placed it on the dresser. He removed the box of Talia's ashes from the pillow of their bed and placed it next to Emma's box. Still quite drunk, he sat in a chair and contemplated the remains of both his wives for some time. In his life, as far back as he could remember, even in early childhood, he had always tried to act responsibly. What did he owe the contents of these boxes? Had he offended the memory of his wives by placing their remains side-by-side? Should he have left Emma in the studio, disposed of Talia, and returned to Emma? Or perhaps he should have first disposed of Emma and returned to Talia?

While he and Talia had waited for her death, he did not have to decide what to do with her body. She wanted cremation and had no interest in the aftermath, which, in her opinion, was simply nothingness. He could not bear the thought of harvesting that beautiful body for science, although he knew she wouldn't have cared. Somewhat guiltily, he had her cremated in the least expensive manner—no service, no fancy urn, no placement in some narrow garden wall niche with a yearly fee. Talia was prudent and would have disapproved of unnecessary expense. More significant, though, she always prized her independence; her ashes would be free on the coastal cliffs she loved, without elaborate ceremony.

As he confusedly mulled over these sober thoughts, the bedroom began to whirl around him: windowed view of the dark bay under dim stars, walls, doorway, bed, and back to windowed view, round and round, window, wall, door, bed, window.... He shut his eyes and felt himself whirling faster and faster. He had to grip the arms of the chair to keep from falling to the floor.

Many hours later, he awoke in the dark. He was lying on the floor in front of the dresser, the gin bottle next to him, completely empty. His head ached, throbbing. He felt he might throw up at any moment, but he could not move. At least the room had stopped spinning. He had a decision to make. What was it? He could not remember what he had been thinking before he passed out. Why was he in the bedroom with an empty bottle of gin? As far back as he could remember, he had possessed a nearly full bottle of Beefeater's in the cupboard. He had ceased drinking heavily many years ago. Lying there, his nausea slowly receded. His memory returned. The ashes. He had been talking to the ashes of his wives and drinking steadily. He had evidently killed the bottle of gin and passed out.

He sat up. The dizziness returned. He placed both hands on the floor on either side of him and waited. He then pivoted slowly to his knees, reached up to the dresser for support and stood. He could make out the gleam of the lacquer of the two boxes, reflecting a dim light from the windows and the sky beyond. Dawn was breaking over the bay. He could not believe that he had slept the entire night on the floor. He backed carefully away from the dresser and let himself slowly down into the armchair from which he had fallen. His body ached. The two lacquer boxes seemed to be staring with annoyance at him. Both wives had been exasperated by the deliberate care he took to make any decision, Emma much more vocal than Talia, who could wait patiently, it seemed, forever, without a remark.

The problem now seemed to be that he had never understood ashes. What really did they represent and how should they be treated, whether they were the ashes of one wife or of two? After the cremation of whatever remained of Emma, he had spent some time in the library researching cremation. The textbook details came back to his mind as he contemplated his wives' ashes. It turned out that cremation by wood was often the custom in ancient societies, but it took a long time, and the remains contained a great many bone parts—hardly what one would call ashes. The Greeks generally cremated; the Romans cremated at first and then turned to burial of the bodies, for no better reason than fashion, led by the wealthy; but even through those years both methods seemed acceptable. It wasn't until the second century of the Roman Empire that burial became the normal way of disposing of bodies until late in the 19th century. Burning was reserved for witches and heretics and traitors and dangerous enemies in order to preserve the living from evil spirits or radical thought. As Christianity took hold, the gathering of the dead in churchyards or within the church itself became a way to assert the community of believers and the understanding that the blessed would be gathered together in heaven. The Enlightenment of the 17th and 18th centuries, in its growing trust in science, began to challenge belief in an almighty God and a community of souls. By the middle of the 19th century, authorities, concerned with scientific hygiene and the danger of epidemics rising from the decomposing bodies in cemeteries, began to search for more efficient ways to dispose of the dead, without the fumes caused by slow-burning wood. The industrial age, after its invention of specially adapted blast furnaces, borrowed from the steel industry, solved the problem of reducing the time cremation took and its fumes. These furnaces were able to turn the matter of a body into its elements: common nitrogen, potassium, calcium, phosphorous, and chlorine with traces of other elements, "nothing but a heap of ashes."

Monty had cringed at these histories of modern ovens of cremation and their diagrams, along with the fanciful architectural drawings of the crematorium buildings that sought to look almost like churches or oriental mosques. When he went to the crematoriums to pick up the ashes of each of his wives, Monty had kept his head down and his eyes almost shut. He did not want to think of either of his wives being incinerated in such absurd semi-industrial surroundings, camouflaged as spiritual edifices. Now looking at the two lacquer boxes, he could only think of those sophisticated furnaces and fanciful buildings. Somehow, civilization had become even more barbaric than it had been before the rise of religions. Of course, he believed that despite all the myths and appurtenances of modern states, they were less compassionate and empathetic than the "savages" who had revered and honored their enemies before they ate them. There had been no honor or empathy in Buchenwald, Hamburg, Hiroshima, Vietnam, or Yemen. And what sort of empathy had led him to place his wives into high pressure furnaces in order to reduce their bodies into flakes? Had it been some vague biblical memory of "from dust into dust"? This morning, in his weakened state, Monty began to doubt that he had ever escaped the Judaism of his childhood.

As if to convert his current dilemma into a more civilized surrounding, he carried the boxes of ashes down to the kitchen and placed them on the kitchen table facing one another. Then he proceeded to prepare breakfast: coffee, fruit, sunny-side eggs and raisin bread toast. By the time he finished breakfast, his mind had cleared. He would take the ashes of both wives to the Headlands and dispose of them, separately, not together. He would simply have to decide where the ashes of each should reside to be dispersed for eternity.

He placed Talia's box on the back seat, because she never worried about precedence. Emma's box seemed to sit smugly on the passenger seat. After all, she had been his first wife and had shared more of his deepest thoughts than had... Monty shook himself violently. Here he was talking to ashes again or rather to the boxes that contained them. The car almost reached the turn-off to the Headlands tunnel, when he decided to take the ashes for a last ride, while they still retained some identity, each in her own box. Once he cast them out... Again, he reprimanded himself for imagining any identity between these products of industrial ovens and his wives, or even their bodies that had been consumed. Nonetheless, he continued on the road to the Golden Gate Bridge, where he slid smoothly into the slow lane.

The sun had risen high over the bay and the city. The waters of the bay and the ocean reflected the clear deep blue skies. The Pacific extended out on a gentle curve to an infinite distinct line of the horizon, broken only by the dim image of the Farallon cliffs breaking that line, thirty miles to the west. If she had been alive in the back seat, Talia would have smiled happily in contemplation of the art deco shapes of the red-orange bridge towers, the powerful hills of the Marin Headlands rising over the bay entrance, and the wide sweep of the Pacific. She would imagine the rich bird and sea life feeding around those far western islands—the images of whales, dolphins, seals, sea lions, and seabirds joining a pastiche in her mind with the bridge and the cascaded building of the city on the bay to the east, a living fabric of the existence in which she had lived. Emma, true to her namesake Emma Goldman, would have been excoriating Monty for taking her on a picturesque ride, when there was so much poverty and suffering in the world, even in that tourist city to the south that hid its poor, and that consumer-happy continent beyond, not to mention the millions of starving peasants under brutal dictators on the continents of Asia and Africa to the west. Almost in the same breath, Emma would be speculating upon which fine restaurant in the city they would eat their lunch, if the prudent Monty would possibly indulge her to lighten the dark mood into which he had drunkenly plunged them with his thoughts of ovens and cremation and ashes. She would be making it clear that he owed her an elegant, tasteful meal with a good wine, before he threw her to the winds in one of his so-called "natural habitats."

For the last ride of his two wives, Monty performed his usual city tour: down the renovated Doyle drive from the bridge, a cut around the absurd Palace of Fine Arts, a remnant of the 1915 Exhibition, through the Marina, with lovely views of the Marina green and the yacht basin, past Fort Mason, and up Russian Hill on Larkin Street, with spectacular views of Alcatraz and the bay, left on brick-lined Lombard and down that curling street past the charming, shingled Victorian houses. He continued on Lombard up Nob Hill with its Coit Tower, rising in the shape of a fireman's nozzle. As he drove slowly around the Tower parking lot, he refused Emma's raucous demand to stop so that she could visit the revolutionary Depression workers' murals on the tower walls, murals inspired by Diego Rivera, one of Emma's leftist heroes. For Talia's sake, though, he regretted not stopping so that she could skip lightly along the stone walls as she had early in their love affair, enjoying the sights of the city skyscrapers and bay, her arms askew in delight. Talia would never ask him to stop, she would simply have leaned eagerly this way and that on the back seat to catch glimpses of the views she had always loved, remembering, he hoped, those wonderful outings they had made before their marriage. Both women had delighted in North Beach, sighing with nostalgia for the old Italian men in their suits and white shirts, who had played bocce on the courts off of Columbus and stood in groups outside the cigar store. Talia would have wanted to stop at either a cheap Basque restaurant off Broadway or at Original Joe's and eat at the counter behind which the good-natured Italian chefs threw together a miner's Hang Town Fry special of onions, spinach, ground beef, and eggs. Emma sniffed and sulked, fearing Monty, the skinflint, would do just that to save money. She was holding out for an elegant meal at Quince or Saison or Coi. Monty knew exactly what would happen if he acquiesced. The moment Emma entered, she would make clear that she disapproved of the pretense of the decor, the place settings of gold and Versace dinner sets with outlandish designs, and the elaborate protocol of the waiters. The almost indecipherable font of the menu with scattered descriptions of the food in French or Italian or Russian would make her laugh. Nonetheless, she would order the most expensive items, along with a wine that she would spend a great deal of time sniffing and rolling around on her palate, before tasting and approving. Talia would settle for a modest salad and coffee. What interested Monty most about his two wives would have been the reaction of the headwaiter and the waiters to each of them. Although Emma had waited tables for years in her teens to earn enough to live and tried to give the impression that she knew as much about serving in restaurants as anyone, the staff took an instant dislike to her and made it clear they only served her because she was a client. Talia, who had served as many meals and washed as many dishes in restaurants in her youth, simply smiled appreciatively and murmured thank you when she was served. The headwaiter and waiters all responded to her with warmth as if they were in the same family. That's how Talia affected everyone. They felt noticed and understood by Talia with common humanity.

Exhausted, Monty headed back toward the bridge. Once again, he changed his mind and turned toward Golden Gate Park. Emma's ashes deserved a final resting place—if even Emma's ashes could ever rest—more to her liking. Before her pregnancy and their marriage, in the full flower of their turbulent love affair, they had attended peace rallies along with thousands in the park, especially a glorious, drugged out day and night at the "Human Be-In" that launched the "Summer of Love." The park was also a refuge for hundreds of San Francisco's homeless, with whom Emma identified and for whom she battled. For his own sake, he thought that Golden Gate Park was also a beautiful place for him to visit in honor of Emma, with its magnificent gardens, redwoods and eucalyptus, and flowering cherry trees, along with ponds where ducks peacefully paddled, and even a rolling field where a herd of buffalo, munched tranquilly on fresh grass. He parked by the Great Meadow and tucked Emma's box of ashes under his arm. Walking slowly over the grassy field, he discreetly removed the plastic bag of ashes from the box, slid the tab open, and allowed the ashes to trickle out slowly. Yes, he insisted, he had chosen correctly for Emma, a place of protest and celebration and caretaking, without authority or pompous ceremony.

Back in the car, he tossed Emma's empty box into the trunk and moved Talia's ashes to the passenger seat, feeling that she would have acknowledged his respectful gesture with a sweet smile, and drove to the bridge. Taking the cut-off onto Conzelman Road, up past the Bridge Overlook, and over the southern cliffs of the Marin Headlands, peaking at Hawk Hill. Now, Talia would be happier to enjoy the landscape without sensing Emma's annoyance. Then the car squirreled steeply down the cliffside road, with gorgeous views of the bay entrance, Point Bonita, and the curving swell of the Pacific Ocean. He ended up at Rodeo Beach where he parked, placed Talia's box of ashes gingerly into a back-pack and began to set off north on a trail. He stopped and returned to the car. From the trunk, he placed Emma's empty box in the backpack too. He then began to hike on the trail along the western cliffs over the ocean. Although he understood that Talia considered death a final end with no care about her body or ashes, he cared. He was determined to do something suitable in a place that he could visit without regret. Luckily, late in the day there were only a few other lone walkers on the trail. The bluff at the end of the trail was empty. He took the box of ashes out of the backpack in the absurd notion that Talia thus would better be able to see that he had chosen one of their favorite sites. They had come here often, because it offered a clear sight of the sweep of the ocean and a series of rough-hewn cliffs north all the way to Chimney Rock at the end of Point Reyes and south past Pacifica to Devil's Slide. Clumps of spring wildflowers had blossomed across the bluff: deep orange poppies, violet-blue iris, blue Brodiaea, and the three-pronged Ithuriel's spear, along with pink mallow, and wide-petalled yellow mule's ears. Today, Monty was happy to see that the stone circular maze, with a diameter of twenty feet or so, that thoughtful souls had meticulously arranged in circles within circles, remained untouched by vandals. On their visits, he and Talia had slowly traversed the maze, and each had made a private wish at reaching the center. Talia had been delighted with that exercise. They never revealed their wishes. His had been for whatever powers there be on this continental coast to watch over and guard the lovely woman who had accompanied him along with their distant children.

He removed the plastic bag of ashes from the box, slid the tab open, and allowed the ashes to trickle out slowly from the bag as he made his way deliberately around the stone mandala, and then over the flowered bluff. He carried the lacquer box that had contained Talia's ashes to the bluff's steep edge. Below, about a hundred yards from shore, was that long black rock shoal jutting out of the ocean, the remains of the cliff that had eroded millennia ago. The ocean waves broke over the shoal with wild crests of white foam. Without thinking, he drew back his arm and flung the box out to sea. He spread his arms out wide to the horizon as he watched the shining lacquer container light upon the waves and sink. Standing there, he imagined Talia's laughter from that nothingness, that nowhere into which she had slipped with such ease.

He began to turn, but then remembered Emma's empty box. "What the hell," he said to himself, "Emma was a feminist. She'd have no complaint if her box joined Talia's in the sea."

He turned and flung Emma's box in the same direction that he had thrown Talia's. As he watched the lacquer container sink, he could almost hear Emma's annoyed groan at his sentimental gestures.

When he returned home and entered the house, once more he paused and listened. Now, indeed, he was alone with the refrigerator and the furnace and his memories. His life was his alone to direct and judge. His daughter Louisa, of course, would criticize, but she was engrossed in the complicated household she had created and wouldn't expect him to listen. It was simply her way of expressing love and interest. Talia had understood him, and probably had opinions about his actions, but never expressed them. And now, with the disposal of Emma's ashes, he had disposed of her judgments.

Monty Wolfe opened a bottle of Sancerre, poured himself a glass, and sat by the window, gazing out at the bay, the city, Alcatraz, the sweeping arches of the Bay Bridge, Yerba Buena Island, and the rising hills of the East Bay. The sun, setting to the west, cast its rays through the narrow opening between the two lands' ends.

A golden light slashed a path across the base of the buildings of the city and reflected brilliantly off the windows of the East Bay. In his inimitable, very slow and methodical way, he began to construct a new story of his life, alone.